To Ann Hoover

Enjoy!!

CREECH

Jim Campbell

To Ann Hoover
Enjoy!

CREECH

A novel by

James Campbell

Copyright © 2016 by James Campbell.

Library of Congress Control Number:		2016901080
ISBN:	Hardcover	978-1-5144-5250-9
	Softcover	978-1-5144-5249-3
	eBook	978-1-5144-5248-6

All rights reserved. No part of this book may be reproduced or transmitted in any form or by any means, electronic or mechanical, including photocopying, recording, or by any information storage and retrieval system, without permission in writing from the copyright owner.

This is a work of fiction. Names, characters, places and incidents either are the product of the author's imagination or are used fictitiously, and any resemblance to any actual persons, living or dead, events, or locales is entirely coincidental.

Any people depicted in stock imagery provided by Thinkstock are models, and such images are being used for illustrative purposes only. Certain stock imagery © Thinkstock.

Print information available on the last page.

Rev. date: 03/17/2016

To order additional copies of this book, contact:
Xlibris
1-888-795-4274
www.Xlibris.com
Orders@Xlibris.com
728431

Contents

Chapter 1   Washington, D.C. 1

Chapter 2   Taos 6

Chapter 3   Trouble in Taos 12

Chapter 4   New York City 17

Chapter 5   London 22

Chapter 6   Chunnel 27

Chapter 7   Normandy 2014 31

Chapter 8   Cairo 37

Chapter 9   Deception 43

Chapter 10 Sao Paulo 52

Chapter 11 Rio de Janeiro 57

Chapter 12 SW Florida Art Colony 61

Chapter 13 Buenos Aires 64

Chapter 14 South American Report 70

Chapter 15 New Assignment 73

Chapter 16 Sao Paulo II 78

Chapter 17 Chicago Art Extravaganza 85

Chapter 18 Water Under The Bridge 91

Chapter 19 Stock Hustler 99

Chapter 20 Lola's Dilemma 105

Chapter 21	Productivity	110
Chapter 22	Branch Work-Chicago	115
Chapter 23	Branch Work-Milwaukee	123
Chapter 24	Branch Work-SW Florida	135
Chapter 25	Gallery Managers	144
Chapter 26	Blue Danube	151
Chapter 27	Lecture Series	162
Chapter 28	'Dance with the one who brung you'	171
Chapter 29	Honorary Doctorate	180
Chapter 30	Two Marriages	188
Chapter 31	Home	198

Dedication

This novel is dedicated to the Taos Art Colony, founded in 1815, two hundred years ago. They're wonderful people whose spirit and essence the author promulgated into a hugely successful international corporation, albeit totally fictional.

Credit is given my first writing instructor and mentor Jeannette Batko. Jeanette is the author of a number of Fun-lovin' Pun-lovin" Vignettes & Verse.

Special thanks to my Caloosa Yacht & Racquet Club friends and neighbors for their input, assistance, and encouragement. Thank you to Gary Green and Marty Freling, my proofreaders. My appreciation is extended as well to Nancy Hall, my most erudite grammarian.

Chapter 1

Washington, D.C.

Art critic Frank Creech had a seasonal condo rental at the Caloosa Yacht & Racquet Club (CYRC) in Fort Myers, Florida. He relished his getaways to the Sunshine State.

His center console boat was docked in the CYRC marina. His yacht in Washington's Potomac River basin was too large for the slips at CYRC.

During their weekly poker game at the clubhouse, artist Marty Freling complained about his earnings to Frank.

Marty told Frank that his last sale was his painting of a girl drinking a Bud Lite on Fort Myers Beach, for a whopping $250. He mentioned that his last exhibition was in 2009 and that only fourteen people visited and no one bought a painting.

Frank sympathized, "Marty, many brilliant, talented artists die in poverty and disgrace. Posthumously, their artwork sells for millions of dollars. The tiny, oil-rich nation of Qatar purchased in 2011 a Paul Cezanne painting, *The Card Players*, for more than two hundred million dollars!"

Frank added, "Paul Gauguin, deceased, died at age fifty-five, never having received the acclaim in his lifetime which he so richly deserved for his beautiful, vivid paintings. Gauguin's friend Vincent Van Gogh, frustrated at his nonacceptance in the art world, cut off his ear and ultimately shot himself to death at age forty-seven."

Marty queried Frank, "In this era of entitlement, why not entitle artists before they are posthumously recognized?"

Frank chortled, "That would take an act of Congress."

"Well, maybe I'll just get that done," Marty responded. He believed in President Obama's promise to be the Champion of Change.

Marty placed a meeting notice in the Fort Myers *News-Press* and the *Naples Daily News*, inviting all the graphic artists in the area to meet at the Hyatt Regency hotel in Coconut Point (halfway between Fort Myers and Naples, Florida) to discuss organizing for the purpose of obtaining federal financial aid for the nation's struggling artists.

Three hundred artists banded together, determined to put their cause in front of the legislators by a march on Washington's Constitution Avenue. Committees took responsibility for obtaining parade permits and notifying news agencies. Buses were rented; placards were printed.

The cause was labeled Save Our Starving Artists, foreshortened to SOSA. The artists taped SOSA placards on their four buses. They were on their way to change, firmly believing President Obama's Champion of Change program would embrace their cause.

On a beautiful Tuesday morning the SOSA buses rolled into DC. Tired but excited, the artists exited the buses, shouldered their placards, and marched down Constitution Avenue, bullhorns blaring "SOSA, SOSA, SOSA NOW!"

People trickled out of the side streets joining the marchers, singing, dancing, and applauding. A few blocks later the trickle became a torrent. As if by magic, musicians integrated the now-enormous parade, and the march morphed into . . . a FLASH MOB!

Walking toward his office at the *Washington DC International Art Critics*, Frank Creech, still clad in his morning karate class attire, heard the music and spotted the dancers and his artist friends from Fort Myers.

In a playful mood, Frank grabbed the bullhorn of one of the marchers and shouted in the general direction of the artists, "Hey, guys, its SALSA not SOSA!"

"Olé! Olé!" responded the flash mob. Some of the Latinos, possibly emboldened by more than a few shots of tequila, wrestled away a dozen SOSA placards and threw them to the pavement.

Frank used the bullhorn again, shouting in his stentorian voice, "Hey, knock that off!"

The music stopped. Marchers and dancers squared off. A few punches were thrown.

The Latinas screamed, "Para! Para!" but the battle had joined.

Frank, six feet four, two hundred forty-five pounds, in great physical condition and never one to miss a good fight, unleashed his forty-two-inch three-row pyramid-studded belt. He waded into the flash mob, wielding his fighting belt. He connected again and again.

He cut a swath through the dancers, until *he* was bayoneted in the navel with a violin bow by one of the musicians!

Cameramen videoed the vicious fight, with voiceover narration by reporters who were covering the mob and the marchers.

When Dick Brooks, managing editor of the *Washington DC International Art Critics*, saw the coverage on primetime six o'clock news—police in riot gear separating the two groups, ambulances loading up the wounded, scenes of Frank slashing Latinos with his fighting belt—Frank Creech's career at the *International Art Critics* promptly ended.

Frank was ambulanced to the Providence Hospital's emergency room.

Dick Boyd, SOSA president, phoned cofounder Marty Freling with the news of Frank's hospitalization. Marty flew to Washington to see Frank. He learned from the resident physician that Frank would need a difficult and costly surgical procedure.

Marty engaged internationally renowned surgeon Dr. Bosco (Bob) Pop-Lazic to perform the operation Frank needed. If Frank's insurance wouldn't cover it, he would pay for it himself.

Frank's umbilicoplasty navigation procedure to repair the damage to his navel was successful.

Marty knew Frank was in desperate straits, so he arranged to sell his boat at CYRC.

The previous year, Regional Southwest Airport in Fort Myers had sponsored a competition for local artists to paint a scene in tribute to American-Iraq War veterans. Frank Creech chaired the awards committee. The paintings were hung in corridor B at RSW airport.

SOSA cofounder Marty Freling won that competition with his beautiful painting *Coming Home*, a soldier in camos, prostate on the floor at RSW. An unforgettable honor was bestowed on Marty due in large part to Frank Creech.

Marty and his wife, Judy, were deeply concerned about Frank's sad predicament.

Frank Creech, thirteen-year senior art critic of the *Washington DC International Art Critics*, had been a genuine and often inspiring art critic. The SOSA membership vowed to help him recover his hard-earned top art critic status.

Dick Boyd visited Frank at Providence Hospital. He gave Frank a money order from Marty for the sale of Frank's boat at CYRC.

Frank thanked Dick and asked him to thank Marty for the favor.

Dick noticed Frank was morose, despondent.

Frank asked Dick, plaintively, "What will I do now?"

Dick told Frank, "Keep your chin up. Marty engaged celebrity headhunter Bill Pringle to find you a new position."

Unfortunately, Mr. Pringle discovered that the video of the fight scene on Constitution Avenue had been picked up by all the TV news networks; the major papers had carried the episode, with photos, in their arts and entertainment sections.

Six months later, Marty and Dick learned from Bill Pringle that Frank had been effectively blacklisted. There would be no opportunity for Frank to gain a prominent position as an art critic.

Frank Creech, former art critic of the *Washington DC International Art Critics*, had sunk to his nadir. Four months after he was discharged from his position, he defaulted on the loan for his luxury condo and had to move to a third-floor walk-up apartment. His society girlfriend had left him within a month of the incident. His yacht had been repossessed. He was bankrupt.

For the first time in twelve years, his once-prized forty-foot yacht, *Artistically Endowed*, had not led the Potomac River annual Holiday Boat Parade.

Adding to his sorrow, his ailing dog Socks had to be put down.

Out of the kindness of his heart, the owner of Frank's favorite restaurant gave him a job as maître d'.

Marty called Frank. He begged Frank not to despair. He promised he'd find him an appropriate career position in the field of fine arts.

Marty quoted Thomas Fuller, the English theologian and historian: "The darkest hour is just before the dawn."

Chapter 2

Taos

Marty's award-winning painting *Coming Home* was purchased. Marty and Judy rewarded themselves with a vacation trip to Taos, New Mexico. He had learned Taos was the first and largest art colony in the United States, due to the glorious light afforded by the New Mexico skies. Light so beneficial to painters. And he learned that there are more artists per capita in the Taos area than in any other city in the world, including Paris, France.

During their visit, Marty and Judy met the movers and shakers in the art colony; gallery owners, painters, art students, and denizens.

Meeting with the directors of the Taos Art Colony, Marty spoke very highly of his friend Frank Creech, furnishing them with a written history of his work for the *Washington DC International Art Critics*. Listed in Frank's résumé were his many contacts with fine art buyers in communities around the world.

He proposed that Frank would be a sparkling addition to the colony. And that Frank, with his connections, could effectively market the colony's art both nationally and internationally.

An accountant as well as an artist, Marty worked the numbers. He came up with an acceptable formula; 2 percent of all sales would constitute Frank Creech's drawing account. Starting draw two hundred thousand per annum, paid biweekly, plus expenses. His contract would be annually reviewed and renewable based on dollar volume of sales made during the fiscal year.

The art colony directors submitted the proposal to their attorney, Vic Lich. Mr. Lich incorporated into the contract the usual boilerplate conditions as to performance, conduct, and other material specifications.

Marty and Judy had already planned a trip to the Washington DC area to visit their granddaughter at a nearby college. Thus, they could contiguously visit with Frank and surprise him with the art colony offer. Frank quickly agreed to the meeting. He arranged to meet them at his place of employment as maître d' in Logan Circle, DC, where he once had a permanently reserved table. He was excited about seeing the Frelings again. He knew Marty would insist on picking up the tab.

Moments after sipping their *le digestif*, Rossala Bianca—a delightful cognac specialty of the restaurant—Marty took the art colony's contract offer out of his attaché case and placed it on the table in front of Frank.

Frank's eyes began to tear. He felt redemption, opportunity, excitement, gratitude, emotion, all competing in a grand rush.

Attached to the contract was a check for fifty thousand dollars, a salary advance. Marty and Judy were so happy for Frank they cried with him.

Frank gave two weeks' notice to his friend, the restaurant owner, thanking him so much for his interim employment.

He shipped his furniture to his sister Eileen in Michigan City. Eileen had a large barn on her property where his furniture would be safely stored. He had contacted several rental agencies and had a short list of rentals to check out in Taos.

Working from a list, he cancelled his lease at his apartment, said farewell to his friends, and made his arrangements with the art colony of Taos to be at work on Monday, two weeks away.

Flying into Taos Regional Airport under a flawless sky, Frank Creech was as eager as he gets about most everything. The first order of business was to satisfy his craving for some good Tex-Mex local food.

Frank asked his cabbie to take him to the best Tex-Mex restaurant.

The driver looked Frank up and down.

"Well, do I measure up?"

"Yes, sir, you do. We're going to the Old Blinking Light restaurant, situated just beside the spectacular Sangre de Cristo Mountains. You'll enjoy great local cuisine and gorgeous scenery."

Frank strode powerfully behind the hostess to his table. Once seated, he immediately noticed an absolute look-alike of Honor Blackman, who played Pussy Galore in the James Bond movie *Goldfinger*, seated at the adjacent table.

He wondered if she was part of the gorgeous scenery the cabbie mentioned.

Trying to think of an introductory line, Frank was startled to hear her sultry British voice, "Hi, handsome. I'm Diane Arnold. Are you expecting company?"

"I'm Frank Creech, and I am not expecting anyone. I would enjoy your company. Please join me."

Frank stood and pulled back a chair for Diane.

In her lilting dialect, Diane said, "Thank you, kind sir. I'm an advanced art student in a Helen Quodomine's acrylic art school. Why are you in Taos?"

"It seems we have something in common. I'm the newly appointed marketing director of the Taos Art Colony. I haven't met my bosses. My appointment is at nine tomorrow morning."

Frank ordered a magnum of Dom Pérignon champagne. Diane fluttered her eyelashes and smiled broadly.

"You're a man of fine discernment, it appears."

They chatted between bites of their delicious Tex-Mex dinners, washed down with their champagne.

As the food and wine disappeared, Frank patted his stomach and shook his head, "I don't know when I've enjoyed a better meal with such a lovely lady."

"Where do you go now, Frank?"

"In my excitement of coming to my new job, I forgot to book a hotel room. I'd better get moving."

"You may be in luck. I'm staying at the Burch Street Casitas, and they're within walking distance of the art colony's headquarters. They probably have a vacancy this time of year."

Diane and Frank cabbed with the driver who brought him to the Old Blinking Light Restaurant then to her residence at the Burch Street Casitas.

She spoke through the voice box in the door to the Casitas' manager. "It's Diane Arnold, and I have a new guest for you."

Diane and Frank heard, "Oh, honey, I'm so sorry. We don't have any openings now."

"I'll find something," said Frank as he waved his arms and whistled. The cab was out of range.

"Looks like you're stuck with me. Oh, don't look so appalled. I have two bedrooms, so you're safe," Diane laughed. She explained, "My sister stayed with me until she had to return to Chelsea last week."

She opened the door to her casita, and Frank wrestled his heavy canvas suitcase inside.

"Are you sure this is OK?" Frank questioned.

Nodding her head and pointing toward an open bedroom entryway, Diane said, "Go freshen up. I'll join you shortly for a nightcap."

After his visit to the bathroom, Frank hung up the suit he would wear tomorrow and placed the other things he would need on the dresser top. He put on his PJs and his tired old terry cloth bathrobe and returned to the sitting room.

Diane, a 5'6" tall ash blonde, came into the room a few moments later; she was wearing a luminous green silk kimono which showed her figure (36" bust, 23" waist, 36" hips) most advantageously, Frank thought.

She poured two glasses of Amontillado from a Waterford Crystal decanter, handing one to Frank.

They touched glasses.

"Here's to you," said Frank.

"Cheers," Diane replied.

After one swallow of their delicious wine, they put their glasses down on the coffee table.

Frank pulled her into his arms, tilted her chin up, and kissed her. She responded with passion. She pressed her body into his body. She put her arms around his neck and wrapped her left leg around his right thigh.

They made love on the sitting room couch.

Slipping back into his PJs, Frank said, "I didn't want to rush you. I, uh, it's been a long time."

Diane responded, "Honey, I had the same concern. It's been two years since my divorce, and I haven't been seeing anyone. Things just seemed to come together."

"They certainly did," chortled Frank.

They snuggled all night in Diane's bed until her alarm sounded.

She made coffee while Frank got ready for his meeting.

They exchanged phone numbers, and Diane gave Frank directions to the art colony.

Under the welcome sign, just inside the colony's entryway, Frank was met by a uniformed armed guard.

"Good morning. You would be Mr. Creech?" asked the guard.

Reading his name badge, Frank replied, "Yes Officer Hasse, I'm Frank Creech."

Bill Hesse picked up the house telephone and dialed quickly.

"Mary Ellen, Mr. Creech is here." Turning back to Frank, he said, "Sit down, Mr. Creech. Mr. Green's secretary will be here in a few minutes to escort you to the boardroom. For security, our cameras have photographed you."

"Thank you, Bill."

Frank thought, *The colony is housing some very expensive artwork.*

"Hi, Mr. Creech. Welcome to the Taos Art Colony. I'm Mary Ellen, Director Green's secretary. Please follow me."

"Anywhere, Mary Ellen," chortled Frank to the vivacious young lady.

"Ha, ha! You and I are going to get along very well, Frank."

Frank met the working directors, Gary Green, Carroll Swanson, and Bud Robitaille. The directors outlined his introductory schedule and assigned Bud to accompany him and fill him in on all colony functions.

They visited the marketing department, the gallery, the financial center, and the employment, restoration, and traffic departments over the course of the week's indoctrination. During their visit to the marketing department, Frank learned from the manager, Leslie D'Alessandro, that he was to be sent to the Louvre in Paris—the largest museum in the western world—to exhibit Colony art following his introductory week.

Leslie gave Frank his business cards and a dozen glossy brochures designed for the exhibition. The literature featured the art to be exhibited and included Frank's bio and current photo taken by Bill Hasse. She explained that the brochures had been mailed to Paris art dealers and private collectors. A hundred show pieces would be in their assigned display booth.

Frank said, "Well done, Leslie."

Leslie curtsied and replied, "We aim to please, sir."

Diane had mentioned that her schedule at the art school was flexible. She was nearing completion of the course. She happily agreed to accompany Frank to Paris.

Frank and Diane met for dinner each evening at a nearby Taos restaurant, Le Cueva Café. They had only casual meals at their Burch Street casita. Frank recognized that cooking was not one of Diane's favorite activities.

Then, again, she was a lovely and so compliant companion.

On the fourth day of his introduction week, Frank stopped in the Burch Street Casitas office and changed the rental to his name.

Frank thought, *It's hard to believe I am so far ahead of where I was before Marty created this opportunity for me. I will be forever in his debt.*

Chapter 3

Trouble in Taos

Frank Creech, six months on the job as marketing director for the Taos Art Colony, believed he had died and gone to heaven in glorious Taos. The scenery was stunning, his work fascinating and highly rewarding.

While they were boating on Blue Lake, Paso del Sur Pueblo, Frank told Diane he recognized two men in a boat near them.

He said, "I remember seeing them at the Taos Art Colony display at the Louvre in Paris." Shaking his head, he continued, "Coincidence, maybe. But why would they be interested in us?"

Placing her hand on his thigh, Diane said, "Don't be paranoid."

Frank responded, pointing to his middle, "My gut feeling is usually right. Something's not kosher here."

The next morning at nine, Frank's cell phone rang. It was Vic Lich, retired district court judge, now an attorney retained by the art colony.

"Mr. Creech," Vic said with authority, "Please come to my office at 1:00 p.m. today. There are some things we need to discuss."

"And what might those things be, Mr. Lich?" asked Frank.

Vic tersely replied, "I prefer going over these items with you in person."

Frank dressed in his blue silk suit purchased from Raja Fashions in Kowloon while he was there for the Asian Art Festival in Hong Kong. Selected by Diane, it was the only silk suit Frank had ever owned.

The receptionist showed Frank into a side waiting room, replete with gallery of colony paintings, including the gorgeous *The Fantasy of Flowers* by Lynda Ortiz. "It will be about five minutes, Mr. Creech."

Frank thought, *Vic Lich has to cost big bucks.* Ten minutes later, he was escorted into Mr. Lich's private office.

Seated in rustic Juniper furniture were Attorney Vic Lich and Taos Art Colony directors Gary Green and Carroll Swanson. He saw seven file folders piled on the sofa table.

Mounted on the back wall was a six-by-six-foot theater screen fronted by a small slide projector. In the far corner stood the New Mexico state flag, the Pueblo Zia Sun.

Vic Lich, casually attired in a Western blazer and bolo tie, said, "Frank, if I may—and please call me Vic—I'll get right to the purpose of this meeting. We are here to examine what appears to be a number of irregularities in your expense account submissions."

Vic began, "This slide shows you and Ms. Arnold boating on Blue Lake, is that correct?"

"Yes."

"The next slide is you and Ms. Arnold at the Folies Bergère in Paris?"

"Yes."

"The next slide is Ms. Arnold in Raja Fashions—in Kowloon, I believe—selecting the suit you are wearing today?"

"Yes."

Seemingly interminable, the slides and narratives continued.

Gary Green said, "Including meals, transportation, housing, leisure, clothing, entertainment, and sundry other expenses, your total reimbursed expenses for the six months you have been associated with the Taos Art Colony amounted to one hundred sixty-five thousand dollars.

Attorney Lich added, "Our auditors, Tim McClary and Bill McDaniels, billed thirty-two hours validating legitimate expenses and isolating expenses which are not within your purview under the reimbursement feature of your contract. Didn't Marty Freling review the details of the contract with you?"

"Well, yes he did, and as Carroll and Gary know, Marty is fastidious about these things. I believe I can show you the expenses were well worth the cost and fall within my purview."

Carroll arose and walked to the screen. He pointed at a photo of Frank and Diane coming out of jewelry store in Hong Kong.

"What about the pearl necklace you billed the colony?"

Frank puffed out his cheeks and exclaimed loudly, "I'm glad you are giving me an opportunity to ask for a traveling secretary to take care of all the things Diane does for the colony that makes my job of selling art so much easier. I need to remind you that's a huge amount of work in small-detail handling which the colony does not pay for."

Carroll glared at Frank and returned to his seat.

Vic asked, "Frank, what possible legitimate end was served the colony by your Folies Bergère party?"

Frank responded, "How could you not notice there were four people at the table?"

"You are begging the question, Frank," said Vic.

Frank stood up, legs trembling, fingers pointing at the two directors. He exclaimed, "You two know those people are the president of the Louvre and his wife. Last year the Taos Art Colony exhibit was in the space next to the men's room, on the third floor. This year we were in the first display area immediately beyond the entryway. That's certainly not a tiny upgrade. Sales were six times the previous year, right?"

Carroll popped out of his chair quickly, saying "OK, we'll give you that one, but show us how much you made for us on that boat vacation at Lake Blue or the hand-tailored silk suit you charged to us."

Reseated and somewhat calmed down, Frank measured his words carefully. "A man who exerts the time and effort I put into my work must have some R&R, sirs. I'll bet you would have paid for an expensive spa, right? And as for my silk suit, that is my uniform for sales calls and for exhibitions. Dress for success, you know."

For four solid hours they bantered, until Vic's secretary quietly entered the room and, after a nod from Vic, said "Janet called. She doesn't want you to be late for her dinner party."

Flourishing his hand and grinning, Vic announced, "Gentlemen, we'll adjourn for the day and continue tomorrow morning at nine o'clock."

Frank was barely seated the next morning. Before he could taste his New Mexico Piñon Coffee, Gary put his own cup down, took a deep breath, and began, "Frank, this could go on forever. And after all, time is money, so let me make a proposition to you for settling this matter. How does that sound?"

"Yeah, I'm due in New York this weekend to arrange the art colony exhibit at MoMA."

Gary continued, "Frank, unless we can get this settled today, you won't be going to New York for the colony."

Shrugging his aching shoulders, Frank said, "Let's hear it, Gary."

"All right, here's the deal. We need to half your salary for the remainder of the six months of your contract."

Interrupting, Frank reverted to his youthful, baroque, Michigan dialect, "Whoa, ain't gonna happen!"

"Hear me out, please," appealed Gary. "At the end of the year, we will adjust your salary as per your contract if we are satisfied with the year's productivity."

"We'll re-contract for the following year. In the meantime, we insist you curtail your expenses. In six months' time you've run up expenses to over half your salary. Now that's fair, isn't it?"

Attorney Lich handed a file folder to Frank. "Frank, you have little choice other than to accept the colony's reduced salary arrangement and to reduce your expenses. We'll need your signature today, please."

Never having even tasted the Piñon nut roasted coffee, Frank rose. "OK, looks like I've been had, and I'm going to need a little time to digest this. You'll have your response from me this afternoon, latest."

Diane, still in her bikini from her sunbathing regimen, came into the casita living room. She saw Frank, a tumbler of Jack Daniel's in his right hand, his left hand holding his head in a peculiar pose.

"What's wrong, sweetheart?" Diane implored.

Frank sighed, "The proverbial shit hit the fan. It seems we've been living a little too high on the hog."

Frank related the session with the art colony's directors and their attorney to Diane. He told her about the salary cut and the colony's demand that he cut back on his expenses.

"What are we going to do, baby?" Diane said, as she rubbed his shoulders.

"Guess I'll sign off on the deal, bite the bullet as it were. We'll need to hold the Dom Pérignon down to a single bottle at dinner, and I'll have to cut back on my short Beli after-dinner cigars," laughed Frank. "Have to get this paper back to Vic Lich now, and when I get back I have an idea."

"May I guess where that *idea* will lead?" cooed Diane as she danced into the bedroom.

Chapter 4

New York City

Shocked and stunned, Frank Creech, Marketing Director, the Taos Art Colony, and Rick Cinotto, Director of the Museum of Modern Art (MoMA), were interviewed by New York City high crimes detective John Loske. They went over every conceivable aspect of the theft of nine colony paintings from the assembly room, three days after their arrival at MoMA.

Frank messaged Marty Freling with the sad news that his beautiful piece *Flamenco*, grouped with the colony's art, was among the missing pieces.

Marty read the *New York Times* morning edition front page story of the MoMA missing art. The *Times*' coverage included a reference to another significant theft of very expensive paintings.

According to the FBI, Marty read, billions of dollars of art goes missing every year. In 2012 men wearing hoods broke into the Kunsthal museum in Rotterdam and stole two drawings by Monet and one painting each by Gauguin, Picasso, Matisse, Lucien Freud, and Jacob Meyer de Hann. The stratospheric number—$400 million! Although the thieves were caught, the art was never recovered.

Detective Loske determined there was no apparent break-in at MoMA. Security was tight; photo IDs together with exhibitor passes were required to enter all nonpublic areas. Many guards, artists themselves, were very agitated, particularly those on the night shift who were suspended without pay while the investigation was ongoing.

New York City police commissioner Robert di Grazia was interviewed outside MoMA by the media. Pointing his finger at the sky, he stated, "Detective Loske and his people would shake the tree until the fruit came down. We're going to get that art back for good. We'll leave no stone unturned. Let the chips fall where they may."

One of the really significant reasons Diane Arnold and Frank Creech were such a good alliance was that Diane was an artist herself. Her partnership with Frank moved her into circles where she could study the techniques of successful colony artists. By employing her upfront gained perspectives and through practice, she had significantly improved her own artwork.

She helped in the display areas and aided artists with their needs. She handled many easily resolved items which allowed Frank to handle the major issues with confidence.

Each day Diane worked on technique, copying established themes and motifs of colony artists. Careful to not get paint on herself, she wore a bulky gray smock. She often stayed past 5:00 p.m., MoMA's closing time.

The MoMA guards were respectful toward their exhibitor friends and were sincerely sympathetic to the great variety of needs of exhibitors and their artists.

Having done all he could to help in the investigation, Frank was tired and hungry.

Diane joined him at the exquisite Todd English Food Hall in the Plaza Hotel where they stayed. They enjoyed a scrumptious lobster dinner washed down with a delightful Chardonnay.

Frank elected to skip his after-dinner treat, a ninety-dollar Trinidad short Beli cigar, in compliance with the colony's order to reduce his expenses.

He was still smarting over having been reprimanded by the directors for inappropriate expense submissions, having his draw halved, and having been put on notice that his expenses must be curtailed.

In their bedroom at the Plaza Hotel, arms entwined, the sweet perfume of love in the air, Diane pondered how to tell Frank the truth about the missing art. Finally, she whispered in Frank's ear, "We need to go to the sitting room for a few minutes. I'm afraid there is something terribly important we need to discuss."

In the sitting room, Diane sipped her Coke, crying, "I meant to return the pieces last night, but I was so tired. I had no idea such a stir would occur, and now I am embarrassed and afraid to step forward. No one is going to believe I just wanted to study those pieces."

She sobbed, "You heard me, Frank. *I'm the thief!* I hid those pieces under my smock, one at a time, and sneaked them into my rental studio which is only two blocks from the museum."

"Don't panic, Diane," Frank said, as he held his index finger against his temple and tried to think of a solution to the desperate dilemma.

Thinking aloud, he ticked off potential solutions, "Sneak them back into the museum? No, the guards are on high alert. Destroy them? No, they're too precious."

While sipping his Jack Daniel's on the rocks, Frank thought of something that might work. *The gracious help of a Good Samaritan!*

"Diane, I think I'm onto something that might work. Let's go get the paintings."

They found a usable crate in the dumpster behind Diane's rental studio and carefully wrapped and packed the paintings into the crate.

Using different cabs to and from Diane's studio, they delivered the crate to the lobby of the Chase Park Plaza and had the doorman summon a bellhop. The bellhop put the crate in the luggage storage area. Frank gave him a generous tip.

Working into the evening, Detective Loske had assembled two hundred sets of photos of the missing paintings for his squad to use in canvasing the pawnshops and interrogating suspected purveyors and buyers of stolen art.

Rick Cinotto called Detective Loske to tell him he'd just received an offer of a reward of one million dollars by Lloyds of London, the insurer of the MoMA, for information leading to the recovery of the stolen paintings.

John Loske asked Rick to get copies of the reward poster to the media for publication and to send him by courier two hundred copies to put in his squad's packets of materials.

Rick said, "I thought you might need copies. My secretary and I are copying the reward poster, and you will have your copies within the hour."

John shook his finger at the wall mirror and exclaimed, "That reward just might do the trick."

Rick Cinotto knew Detective Loske and his squad planned to go through the museum, room by room, beginning at 8:00 a.m. tomorrow.

John told Rick, "If the artwork is not found at MoMA, my squad and I will go to the streets posting the reward posters and seeking information about the stolen artwork."

Rick would have to close the museum to the public, possibly for the entire day. He could just imagine there would be an angry uproar from the visitors who were denied entry. He was concerned that any negative press coverage of the disruption coupled with the theft of the paintings would likely end his career at MoMA.

He called his wife, Therese, and advised her to hold up on the purchase of the new drapery she wanted for their living room.

Late in the evening, just as John Loske pulled down his pants, preparing to sleep on his couch so as not to disturb his wife, his phone rang.

"Hello, John. Frank Creech here. You said to call if something important developed, and it has."

"I'm tired," warned John, "and my back hurts, so this better be good."

Frank's voice sounded matter-of-fact. "I have some good news for you. An acquaintance delivered the missing paintings to me ten minutes ago and does not want the reward. The Good Samaritan wishes to be anonymous. And please don't mention that I was involved in the return of those precious pieces."

"Are you sure you don't want to share the credit?"

"No, I do not. This was the first time under my directorship of the art colony's marketing that something like this has happened. I certainly don't need to draw any further attention to myself. I'm so thankful a Good Samaritan had the courage and good heart to bring those missing paintings to me.

"Meet me in front of the Plaza Hotel in twenty minutes and collect the paintings. You can claim the reward."

John Loske brightened, pulled his pants back up, and muttered, "This is good, very, very good."

Commissioner di Grazia made a public statement extolling Detective Loske for having closed the case in twenty-four hours and for the detective's generous donation of the million-dollar reward to the New York City Patrolmen's Benevolent Association.

The commissioner said, "Detective Loske will receive an NYPD commendation medal."

He added, "All's well that ends well."

When Rick Cinotto heard the good news, he called his wife. "Therese, you can buy those draperies. Detective Loske somehow got those paintings back. He saved my job."

The media broadcast the news that the missing art was recovered and back on display. The line of people at the MoMA wrapped around the block three times with people anxious to see the colony's art.

Frank had the paintings and the story of their recovery displayed along with a photograph of a beaming Detective Loske.

The art colony's complete array of fine art paintings, including Marty Freling's *Flamenco*, were sold by 2:00 p.m. at no bargain prices.

At twenty minutes after noon, Taos time, Director Carroll Swanson phoned Director Gary Green. "How did that SOB pull that off?" he asked.

Gary stuttered, "I-I-I haven't the foggiest idea, but we need to restore his draw in full, and we had better lighten up on the expense account issue as well."

Carroll hesitated for a moment and then replied, "You don't think . . ."

Gary interrupted, "Uh, let's not go there."

Chapter 5

London

Colony director Carroll Swanson accepted the Taos Chamber of Commerce offer by President Betty James to pay for half of the exhibition room rental in London. They would ship a display booth to the colony's exhibition site. The chamber would send their own representative to London to distribute literature offering reduced air travel, reduced hotel, and reduced car rentals to induce British tourists to visit Taos.

Carroll had a copy of a *Naples Daily News* article, sent to him by Marty Freling. The article stated that Collier County (Naples), Florida, collected almost four million dollars from their 4 percent bed tax levy in the month of March 2014. Many of the tourists were German citizens. The article credited the Fort Myers and Naples chambers of commerce, with help from Lufthansa Airlines North America director Wilhelm Verhufen.

Carroll phoned Gary, "As we are members of the Taos Chamber, I had to recuse myself from the vote to pay for half of the display room in London. We'll owe some favors."

Gary replied, "No problem, young man. Well done."

Without verbalizing it, they both understood the art colony would gain by fine art sales to the British tourists.

Two months before the exhibition target date, the colony's travel agent, Jack Murtha, told Frank there were 2,730 hotels in London with over seven thousand rooms.

Since Diane would be on her home turf, Frank asked her to select the colony's exhibition site. She chose the ME London, five stars, in the heart of the city and within walking distance of fourteen art galleries.

Frank had the marketing department book the ME London conference center, which had a three-hundred-person capacity; they would use it during the second week of their stay to exhibit and sell colony art to the general public and to London galleries.

The marketing department placed ads in the *London Times*.

Frank planned to use the first week to contact the three current art colony customer gallery owners, and he needed to personally contact as many of the 240 galleries who had received invitations to the exhibition from the colony's marketing department, as time permitted.

Diane and Frank were seated on white leather sectional furniture in the ME London's exquisite lobby, while their room was being readied.

Arlene Anderson, Diane's sister, hurried in from the hotel's entryway to join them.

She hugged Diane. She kissed Frank's cheek as he stood up to greet her, asking, "Are you *the* Frank my sister has become infatuated with?"

"I am indeed *that* Frank, *the* one who is infatuated with your sister."

Her eyes riveted on Frank, having apparently heard so much about him.

"Everyone calls me A.A., Frank. Am I in time for lunch?"

"That you are, A.A. We have reservations at Radio, here in the hotel."

Diane laughed as she watched Frank's puzzled expression as he read Radio's lunch menu.

"What is it, honey?"

"So many things I've never even heard of."

He ordered horseradish soup, Korean fried cauliflower, chicken livers with foie gras parfait, and dark ale.

The girls ordered monkfish fingers with chips, flavored with chili, vinegar, and mayonnaise. They had pale ale.

After lunch, A.A. and Diane went shopping for wedding dresses for a cousin's wedding.

Frank went to the suite and began calling art gallery owners. He knew many of them from his thirteen years as art critic for the

Washington DC International Art Critics. He made forty-four calls, asking the owners to come to the exhibition next week, checking off responses on his contact sheet. He had sixteen *yes* responses and five *no* responses. The rest of the contacts weren't in or "would think about it." He made appointments with the three present colony clients.

Frank arranged with the concierge for a London black cab to meet him at 8:30 a.m. in the lobby. He had mapped the contacts he needed to see in person. The last appointment was a lunch date with one of the present gallery owner in the colony accounts, after which he would return to the suite and continue his telephone survey.

Long day tired, Diane and Frank ordered a room service light dinner. They enjoyed the late night snack invented by the Earl of Sandwich in the 1750s, and hence called a sandwich. It consisted of meat and cheese between slices of bread. Their side dish was cottage cheese.

They watched a rerun of BBC series *Boys from the Blackstuff* (an authentic snapshot of Britain in the early 1980s) while sipping their champagne and nibbling their Walkers Shortbread cookie desserts.

Arms around each other, they slept soundly until the too early alarm sounded.

The next morning, at the café off the lobby, they enjoyed "the English," a typical heavy British breakfast. It was a giant assortment of eggs, bacon, beans, toast and fried bread, juices, milk, tea, and coffee.

Frank and his hack left amid the London morning rush-hour traffic.

Diane went to the hospitality suite to make arrangements for items required for the exhibition. These items included the mic system, the art backboards, special lighting, and show hours marquee information. Assistance in hanging the two hundred precious pieces of art to be displayed was also included in the agreement. The things she did in all the exhibitions helped Frank immensely as they took away many last minute potential problems.

The exhibition room would be open to the public each of the seven days from 2:00 p.m. until 7:00 p.m. It would be open for gallery owners and their staffs from 11:30 p.m. until 1:30 p.m. A buffet would be catered in the exhibition room by Radio during the gallery owner periods.

Frank finished his seen contacts and telephone survey work Saturday afternoon. 160 contacts made either by phone or in person, sixty-eight *yes* check marks, nineteen *no* check marks, and seventy-three "we'll try to get there" responses. All in all, it looked good to him.

Diane and Frank went to Chelsea to visit A.A. They stayed overnight, returning in time to greet Director Bud Robitaille and his wife, Kathleen, who came to London to help at the exhibition.

Things went as expected on day one and day two. Some purchases were from individuals. There were several nice volume orders from galleries, six of them new to the colony.

On the third morning, only a few people trickled in.

Frank said, "Something's wrong here. I'll check it out."

Diane said, "Stay here, honey, I'll go find out what's happening."

He knew she would do exactly that.

Ten minutes later she called Frank. "Uh-oh, there's a group of men gathered in the hotel approach lane waving placards and shouting."

Diane understood the tortured cockney language. "Yankee scarpers (go away)."

After she heard more of the less than polite comments, she called Frank back. "Frank, there is a disturbance. Maybe you'd better come down here."

Frank, having handled disruptions at exhibitions previously, went to his room, grabbed his studded belt and his money belt, and raced to the hotel entryway.

On the curved walkway to the hotel entrance he faced the eight poorly dressed, scowling, unshaven men. Pointing at the *Buy British* placards, Frank angrily asked, "What the hell's going on here?"

The man in the front of the group laughed and said, "Cor blimey, a bloody Yank on ees muscle."

Frank uncoiled his fighting belt, bent slightly, moved closer, glared at the men, and waited for a reaction.

The gang backed up a few feet, looking at each other with troubled glances.

Diane saw through her binoculars two men putting their placards down. She felt a tingle of excitement in her groin area. She screamed out the window, "Now, Frank, now!"

Frank opened his money belt in his left hand. His right hand was still brandishing his fighting belt. He spoke in his stentorian voice, "How much are you getting paid for this little demonstration?"

There was no response. The wide-eyed men just glanced at each other.

"All right," Frank said, "Here's my deal. Twenty quid for each of you, you leave, and not come back or . . ." He didn't finish the sentence. He flicked his fighting belt.

The men took their caps off, brims up, arms extended. Frank doled out the money.

Diane and the exhibition team saw the men pocket their money and scatter.

Bud looked at Kathleen. Shaking his head he said, relieved, "Phew. Glad that's over."

Bud exclaimed, "I've seen a lot of things, but this one takes the cake. We just saw Frank Creech back down eight tough-looking thugs in five minutes flat."

Frank walked back to the hotel. In the entryway he saw a bobby dismount from his bike. He heard the bobby tell the doorman his stationhouse had a call about a hostile group in the hotel's entryway. The bobby asked the bell captain what had happened.

Frank heard that discreet British gentleman reply, "Why, nothing at all officer. There was a little disagreement which appears to have been settled."

Business picked up. Individual collectors and gallery owners wanted to meet Frank. It seemed to Diane that they wanted to do business with the man who stood up to the thugs. The exhibition was a huge success for the colony.

Chamber of Commerce president Betty James had made a number of contacts with travel agents as well as exhibition visitors, passing out pamphlets and explaining the special reduced airfare and lodging and attraction discounts. She was excited by the response and expected that British tourists would be coming to Taos in throngs.

Carroll walked past the marketing department tote board and saw the numbers were surging in sales of colony art at the London exhibition.

Gary said, "I know, I heard it from Bud. Frank seems to have an uncanny way of turning adversity into profit."

Chapter 6

Chunnel

Frank told Diane he wanted to experience traveling from London to the continent via the Eurotunnel, popularly named the Chunnel, on their way to Normandy.

He had read in *Frommer's London* that the Chunnel had been inaugurated in 1994 at a cost of more than twenty-one billion dollars. It is seventy-five meters under the English Channel. Its underwater distance is twenty-three miles. With the addition of high-speed track from Dover to London in 2006, passengers can travel between Paris and London in two hours and fifteen minutes using Eurostar rail service.

Diane was concerned about their safety. Living in Chelsea, a suburb of London, she recollected the 2009 incidents in the Chunnel. Over two thousand people had been stranded in the Chunnel due to weather-related issues, illegal immigrant disruptions, or rock slides. She recalled that one train was said to have been left underground without food, water, or information for eighteen hours.

Diane said, "Honey, I'm very leery about traveling through the Chunnel, but if you really think it will be all right, I'm with you."

The waiter in Eurostar's dining room watched Diane and Frank enjoying their lunch of Scottish smoked salmon and pumpernickel bread with mustard sauce. Their dessert was fruit-filled Belgian waffles, topped with fluffy Irish whipped cream.

Diane's hot Tetley tea spilled onto her lap as the train, with a frightening screech, lurched to a stop.

The car's speaker blared, "Remain in your seats, please. A repair crew is on the way."

"Stay here, Diane, I'm going to check out the situation," Frank said, as he rose from the table.

As he approached the vestibule, the conductor put his hand up in a halting manner and yelled, "You can't go out there!"

Frank thought differently. At 245 pounds, he easily muscled past the conductor and hopped off the diner car.

He ran up the walkway to the Eurostar locomotive where he spotted two uniformed men inspecting the drive wheels.

Frank asked authoritatively, "What's going on here?"

One of the men said, "There was a rock slide. A rock's wedged between the lead drive wheel and the rail."

"Get me a heavy-duty crowbar," Frank growled.

"Sir, you can't move that rock."

"Maybe not, maybe so. But we won't know that unless we try, right? Now, please get me that crowbar."

One of the men said, "I'll need my supervisor's approval, sir."

Frank, eyebrows lowered, balled his right fist. Shaking it at the men, he announced, "Your supervisor's approval will be the least of your problems unless you get me a crowbar right now."

Pointing at what appeared to be a toolshed about fifty yards ahead of the locomotive, Frank cupped his mouth and shouted, "Go! Go! Go!"

The conductor had called the on-duty maintenance supervisor, and both he and the conductor ran to the locomotive.

The supervisor began videoing the scene with his cellphone, thinking that he might need visual evidence in the event of a legal action against the man who seemed to be aggressively commanding his crew to go to the toolshed.

On a dead run, the crewmen returned in seconds.

The first man back handed Frank a crowbar. Gasping, he said, "This is a Stanley FatMax Xtreme, very heavy duty."

The second man, panting, hand on his hips, said, "Let's hope it does the trick."

Frank chipped a small piece of the rock away. Recalling a geology class he took as an undergraduate at Michigan State University, he determined that the rock was soft sandstone and was of only slightly stronger rock strength than chalk. The rock was only about four inches in diameter; and because it was sandstone, he felt he wouldn't have to dislodge it but simply shear it so that it would crumble away from the rail.

Using the crowbar, he pushed away the rock debris from the rail sides and studied where and how to apply the crowbar so that the rock would fall away to both sides of the rail.

Realizing he would have only one shot at dislodging the rock, Frank flexed his muscles, set his legs, carefully situated the crowbar, sucked in his breath, and heaved.

Exactly as he had planned, the rock crumbled and fell away from the rail. The locomotive's flanged wheel settled perfectly on the rail.

Frank wheezed and mopped his brow with his shirt sleeve.

The conductor, the supervisor, and the crewmen shouted, "Bravo! Bravo!"

The conductor put his arms around Frank and said, "You've saved us hours of time. Thank you, sir."

The supervisor, still videoing, asked Frank's name, his nationality, and why he was traveling on Eurostar through the Chunnel.

Frank obliged, "I'm Frank Creech, marketing director, the Taos Art Colony, New Mexico, United States of America. We're going to Normandy to the American Cemetery and Memorial to commemorate the seventieth year of the Allied invasion of Normandy."

Diane joined the happy group, as Frank continued, "We chose the Eurostar because we wanted to experience the Chunnel. We heard the food and service were excellent, and so they were. Equally important, the Eurostar's station at Coquelles is near the cemetery."

The video/audio action secured by the supervisor on his cell phone was entitled "Chunnel Hero," with a still shot of Frank, and it included praising commentary from the Eurostar Corporate Social Responsibility (CSR) department. The chairman of CSR announced Eurostar would award Frank with a medal of honor.

BBC's helicopter whirred overhead as its crew filmed Frank and Diane stepping off the Eurostar train onto the Pas-de-Calais railway station platform in Coquelles.

Television cameras panned an excited crowd at the terminal as they waved American and French flags while cheering for the smiling couple.

Frank waved back.

Diane curtsied to the crowd, to the helicopter, and to the TV camera people.

Gary Green, spokesman for the Taos Art Colony, told the media how proud the colony was of Frank and how they looked forward to the colony's commemoration of the seventieth anniversary of the Allied invasion of Normandy.

Carroll Swanson texted Gary: "There's a big upswing in Colony sales apparently due to media coverage of Frank dislodging a rock from the locomotive's drive wheel after a rock slide in the Chunnel."

Carol shook his head while reading the *Wall Street Journal* coverage. The article included a photo of the Eurostar conductor and its maintenance supervisor, Diane, and Frank in a group hug.

Carroll nodded and said to himself, "He's invincible. Frank Creech is invincible."

Chapter 7

Normandy 2014

Prior to his European tour, Frank recalled reading in *Time Magazine* about the seventieth year anniversary of the Normandy American Cemetery and Memorial and that one million people visited the cemetery each year.

Time's article attributed the immaculately maintained cemetery and its memorial grounds to the exceptional care provided by the American Battle Monuments Commission. A cemetery plaque listed the 9,387 United States men and women buried in the cemetery, many of whom had died in the D-Day invasion, June 6, 1944.

In his research, Frank learned that only 39 percent of fallen American servicemen and servicewomen are interred in foreign soil. The remains of the majority of American service people killed overseas were transported home, accompanied by honor guards.

He put forward a plan to art colony director Gary Green and to SOSA president Dick Boyd to assemble as many artists as possible at Normandy to commemorate the seventieth anniversary of D-Day.

Frank proposed to the art colony directors and to President Dick Boyd a contest for best paintings depicting the D-Day invasion at Normandy. The first prize would be $10,000; second prize, $5,000; and third prize, $2,500. Award money was to be paid equally by both associations. There was a lot of "We'll get back to you" until Frank threw in the profit motive.

Diane Arnold, Frank's companion, spoke French fluently. She opened an art gallery in Colleville-sur-Mer, a town near the cemetery. She hired a well-known curator to run her gallery. He would display and sell the commemorative paintings. Proceeds, less 10 percent, would go to the artist's association for their redistribution.

The marketing department put her gallery on their client list and furnished the gallery with current colony catalogs.

Frank was learning the corporate game: put the directors in the loop. Better still, let them believe it was their idea, and they tended to cooperate more fully.

He went over the plan with Director Carroll Swanson, stating, "This fits in with Director Green's concept of expanding our markets in Europe."

Carroll responded, "Sounds like a plan. Go for it."

Frank laid out the plan for SOSA president Dick Boyd. Dick agreed to the plan.

He told Frank, "SOSA is up for anything that increases our sales."

Having received the OK from the two top managements, Frank asked Carroll and Dick to poll their people regarding using Diane's art salon to market their paintings.

The artists 100 percent OK'd the consignment of their pieces to Diane's art boutique. They did so for three excellent reasons in Dick's opinion.

First, the artists had experienced the unimaginable difficulty in transporting their art as baggage. Too many beautiful pieces were damaged beyond repair.

Second, commercial packaging and shipping was prohibitive because of the high cost of insuring the expensive artwork.

Third, the museum staff would refer visitors who wished to purchase commemorative paintings to Diane's nearby gallery.

The artists knew Diane's gallery would be the best outlet for their paintings.

The marketing department sent press releases to travel agencies and to major newspapers both in the United States and in the Allies involved in D-Day. They were notified that on the seventieth-year anniversary of the invasion of Normandy, the Taos Art Colony would conduct an art contest depicting scenes from D-Day at the Normandy American Cemetery and Memorial.

Frank, utilizing the knowledge gained in his thirteen years at the *Washington DC International Art Critics*, had instructed his marketing department manager Leslie D'Alessandro in the wording of the releases so as to catch an editor's attention.

Leslie's press releases included directions from the cemetery to Diane's Colleville-sur-Mer art gallery for those who wished to buy the commemorative paintings.

Frank was thoroughly impressed with Leslie's quick learning curve. Once she grasped what he wanted, it was quickly accomplished. He had seen that she arrived early for work and stayed until there was nothing further she could do.

Many of the artists and their families visited Diane's gallery, and Frank learned they liked the colorful and dynamic display of the art consigned to her.

Altogether, four hundred twelve colony and SOSA artists and their guests came to honor the fallen Normandy heroes.

Dick Boyd told Frank that prior to SOSA, freelance artists' earnings in Fort Myers had been near the federal poverty level. Unfortunately, neither the president nor the congress had espoused the SOSA (Save Our Starving Artists) cause.

Dick mentioned that since SOSA's organization, however, certain minimums for pricing were set and SOSA artists' income became closer to the national average. Still, it was not within everyone's economic comfort zone to make the journey to Normandy.

The competing artists brought the tools of their trade: palettes, brushes, smocks, stools and easels, paints, charcoal, pencils. They very much wanted to create something prizeworthy. Frank gave the contestants forty-eight hours to complete their paintings for the contest.

Non-entrant artists had been selected to judge the submitted art. They were people of totally equitable reputation. The contest rules provided that tied scores would split the prizes.

Frank walked among the competing artists while they were working. He asked, "Does anyone need anything?"

One of the Taos artists raised his hand and said, "Yes, I do."

Frank asked, "What do you need?"

He answered, wryly, "Talent."

Diane stopped by her gallery. She wanted to know where she could buy picnic food and supplies. Her gallery manager took her arm and walked her to the door, pointing to a little deli a block away.

She purchased a picnic basket, napkins, plastic cutlery, a bottle of cabernet, and a picnic blanket. She waited while the chef prepared one of Julia Child and Diane's favorite foods: quiche. It was a bacon and leek quiche whose aroma while baking was breathtaking to Diane.

She called Frank. "Honey, we're going to picnic in the French countryside. I have borrowed the gallery manager's car. I'll meet you at the gateway to the cemetery in twenty minutes. OK?"

"That's a great idea! I'm almost finished labeling the entries to ensure that no one substitutes an earlier painting."

They drove through the scenic countryside until they found a grassy knoll near a bridge overlooking a sparkling stream. They savored their delicious picnic.

Wiping their chins, Diane and Frank kissed.

They gathered up their picnic remnants. Frank said, "I have an idea."

She said, "I know where that idea will lead," as she picked up the picnic blanket and danced over the hill to the side of the knoll unseen from the road.

Tired and happy, the couple returned the car to her gallery manager and walked to their rented villa.

The next day, Diane went to her gallery; Frank stayed in the villa to work.

He returned phone calls and inquiries from potential gallery owners and fielded questions from artists around the globe.

Carroll sent a message to Frank advising him that Gary and wife Susan would come to the Normandy Memorial for the prize presentations. Frank thanked him for the heads-up.

When he was caught up, Frank called Leslie. They went over his reservations and travel details for his upcoming visit to Cairo, Egypt. Once again he was somewhat awed by the detail covered by his efficient marketing department manager.

"Judgment Day," Frank laughed as he cabbed to the Normandy American Cemetery and Memorial.

The artists, their families, and their guests gathered in the Visitor Center. One hundred twelve paintings were presented. The judges paced back and forth, making notes, talking among themselves. They consulted with Frank on particularly critical issues.

Diane Arnold and her volunteers served very much appreciated refreshments during the arduous judging procedure.

Frank observed that the display was an amazing array of paintings; high skies and brilliant color schemes were used by the Taos Art Colony contestants, and the SOSA members' artworks were much cooler and more solemn. All of the pieces depicted an aspect of the heroic battle of D-Day.

The winning paintings would be on display in the museum for a year. If not sold, they would be sent to Diane's gallery. The remaining paintings were sent to her gallery the following day.

Everyone stood when Frank, using a mic, welcomed them and asked, "How many of you have relatives interred in this cemetery?" Thirty people raised their hands.

Frank lowered his head and solemnly said, "God bless you and your families."

He continued, "You can tell from the time it took for the judges to find the winners of this contest, the competition was very close. There are many, many beautiful paintings on display in this building.

"Here to award the prizes are colony director Gary Green assisted by Dick Boyd, president of SOSA."

Frank led the applause.

While Dick held up each painting in prize order, Gary read the presentations.

Third prize: John Miller for his painting of two smiling young British soldiers, fingers splayed in the familiar Winston Churchill *V*, posed in front of a destroyed German Panzer tank on the heights above the beach.

Second prize: Suzanne Boemer for her painting depicting brave American nurses setting up IVs at their stations on the beach while shells burst around them.

First prize: Marty Freling for his haunting painting of the Christian crosses and Jewish Star of David granite markers. The background was a huge American flag and sunrays beaming on the hallowed grounds.

Each prize winner stepped up to applause and received their checks from Frank.

Gary said, "Today's program is our final day of this commemoration. I'll close our program with the inscription on Marty's painting.

"It's a quote from the American Battle Monuments Commission's first chairman, General John J. Pershing. 'Time will not dim the glory of their deeds.'"

Everyone left the Normandy American Cemetery and Memorial a little taller and a great deal prouder of their forefathers' sacrifices for their freedom.

Chapter 8

Cairo

Frank and Diane were in Cairo principally so Frank could call on the three galleries that purchased colony art.

Cairo was listed on the travel warning list posted on travel.state.gov. Frank routinely ignored such warnings.

Recognizing the lack of sustainment in women artists, the Taos Art Colony directors had asked Frank to visit the National Museum of Women in the Arts in Cairo. Women artists made up over 40 percent of Egyptian artists.

Gary explained to Frank that women made up 60 percent of classes in art schools in Taos. Yet they faded away in their twenties and thirties, and ultimately, the colony women artists were only 30 percent of the Taos artist population.

Although Taos art school owner Helen Quodomine proffered to the board that it might have a great deal to do with their childbearing ages, the directors wanted to learn how the Egyptians kept their women artists in the fold.

Frank texted the directors with what he had learned: The Egyptian art community had a maternity leave arrangement whereby pregnant artists were provided with monitors and ongoing art education in classrooms during the women's early terms and with an in-home continuing art education during their later stages of pregnancy. Evidently, from the number of women returning to the world of Egyptian art following the births of their children, the program worked.

With very little debate, the Taos Art Colony board adopted the Egyptian program. Bud Robitaille was asked to set up the program for pregnant Taos women artists and to monitor its results.

Over the next two days Frank called on the three gallery clients, private collectors, and art galleries not yet contracted with his *Art of the New World* catalogs especially prepared for Middle East galleries and private collectors.

He sold twelve pieces to the first gallery visited, a $300,000 net sale.

The second client gallery manager was interested in the new art, but the owner was out of town and wouldn't return for several weeks.

Frank had an appointment with the third client gallery for the following day.

Diane had vacationed in Cairo three years ago, visiting all the historic sites, so she spent her time shopping and sunbathing. Her birthday was two weeks away. Frank had provided her with her own credit card for joint expenses.

She reminded Frank that her birthday was two weeks away. He told her to buy something nice for her birthday.

She was interested in either an amulet or collar with the emerald green *wadj* design—which in ancient Egypt, she had learned, meant "good health."

Ever the food connoisseur, Frank asked the concierge at their hotel, the Pyramisa Cairo (overlooking the river Nile in Cairo's city center), where he might enjoy some good local cuisine. He suggested the Hello Lounge, a popular spot for American tourists, with a very good reputation.

The concierge told Frank that the Hello Lounge featured *Feteer*, a flaky, bubbly cushion of crispy pastry filled with anything from honey to beef and olives. Diane and Frank looked forward to dinner there.

Diane had gone to Khan el-Khalili bazaar to shop and to purchase a necklace she'd seen earlier in the week. It was Frank's birthday gift to her. She was late, and Frank was concerned.

After several unanswered phone calls to Diane, Frank became irritated at the general idea of women "shopping till they drop" and texted her to meet him at the Hello Lounge.

He ordered two *Feteer* meals. He ate his dinner, washed down with a mint tea, Shay bil na'na. The meal was delicious, but Frank was worried; he continuously eyed the entryway, hoping she would soon appear.

No Diane.

Frank had Diane's dinner boxed, left the Hello Lounge, and cabbed to their hotel.

It grew late in the evening. Frank's concern grew close to panic. He began to listen to the footsteps in the hallway.

Frank finally called the concierge, who immediately came to his room and listened to the details of Diane's absence. Concerned, the concierge phoned hotel security. Security sent two armed guards to the bazaar.

They reported they had canvassed the shops showing Diane's photo. Only one shop remembered her, the one where she had purchased her necklace.

Frank suggested they call the police. The concierge said there was no way the Egyptian police could help. He explained to Frank that the Egyptian police had their hands full due to the toppling of the Morsi regime by pro-Mubarek forces. There were riots, one of which killed twenty-four policemen.

Frank's focus was on finding Diane. He made calls to the U. S. embassy, his congressman, his senator, and to influential friends in Washington. Biting his lip, he also called Dick Brooks at the *Washington DC International Art Critics*. They were all sympathetic and promised they would do whatever they could to help him.

The next day he called the gallery owner with whom he had an appointment. He explained that he had to cancel because his lady friend had gone missing, and he was working hard to find her. The owner understood and wished Frank good luck.

Frank contacted Egyptian authorities, who politely listened to him and promised they "would look into it."

Then he began calling personal friends and acquaintances, pleading for help.

He was near exhaustion when Marty Freling returned his call. Marty advanced the theory that Diane could have been taken by Arab nomads to sell into white slavery.

He suggested Frank contact Barbara Orr. The Orrs were in Tel Aviv with a group of LTA (lighter-than-air craft) enthusiasts from Fort Myers to see the new Kothmann LTA Airship at Ben Gurion Airport.

Marty thought that maybe, just maybe, the new airship could be used in a searching for Diane.

Ladd, an LTA pilot, had read in the Fort Myers *News-Press* that the Kothmann Airship Company—which was known for the introduction of very successful LTA freight-handling airships—had developed an airship designed for passenger flight.

The airship was to be experimentally flown the day after their arrival in Tel Aviv.

Marty told Frank he'd call Barbara to explain the situation and to tell her that Frank would join them at Ben Gurion Airport the next day.

Marty told Frank that Barbara Orr was very persuasive in most situations that called for immediate action; if anyone could persuade the Kothmann executives to use their airship to search for Diane, it would be Barbara.

Frank booked the first flight from Cairo to Tel Aviv and joined the Orrs and their friends at the Kothmann private facility at Ben Gurion Airport.

After an hour of pleading with Kothmann's manager Fred Zebley, Barbara had convinced him to use the airship to search for Diane Arnold.

Fred sold the idea to the Kothmann owners. His argument was that the publicity would be profitable.

Joining Frank, Barbara, and Ladd Orr were friends Derrill Dare and Tal and Kathy Leonard, who would be spotters. Nona Bennett, Derrill's close friend, agreed to videotape the daring adventure. They joined hands, vowing to seek and to find Diane Arnold.

Fred checked the weather and told the rescue group that there was no severe weather in the area selected for their search, but he warned them sandstorms were a recurring event in that locale.

As the airship approached the outskirts of Cairo, traveling along a known smuggler's route, Barbara spotted a caravan.

Suddenly the sandstorm Fred predicted swirled around the airship, severely limiting their vision.

After twenty minutes of circling, the sandstorm abated.

Kathy shrieked, "Someone's waving a red bandana in the back of that old canvas-covered wagon!"

The airship reduced speed, descending to just twenty feet above the desert floor. Frank verified that the bandana was the one Diane had covered her head with for her trip to the bazaar.

The crew watched as the caravan's cantankerous camels, apparently frightened by the airship, broke free from their reins and scattered in different directions.

Pop! Pop! The renegades fired a couple of ineffective rifle shots in the general direction of the airship.

The pilot set the airship down forty yards from the caravan.

Tal Leonard, an ex-Marine, leaped out of the airship and waved his Colt .45 at the wagon driver while signaling him to release Diane. The nomad swung out of the driver's seat on the wagon, ran to the back of the wagon, and released her.

She ran to the airship. Tal helped Derrill and Ladd pull Diane inside the airship. Tal fired two shots in the air, and they pulled him into the airship and closed the door.

Barbara saw the Arabs had regrouped; they had mounted their camels, rifles in hand, and were charging the airship. She yelled to the pilot, "Go! Go!"

Joyfully reunited, Frank hugged Diane. He told her what Marty had suggested the Arabs had in mind for her.

He asked her, "Did they hurt you? Did they—"

Cutting him off, Diane said, exasperatingly, "If Marty was right they were probably transporting me to a desert sheikh. I was consigned goods."

"Well," Frank said with a wry grin, "I'll give the sheikh credit. He made an excellent selection."

Clinging to his arm, Diane cried softly. Shaking her head, she said to Frank, "You may find this humorous, but you weren't the victim. I doubt you'll find this humorous. *They stole my bracelet.*"

The pilot radioed Fred Zebley and excitedly reported the successful rescue.

Fred shouted, "Yahoo! Payback time!" He called his media friends and notified them of the rescue and gave them the airship's ETA.

When the airship taxied to the Kothmann facility, the reporters and photographers were waiting.

Barbara Orr was elected the spokesperson. She fielded the reporter's initial questions and then suggested, "Please look at the videotape Nona Bennett will share with you."

Diane took a few minutes to repair her disheveled clothing. She borrowed Kathy's makeup. When she emerged from the airship, the media interviewed her.

During the media interview, she had explained why she and Frank were in Cairo and mentioned the names of the three art gallery clients which stocked colony art.

Colony director Carroll Swanson walked past the marketing department tote board on his way to his office. He noticed an upswing in sales volume following the media coverage of Diane's abduction. He called Director Gary Green. "Gary, did you see the increase in sales?"

Chapter 9

Deception

Frank, comfortably settled in his seat, sipped his Jack Daniel's nip. Diane slept next to him on their way home to Taos. He checked his calls and messages using his smartphone's airplane mode.

His bank president called with an urgent request he call immediately. He pressed the call-back button. David Pohl got right to the point. "Frank, Diane Arnold called to report two necklaces she purchased in Cairo were stolen. Diane's credit card does not have a purchase protection feature. I'm sorry to tell you we cannot cover your loss."

"Dave, did you say two necklaces?"

"Yes, one for $16,047.50 and a second one for $12,500.07, purchased from the same jewelry store in Cairo on the same date."

Frank thanked Dave for personally calling him with the bad news. He decided not to awaken Diane. He reasoned, "She's had a traumatic experience. We can talk about the stolen necklaces after she's rested."

They rested the entire day of their first day home. The next day Frank had to go to his office in his marketing department. Diane had a required class at her acrylic art school.

Something was bothering Frank. He had that all too familiar gut feeling when his instincts told him something was amiss.

He had not broached the two and not one necklace issue with Diane. Both his and Diane's credit cards were auto paid from his checking account. His banking was paper free, and he had never questioned any charges.

He called David Pohl and asked him to furnish a summary of Diane's charges since the inception of her own credit card. Mr. Pohl said he could stop by the bank and pick up the monthly summaries later that afternoon.

Leslie went to lunch with Frank at Le Cueva Café, so they could continue his update on colony marketing activities.

His cell phone rang, and he allowed the call to go to voice message so as not to interrupt his work with Leslie.

After lunch, Leslie had an errand to run and left quickly at her brisk pace.

Frank sat down on the weather-protected bench in the Taos Chile Line Transportation stop and listened to his voice mail.

"Hi, Frank. It's Fred Zebley, Kothmann Airships in Tel Aviv. I have some bad news. We received a formal complaint from the Egyptian interior ministry stating that our airship had attacked the Bedouin Camel Caravan tour and abducted a tourist at gunpoint."

Fred continued, "The complaint states that the attack was in violation of the peace pact between Israel and Egypt and may have dire effects on that pact. A copy of the complaint was sent to the Israeli government. Please call me."

Frank took a sip from the water bottle he bought at the café. A bus stopped, and he waved it on.

Frank called Fred Zebley and was routed to voice mail. At the tone he left a message, "It's Frank Creech returning your call. I'm stunned and don't know how to respond. Please call me back."

He finished his water and put the bottle in the recycle container. Walking back to his office, he muttered, "Bedouin Camel Caravan tour. Tour, tour?"

Checking his watch, Frank walked to the bank to see if Diane's credit card activity summaries had been printed.

As he entered the bank, David Pohl waved him into his office. "Here's your requested printouts, Frank. Included are Diane's charges for the month to date."

Frank reflected, "David is a typical bank executive. If he saw anything suspicious in Diane's charges, he kept it to himself." He thanked Dave and went across the street to his office.

"Leslie, unless you need me for something, I'm working on a project that won't keep."

"No problem, boss."

Frank started from back to front. He slapped his forehead, "There it is—a charge for tour 12, Bedouin Camel Caravan Tours, Ltd. $212.50. She knew I never looked at her credit card charges."

He highlighted the item and continued to read the entries, his eyes getting larger while his jaw began to tighten as he continued to highlight charges that were inexplicable.

He put a bookmark between the report pages, got up, and hurried to the restroom. After using the urinal, he washed his hands, splashed his face, and wiped it with a paper towel. On the way back to his desk, he stopped at the water cooler and had two cups of cold water.

Frank disliked hearing men using cell phones in restrooms, considering it an intrusion on the privacy of other restroom users. He realized he could miss Fred's call and ran back to his desk.

The missed call message was on his phone. There was no voice mail, and Frank quickly inserted a memory stick in the phone's USB port and touched the call-back button.

"Hi, Frank, I apologize for the phone tag—"

Frank interrupted, "Fred, I have a memory stick in my phone. Please tell me again, from the top, how you received the complaint from the Egyptian interior ministry and its content. I may need to share the information with my bosses here at the colony."

"Sure thing," Fred replied. He recited the original information he had given Frank and added it was sent certified mail, date and signature of recipient required."

Fred continued, "There is a damage section in the complaint—the amount demanded is $250,000 U.S. to recover the caravan tour's losses which are detailed in the complaint. An additional $1,000,000 U.S. is demanded for punitive damages.

"There is—in addition to the damages demand—a threat of civil action, a citation for an 'act or war,' and a thinly veiled threat of retaliation. Maybe I should send you a copy?"

"Oh, please do, FedEx if you will."

"I certainly will send a copy of the complaint to you today. My Kothmann Airships owners are very upset with me, as you can imagine. We've turned the complaint over to our law firm. I have an appointment with the lead attorney tomorrow morning to go over my role in what we were told was a rescue attempt of your kidnapped companion, Diane Arnold. You can imagine the spot I'm in."

"Yes, I regret very much having put you into this deplorable situation. And you have my word, if there is anything I can do to ameliorate this unfortunate exposure to you and Kothmann Airships, it will be done. Thank you, Fred."

Frank decided to wait for the copy of the Egyptian complaint before sharing the information with the colony directors and facing the music.

"Oh my, double whammy, and they both appear to have been caused by Diane. The primary one being the complaint filed against Kothmann Airships wherein I think the colony may be a complicit party because of my role in the 'rescue' of Diane. The second one is the credit card I gave her seems to have been used routinely to steal from me."

Frank excused himself from the marketing department and walked to the casita.

He went to the management office and told them he had misplaced the key to the safety deposit box mounted on the wall in the master bedroom. The casita's clerk charged him $2.00 for the new key.

Before he left the office, something occurred to him. "Oh, by the way, I have some friends interested in renting here. Do you have any openings?"

"Maybe in September, we'll have something. We have a waiting list for the casitas. We've been booked full for over three years, and we're working on an expansion into the open lot behind us."

Frank realized Diane had lied to him about the likely availability of a casita on the night of his arrival in Taos.

He opened the safe, took the two thin boxes off the top shelf to the sitting room, and opened them. He stared at the two necklaces. Shaking his head, he uttered, "What might have been unbelievable has become a reality."

He checked his emails, responded where he could, and placed the others which required research in the reminder app.

Frank called Leslie. He left a message: "We need to review the plans for the South American campaign—it's only two weeks away. I'll see you at nine in the morning."

He opened a new bottle of Jack Daniel's and poured two ounces over ice into his tumbler. He continued looking through Diane's charges, stopping to highlight suspicious purchases. The last one highlighted was the purchase of *two* wedding dresses in London. He assumed one was for her sister, A. A.

Diane came home with their takeout dinners from the café. She saw Frank in the sitting room. "Long day with a paintbrush, but I'm making progress. I've got our dinners from the café, honey. I'll bet you're tired and hungry, aren't you?"

"I'm tired but not hungry yet. Pour yourself a glass of wine and join me. We need to talk."

"Well, yes, we do. I'll put our dinners in the fridge and be there in a sec, my love."

Frank heard the toilet flush and the sink being used. He took a sip of his drink and thought, *I wish it weren't necessary to have this confrontation. I enjoy Diane's company so much."*

Then he remembered the stolen paintings from the MoMA and the taped conversation on her answering machine. He sighed deeply, clasped his hands together, and muttered, "Need to get this over with."

In her bathrobe, glass of wine in her hand, Diane came into the sitting room. When she saw the necklaces displayed on the table, she sat her glass of wine down, looked at Frank quizzically, and asked, "Am I in trouble?"

"We're both in trouble." He put the memory stick in his laptop and let her listen to Fred Zebley's recital of the Egyptian interior ministry statement.

Wordlessly, Frank gave her the bank's summary of her credit card charges, page turned to the highlighted purchase of the Bedouin Camel Caravan Tours tour 12.

Diane began to cry. "I love you, Frank. I was planning on our being husband and wife. I searched for a suitable location for our home together here in Taos. I needed to stimulate your interest in me. I wanted to make you more aware of my importance to you. I see now that I went too far."

"Why did you purchase two necklaces?"

"Rather than my buying a necklace for my birthday gift from you, I purchased two necklaces so that you could choose one for me. I would have returned the other one."

"Then why did you report them stolen?"

"I panicked," she said, wiping the tears from her cheeks with a tissue from her bathrobe.

"I hope you realize that you and I are in serious trouble because of your deception, Diane. I have to take the statement together with Fred Zebley's conversations with me to the colony's directors tomorrow. It's not going to be a pleasant experience, I'm sure."

Frank took a sip of whiskey. Diane closed her eyes and drank half of her wine in a single gulp.

"Do you want your dinner, Frank?"

"Yes, please join me."

"OK. Can we forget about the trouble I've caused just for tonight?"

"We can try."

After dinner they retired. They made love, both feeling it might be for the last time, and then fell asleep in each other's arms.

In the morning, Diane prepared Frank's coffee and put the churros from the café on the kitchen table.

Frank cocked his head to the right, smiled, and asked, "Diane, one more thing, and I promise to shut up. Was that a setup at the Old Blinking Light?"

"Yes. I wanted to meet you after reading the announcement of your new position with the colony, because I am an aspiring artist. I showed your photo to the cab driver and the hostess and paid him a hundred dollars and her twenty dollars. And I'm not sorry!

"I know you care for me, Frank, or you would never have gone to so much trouble to get me back."

"Yes, I do care for you, Diane. Pick out the necklace you want."

"Oh, Frank, thank you so much," Diane said as she hugged him.

The moment he left, Diane called her sister. "A. A., I could be in big trouble. Are you still seeing your barrister friend? I'll need his advice as quickly as possible."

Without asking Diane what the trouble was, A.A. replied, "Yes, we're quite close. Chester should be back from court now. I'll ask him to call you."

Diane recited to A.A.'s friend Chester all the details, including her role, in the Egyptian affair. She asked, "Could I be in trouble?"

Chester pondered for a few seconds, "Yes, you could be complicit in an illegal activity or wrongdoing."

"What should I do?"

"Do you still have your British citizenship?"

"Yes, I am a dual citizen."

"I didn't tell you this, OK? Leave the United States as quickly as possible, return to your home in Chelsea. Make up an excuse—your mommy is sick, whatever. Extradition from Great Britain to the U.S. is becoming quite difficult due to the harsh prison sentences imposed by U.S. courts on those who are extradited."

"Thank you, Chester. Please tell A.A. I'll call her with my ETA at Heathrow as soon as I can."

Diane packed her suitcases, surprised at how much clothing she had to pack. She left the very light summer things in a box marked "give to Salvation Army." Her luggage was down to one bag, less than fifty pounds which she would check, and her large carry-on tote.

She wrote a note to Frank and left it on the coffee table in the sitting room:

> *Honey, I'm so sorry. My mommy is sick, and I have to return to Chelsea at once.*
>
> *I didn't want to bother you at work, knowing what you have in front of you today.*
>
> *The other necklace is in the safe. My flight will be my last use of the credit card you gave me.*
>
> *Please let me keep my little gallery in France, it's my only source of income.*
>
> *This is probably for the best. Think of me sometimes.*
>
> *Love,*
> *Diane*

She cabbed to the bank, had the cab wait, closed her checking and savings accounts, and went to Taos Regional Airport where she was booked on a flight to Santa Fe to make her connection to London.

Frank sipped his now-cool second cup of coffee, reading his South American campaign structure, watching the clock, waiting for the FedEx delivery.

M.E. called, "Frank, hold the line. Gary needs to talk with you."

Gary said, quickly, "Frank I just had a call from a London gallery owner who told me he heard on a BBC news program that the Egyptian interior ministry claims a Kothmann Airship attacked a caravan tour and abducted a tourist at gunpoint. Please tell me that wasn't your rescue of Diane?"

"One second, boss, I'm signing for a FedEx package sent from the Kothmann Airship manager in Tel Aviv." After a moment, he said, "Yes, it was our rescue mission. May I come to your office?"

"Yes, immediately, Frank."

Frank arrived at Gary's office at the same time Bud, Carroll, and Ken were walking to the door.

Frank put his memory stick in Gary's laptop. "Gentlemen, please listen to this, and then we'll open the package from Kothmann."

Before they read the statement, Gary called M.E. into the office. "See if Vic Lich is in his office now."

They grouped closely and read the statement together.

M.E. popped her head in the door. Holding the phone, she said, "Vic's on the line now and has open time after lunch."

Gary said, "Fine. Carroll and Frank will be there at 2:00 p.m." He explained, "I have an appointment, and Ken needs to watch the store. Let me know what our exposure may be in this affair as soon as possible."

Vic read the statement and listened to the memory stick conversation.

He looked up at the ceiling. Then he rolled his chair forward, looked at Carroll, and said, "Tell Gary the colony is in the clear. The action taken by Frank to rescue Diane was on his own. He is not an employee of the colony, he is a contractor. The colony has no liability."

"And Frank, if you were my client, I would tell you to not engage in any further discourse with Kothmann Airships."

Carroll tightened his lips, pointed at Frank, and said, "And I'm telling you to button your lip," while he made the zipper motion.

Chapter 10

Sao Paulo

Frank realized his coming trip to South America would be his first trip without Diane since he had met her over two years ago.

He had not heard from her since the day she left to return to her ancestral home in Chelsea. He cancelled her charge card and, per her request, donated the box of clothing she left to the Salvation Army.

A week after Diane left, Leslie D'Alessandro, his marketing department manager, had a talk with Frank. "Boss," she said, "I don't mean to interfere, but may I make a suggestion of a personal nature to you?"

"Leslie, I value our relationship and your judgment. I'll appreciate any suggestions you may have for me. It shows, huh?"

"Yes, you're usually up and excited about a new campaign, but you've been in a solitary mood and appear somewhat dispirited. The ad people have produced a terrific program to get us off to a head start in South America. We need to utilize that program and make a good showing for this important campaign.

"Something that will definitely help, in my opinion—when you go back to your casita after work, gather up all the feminine things, Diane's personal touches, and any other reminders of her and get rid of them. Cheer up, get over it, and get on with your life."

"Leslie, that may be exactly what I needed—a swift kick in the ass! I'll do exactly what you suggested, and thank you."

The Taos Art Colony marketing department was eager to trial run their new sales agenda in one of their toughest markets, South America, beginning in bustling São Paulo. The program paired groups of paintings by content: mountains, ski resorts, trees, flowers, lakes, and tourist attractions.

Their aggressive plan included floor planning and volume discounts.

The advertising package was designed by the prestigious ABC's of Advertising, Inc., Clio Award–winning firm, whose owners—Cecilia Albrecht, Ron Bradley, and Neil Chartrand—are residents of Caloosa Yacht & Racquet Club in Fort Myers. The firm was considered tops in the field of advertising for the arts.

The package included a trip to Taos, airfare, and hotel accommodations for São Paulo art gallery owners, sponsored by the Taos Chamber of Commerce.

Frank had read in the *New York Times* travel section that São Paulo is the megatropolis of South America, with a population of over twenty million people. In 2005 there were forty-one art galleries. In 2014 there were 110 art galleries. The time seemed right to open this important market.

Each art gallery received three serial mailings from the colony, outlining the new marketing plan.

"Brazil, where hearts were entertaining June . . ." Frank hummed, as his plane cruised at close to five hundred miles per hour on its way to São Paulo, Brazil.

It took Frank a solid week of work to contact the gallery owners. His cell phone had an app which translated English to Portuguese and, if required, Portuguese to English. He followed the RSVP invitations with both seen calls and phone calls and secured 136 confirmations for the art colony presentation and dinner the next Saturday evening.

Frank chose the Figueira Rubaiyat restaurant for the Saturday night presentation and dinner. The restaurant, built around a fig tree, had the local reputation by Paulistanos as the very finest dining and entertainment in São Paulo.

São Paulo's mayor graciously accepted Frank's invitation to dine with the city's art gallery owners. The dignitaries at the mayor's table appeared to enjoy the presentation.

Frank walked over to their table and introduced himself just as the musicians began to play the traditional music of Brazil, the samba.

"Samba?" asked the beautiful Latina, as she rose from the mayor's table.

Frank looked around and realized she was asking *him*.

"I'll give it a try," chortled Frank, as he took her hand, leading her to the dance floor.

He led with a left toe double tap followed by a left heel double tap, then switched to right foot, alternating. His partner looked once at his moves and followed expertly. They began to make turns, continuing the tap pattern. His moves were solid with the rhythm of the drums, hers artistic and flowing, her beautiful white dress reflecting the pink light beams searching the dance floor.

Frank looked at her as they swirled, she circling around him. She was at least five feet ten and, with her three-inch heels, only an inch or so short of his own height. Her hair was an onyx black weave, her sparkling eyes golden tan, her skin almost the color of her eyes. She was stunningly beautiful, svelte, sweet, and sensual.

As they left the dance floor, Lola said, "Frank, you're not a good samba dancer. You're an excellent samba dancer!"

Frank nodded his head and flourished his hand, "Well, I just led, all the beauty of the dance was you. I am disadvantaged, however. I don't know your name."

"I'm Lola DeLicio, the mayor's niece."

He walked her back to her table. As he pulled her chair out, she gently touched his hand. "One second," she opened her clutch purse and handed him her Samba Troupe business card, "Please call me tomorrow, after nine."

Frank took the card, nodded politely to Lola and to the other guests, and left them. His hand raised in a salute, he said, "Have a pleasant evening."

He wanted to dance with Lola again, but he needed to thank his guests and wish them a good evening.

It was a great evening; everything went well. Frank was confident orders would flow to the art colony.

At nine fifteen the next morning, which was as long as Frank could wait, he called Lola.

"Thank you for the great samba. I'm too tall for most of my dance partners, but not for you." Her voice sounded like music. "What are you doing the next couple of days?"

"I have two days of follow-up calls to make on the art gallery owners, lunches and dinners and cocktails, and some forty people to see before I leave for Rio."

"In time for the World Cup, I'll bet."

"Yes, and I'll delight our customer base there—I have thirty select seats to give to them."

"Have you ever been to Rio?" Lola asked.

"No."

"I grew up there and have family there. Could you use a guide?"

"Oh yes, I could. That would be wonderful! I'm booked on TAM flight 401 arriving Wednesday at 1:15 p.m."

Lola noted the flight number and ETA in her phone's calendar.

"Frank, one of my attractions to you is your dancing skill. Outside of professional dancers, many men I know pretty much just shuffle their feet. May I ask where you learned to dance so skillfully?"

"Long story short, I hope. After my tour of duty in Vietnam, I returned to my family's home in East Lansing, Michigan. Using my GI Bill education benefits, I was accepted at Michigan State University for the fall semester. My sister couldn't abide anyone sitting around all summer.

"She managed a Fred Astaire dance studio. It was back in the day when you followed paper step patterns taped to the floor.

"After a couple of months of instruction, I began to teach dance. I taught dance, increased the complexity of the dance steps and the different dances, and earned my spending money during my five years of college.

"I was in the athletic program at MSU. There are steps in athletics as well as dancing. I know that the two things complemented each other."

"Did you keep up with dancing after college?"

"When I was a stringer for the *Washington DC International Art Critics* I attended Latin dance classes as time permitted. In fact, I met two of my three ex-wives on the dance floor and danced my way out of three marriages."

"I'll pick you up at the airport in Rio, dancing man," Lola said enthusiastically. They ended the call.

Frank sang, "We stood beneath an amber moon and softly murmured. Someday soon, we'll kiss and cling together. Brazil, Brazil."

Chapter 11

Rio de Janeiro

Lowering the TAM airliner landing wheels, the pilot began the plane's descent into Rio's international airport. Frank looked out the window at the Christ the Redeemer, a 130-foot statue on top of Corcovado Mountain, once considered the largest Art Deco statue in the world.

What a sight, he thought. *Almost worth the trip itself.*

Lola DeLicio watched Frank stride toward the baggage carousel and reflected, *He walks like John Wayne walked, strong, purposeful!*

The airport handled 230,000 passengers each day, and that made it easy for her to sneak up behind Frank.

She put her arms around his waist and said, "Welcome to Rio."

Frank spun around, placed his hands gently behind her neck, pulled her to him, and passionately kissed her full on the lips.

Lola gasped, "Is that how you greet all your tour guides?"

Grabbing his heavy suitcase off the carousel, Frank responded, "Only if they look like you." His canvas suitcase was worn but still serviceable. He traveled so frequently he had commissioned SOSA artist Rickie Carter to paint two palm trees on each side of his suitcase for quick identification.

They walked out of the terminal and over the trestle to the parking garage. It was a very comfortable seventy degrees. Frank wore his leisure travel khaki suit. Lola had on a silk yellow cling dress. Frank thought the dress defined her figure most advantageously.

As they drove away from the airport in her gold Beamer, Lola told Frank, "The City of Samba will be our first stop. We'll have lunch at the Brazilian Steakhouse and watch the rehearsal of my Samba Troupe performers for Carnival in Rio, unless you have calls to make this afternoon?"

Frank said, "My calls start tomorrow morning. You read my mind, I was thinking of a Brazilian steak and would like to see your dancers samba. Do you own the Samba Troupe?"

"I wish I did. My uncle Fernando, whom you met in São Paulo, is the owner. I have 20 percent interest. I book our performances, teach our new people, choreograph their dances, and chaperone the young ladies."

"I should have guessed that, Lola. You picked up my samba steps immediately. And in case I haven't mentioned it, you are unquestionably the most beautiful woman I've ever seen."

"Flattery will get you everywhere," laughed Lola, playfully patting his cheek.

Lola ordered their lunch: costela, tender and juicy beef ribs slowly cooked and seasoned to perfection, accompanied by a Brazilian baked potato dish, washed down with a Rio Grande do Sul merlot.

After lunch they enjoyed the polished rehearsal of Lola's samba dancers. The costumes, the brilliant colors, and the perfect choreography delighted Frank.

Lola drove Frank to his hotel, Belmond Copacabana Palace, Avenida Atlântica. He needed to register and freshen up. She said, "I'll call you later. Maybe we can have a light evening meal?"

He said, "Do that, *mulher bonita* (beautiful woman)."

"Ola, bonito. (Hello, handsome.) Buy a Speedo swim suit and Ipanema flip-flops from the men's shop in the lobby. Put them on and meet me in the hotel bar in, say, an hour?"

Frank worked the translator app. "Dar o sim a. (I approve.)"

At dinner the waiter explained that while the Brazilian wines were as good, if not better, than those of Argentina, they had only come into world markets recently.

Frank and Lola relaxed and enjoyed their feijoada (pork and beef stew with beans), paired with an excellent Brazilian Cabernet Sauvignon, Pizzato Concentus.

Afterward, they walked hand in hand on the white sandy beach, a few yards past the hotel's beachfront area. Lola spread her shawl on the sand, and they sat on it.

Frank looked at her black bikini and thought to himself, *How many women could wear that swimsuit?*

They savored the breeze off the Atlantic, listened to the breakers, held hands, canoodled.

A nearby couple, Americans, laughingly shouted, "Get a room."

Frank began to rise. Lola pulled him back down, saying, "They're just being cute, honey. Be cool."

She tossed her long right leg over his thighs, her right arm over his chest, her head cuddled into his neck. Her frangipani perfume titillated his senses. They lay quietly, not speaking, watching a freighter on the horizon slowly sailing north.

"We, uh, I have a room."

"Frank," she said, hesitatingly, "I'm very tempted, but I am so well-known. If I went to your room, everyone in Rio would know it by 10:05 a.m. tomorrow morning and that can't happen. Let's call it an evening. Please, please, don't be upset. The right time and place will come soon. I'll work out a plan, honey."

The next day Lola drove to São Paulo to register new students in her Samba Troupe school. Samba dancers were part of her business. She told Frank the troupe's turnover was similar to the art colony's loss of young women in their twenty's and thirty's.

Frank spent the next two days calling on his art gallery customers and contacts, delivering the World Cup soccer tickets, selling the new Taos Art Colony South American marketing plan. He crammed a week's work into two days, in the hope that he would have time to spend exclusively with Lola before his flight on Sunday afternoon.

On Friday evening, Lola called. "Frank, check out in the morning. I'll be at your hotel by eleven thirty. I have a plan I think you'll like."

She spotted his palm-painted suitcase under the canopy at the Belmond Copacabana Palace before she saw Frank. The doorman put the suitcase in the trunk of her golden Beamer, next to her pink suitcase.

Frank hopped into the car, big smile on his face. "Where are we headed?"

"Ola, bonito. We are going to Búzios, about a two-hour drive. I reserved a seaside villa for us. It is stocked with fine foods and wine, and has its own private beach."

After they settled in the villa, they enjoyed a light lunch of cold lobster tails and fresh fruit, paired with Santiago Sauvignon Blanc on their balcony overlooking the Atlantic Ocean.

He couldn't help appreciating Lola even more than before. He thought, *She paid for this beautiful hideaway. I don't remember Diane ever buying anything for me. Whoa, almost forgot that tuna wrap she bought me in New York City at the deli that didn't take credit cards.*

They walked down to their private beach. Lola put her shawl on the sand. She inserted Brazilian Luiz de Aquino's CD *Noites Claras* (Clear Nights) in her portable CD player.

They escalated the passion begun at the Rio beach. Lola slipped off her bikini; Frank dropped his Speedo. Their flip-flops were tossed aside. Lola straddled Frank, and they made love, and they made love, and they fell in love.

In the shower, Frank sang Taio Cruz's "Telling the World."

"She's the one, she's the one. I say it loud, I'm telling the world. She's the one I can live for, I've found the girl, the one who deserves every part in my heart, the one I can live for, a reason for life."

They were quiet on the drive to the airport. Each reflected on the love they had found together and the problems they would likely encounter.

At the airport, after many goodbye kisses, they promised each other they would be together again soon.

On the American Airlines flight home, Frank lined up on his tray table a row of empty little nip Jack Daniel's bottles. He thought, *I've enjoyed this bourbon on so many occasions—some bad, some good. There's no solace needed tonight. I'm a happy man.*

Chapter 12

SW Florida Art Colony

Frank Creech thought it was going to be a long month; he so missed his beloved Lola DeLicio. He determined the best thing to do was to continue his productivity.

He had kept in touch with Marty Freling. Marty advised him that the SOSA group of Fort Myers would disband, having failed to gain congressional grants for its artists.

Frank phoned Director Gary Green. "Gary, I've just learned that SOSA is going to disband. We will lose the income generated from sales of their art unless we act quickly."

"What do you have in mind, Frank?"

Frank kept it short. "Make them a branch."

"Hmm . . . I'll get back to you."

Three days later, Gary updated Frank. He told him the directors had met with their attorney, Vic Lich. Vic had amended the colony's charter. The master corporation had become the Art Colonies of America. The new branches would be the Taos Art Colony and the SW Florida Art Colony.

Vic Lich advised Gary that the SW Florida Art Colony entity would require certification by the SOSA members. Gary passed that on to Frank to handle.

Frank called Marty Freling. Marty and SOSA president Dick Boyd arranged to have as many of the SOSA members as could be gathered at the Hyatt Regency Coconut Point Resort and Spa, Bonita Springs, Florida (halfway point between Fort Myers and Naples). They would be asked to vote on becoming a branch of the Art Colonies of America at a set cost to them of 10 percent of sales. They arranged for a Saturday morning meeting.

Marty called Frank from the Hyatt lobby at 2:00 p.m. on Saturday. "Two hundred forty-six artists voted unanimously to accept the proposal. It was a win-win situation, a no-brainer."

"Well done, Marty. Stay for a few minutes. I'll need to call you back."

Frank called Gary. "Gary, we got the deal. May I ask Marty if he would like to head up the SW Florida Art Colony?"

"By all means, do so. Marty has been an important part of the colony's success. Tell him the salary will be $120,000 plus expenses."

"You can OK that?"

"I believe I can. There have been some management changes. I've been named chairman of the board of the Art Colonies of America. Oh, and Carroll Swanson has been appointed president of the corporation. We appointed Ken Geelhood, longtime secretary/treasurer of the colony, to the board of directors. I believe you know Ken. Also, for your information, Bud Robitaille, a former director, has accepted the presidency of the Taos Art Colony. He feels he can grow the branch."

"Congratulations to all of you. Your hard work has paid off!"

"Frank, remember what I told you sometime ago? 'Time is money.' Get on with it."

"Yes, sir."

Frank called Marty back. "Marty, we'd like to have you head up the SW Florida Art Colony."

"I'm flattered, but I believe you know the answer has to be no. My art is selling well, with thanks to you for the markets I am now enjoying. Judy and I just want to relax and enjoy our family and friends. Of course I'll continue to be helpful whenever I can. Dick Boyd can handle it quite well."

"I'll call Dick. Thanks, Marty, for everything."

"You're entirely welcome, Frank."

Frank called Dick next. "Am I speaking to Dick Boyd, president of the SW Florida Art Colony, whose annual salary is $120,000, plus expenses and employee benefits?"

Frank explained the corporate reorganization to Dick.

"Oh my goodness, thank you and the colonies so much!" Dick exclaimed.

"No, Dick. You need to thank Marty. He pulled all the right strings, as usual. You'll need to come to Taos next Monday for a week of indoctrination conducted by Director Ken Geelhood. Gary said to bring Gail."

He continued, "Travel and transportation will make your reservations and FedEx the information to you, and the colony's limo will transport you and Gail from the airport."

Frank left a voice mail for Gary. He related his conversation with Marty and Dick.

Then he called the colony's personnel department. He spoke with Marion Jones and asked her to send Dick his employment papers.

Oh my, my, pondered Frank. *In light of my disruptive involvement in the melee on Constitution Avenue in Washington, D.C, during the SOSA march, I do feel a sense of atonement in helping the new SW Florida Art Colony get off the ground.*

Chapter 13

Buenos Aires

The colony's team would depart for Buenos Aires in one month, after the three consecutive mailings to targeted area galleries, with the same plan which worked so well in São Paulo.

Frank and the marketing department people chose the Hilton Buenos Aires because it had the largest convention center and a convenient downtown location near a number of high-end art galleries. The hotel's spacious conference room would serve as both the display area for paintings and for the presentation dinner party.

Not quite coincedentally, Lola DeLicio had booked her Samba Troupe at the Teatro Colón, a high-end performing arts theater in Buenos Aires, for the same week as the colony's art exhibition.

The Hilton staff had arranged a car and driver for Frank for his seen calls, and Frank had installed a translator app for Spanish-English on his cell phone.

He was told the temperatures would be in the nippy 50°F–60°F for Team Bueno's visit to Buenos Aires.

Team Buenos was comprised of Dick and Gail Boyd, Bud and Kathleen Robitaille, and Frank Creech.

Gary approved Frank's request that the wives be paid per diem wages equal to their husband's salary for their assistance.

Although it was a lengthy trip—twenty-two hours for the Taos people, sixteen hours for the Fort Myers people—they were all excited for their opportunity. The LAN flight from Miami set down at 2:35 p.m. on Wednesday at Ministro Pistarini International Airport.

After checking in, the team went to the display room. They uncrated the art and mounted half of the hundred pieces selected for first display on racks. Held in reserve were an additional one hundred paintings.

A tired Team Buenos elected to break for dinner. Frank wanted to try the "Food with an Argentine twist," advertised by the hotel's El Faro Restaurant. The specials were *bife de chorizo Argentino* (juicy steak) and salmon with a caprese salad. The *bife* was paired with an Argentine pinot noir, while the salmon was paired with a superb Riesling. Dessert was dulce de leche with churros. Dick nodded his head. "Good choice, Frank."

After dinner, the team walked to the Rio de la Plata harbor. They sat on park benches, enjoyed the breeze, and talked about what they needed to do the next day.

In the morning, the team returned to their display room work.

On Thursday, Frank saw the owners of six of the eight art galleries targeted. The remaining two owners would see him on Friday. He inked a contract with an art gallery in Montevideo. He'd follow up with all the next day. He felt it was a good day.

Team Buenos visited one of the prestigious art galleries near the hotel. On display they saw several pieces of art produced by Buenos Aires' deceased surrealist painter, Roberto Aizenberg, the most noted surrealist painter in the world. The team now understood why South America was such a tough market for imported art.

Dinner on Thursday evening was at Cabana Las Lilas, a short walk from the hotel. The restaurant was noted for its Argentine barbeque. They tried the local beer, Quilmes. The label read, "Established in 1888."

During dinner, the team reviewed its day and its plans for Friday's activities, which included receiving and placing the lobby signs, setting up cash boxes and credit card devices, and arraying the necessary sales documents. And they needed to test the audio system.

On Friday, Team Buenos had two more days remaining before the exhibition. With the new corporate structure, the team would be with him for all major exhibitions. He felt they needed solid grounding.

Frank made ten seen calls (in-person visits) on art gallery owners. Three contacts were very interested, and he felt certain at least two would place orders. He consigned twenty paintings, using his catalog, to a shop in suburban Buenos Aires. Two of the day's contacts were branches of a São Paulo gallery with several colony paintings on display. They told Frank that they anticipated continued growth in art sales, despite Argentina's brash default on monies owed hedge fund creditors.

RSVPs for Saturday's dinner presentation by mail and in person now totaled fifty-eight. Frank wanted a hundred.

He thought, *There's a lot more work to be done.*

As he walked into the foyer of his suite, Frank nearly stumbled over a large carton. It contained the suits he had ordered for Team Buenos. He checked the spelling of the individual's names embroidered on the pockets, under "The American Art Colonies." The soft wool slacks, skirts, and jackets were light gray; the embroidery on the patches was bright gold.

After trying on his suit, Frank had the bellhops deliver the rest of the exhibition suits to the team.

His cell rang, "Ola minha linda mulher!" (Hello, pretty woman!)

"Ola, bonito," she anxiously replied. "I will be about fifteen minutes late. I just got my Samba Troupe settled in."

Sheathed in a mid-length mauve dress, accented with a three-row pearl necklace and matching bracelet, Lola DeLicio scanned the El Faro dining room. Sighting Frank, she walked purposefully toward him, eyes straight ahead, riveted on Frank's beaming face.

Frank noticed the room had suddenly become silent. No clatter of utensils or plates, as everyone watched the stunningly tall beautiful woman stride across the dining room.

Team Buenos and Lola chatted and happily devoured their typical Argentine dinner of asada (grilled meats with a garlicky green chimichurri sauce) and roasted vegetables, washed down with an excellent Argentine Malbec wine.

Frank was happy that it seemed everyone was in good spirits.

Dessert was the popular dulce de leche made with quince, sweet potato, fig, and chayote jams, over a slice of Port Salut type cheese.

Finally alone in the elevator, Lola and Frank kissed passionately, he with a hand on her buttocks, she with a hand on his crotch.

"Wanton woman," Frank chortled (a gleeful chuckle and snort sound).

Lola went to the bathroom. As Frank began to undress, he remembered the white silk sheer nightgown he bought her. He took it out of the chest of drawers and hung it on the bathroom doorknob. "Honey, something for you on the doorknob."

Her golden tan arm snaked out of the bathroom door and snatched the nightgown.

After she came out of the bathroom, Frank took his turn.

When he came out, Lola was lying on the bed in her new nightgown. She curled her forefinger and said, "Come here, bonito."

Basking in the afterglow with her legs over Frank's thighs, Lola said, "Regrettably, I'll have to go now to chaperone my young ladies. Eu te amo." (I love you.)

On Saturday morning, Team Buenos met for their Argentine breakfast: strong coffee, cereal, juice, and pastries. They thanked Frank for furnishing their exhibition attire.

Following up with three of the art gallery owners, Frank secured orders from one gallery.

He said to himself, "I went one for three. Good enough, for the major leagues."

He called on a few high-end boutiques. They were very receptive to original art. He learned that boutique patrons would buy art to match the color of a couch or for a variety of other reasons not related to beauty or appreciation. Two boutiques ordered a half dozen of each pieces from the colony's catalog.

Lola called Frank. "Honey, don't expect me tonight. I've just learned we are going to have an opening night party after the performance. I'm so sorry."

"That's OK, baby, you wore me out last night. I'm not Superman, you know."

"You could've fooled me," giggled Lola.

At 10:05 on Sunday morning, the first seven people arrived. They strolled through the room and spoke with the representatives.

One man returned to a particular painting twice. He cupped his chin and nodded.

Bud waved the rest of the team to his vantage point, he whispered, "Watch this."

Frank said, "It's really beautiful, isn't it?"

The man spoke English, "Yes, but priced way out of my customer's range."

With his arms raised, Frank said, "Oh, you're an art dealer."

"Yes, I have a small gallery in San Isidro."

"Your dealer cost is 60 percent of list. What you charge is your business. I have a feeling you already have it sold? Take it with you."

"OK, it's a deal."

Frank completed the paperwork, while Gail wrapped the customer's purchase.

After the customer left with his precious art, Frank assembled the team.

Bud said, "You make it look so easy."

Arms up and palms cupped, he said, "That's how it's done, folks. Assess the opportunity, ask for the order."

In Taos, President Carroll Swanson visited the marketing department. A tally board had been set up for the Buenos sales and contracts. Carroll's eyes widened.

He called Gary. "Team Buenos is doing very, very well."

Sales, contracts, and consignments exceeded their expectations. The Art Colonies of America's executives were delighted with Team Buenos' performance.

Later that evening Frank excused the rest of the team. He and Lola practiced tango steps in the exhibition room.

At the dinner presentation Frank mounted the dais. He greeted his 126 guests and glided easily into the presentation, pointing out the benefits of contracting with the Art Colonies of America.

Arms extended and palms up, Frank said, "It has been a pleasure for all of us to meet all of you." Bud, Kathleen, Dick, and Gail rose and joined Frank on the dais. They applauded the audience.

Frank concluded, "The El Faro staff will now ask you to select either the empanada de pescado or the carne asada entree. Enjoy your meal. The tango musicians will be here around eight o'clock."

Lola, who was dressed in a luminous tan and gold flowered dress with matching gold-laced tan dancing shoes, watched Frank.

Silently she reflected, *He's made for this role, and he's playing it perfectly.*

The team circulated among the guests—smiling, shaking hands, asking questions, answering questions. They wrote nine new contracts during the course of the evening.

Frank knew Argentines loved their national dance, the tango. He instructed the tango band leader to play ten tango dance pieces and then summon Lola and him to the dance floor.

The tango band leader addressed the audience. "Damas y caballeros, asistiandonos esta noche es la encantadora Lola DeLicio, la bailadora lidor de la Samba Troupe. Ella bailara con su anfitrion, Frank Creech." (Ladies and gentlemen, here with us is the leader of the famed Brazilian Samba Troupe, Lola DeLicio, who will dance the tango with our Art Colonies of America host, Frank Creech.)

The band leader waved Lola and Frank to the center of the floor.

They tangoed to "Por una Cabeza," a la Al Pacino and Gabrielle Anwar in the movie *Scent of a Woman*, ending with Lola's sensuous leg wrap.

The audience and the team applauded. Lola and Frank returned the applause.

At the airport on Sunday, Frank expressed his thanks and appreciation to Team Buenos. He bid them and his beloved Lola a happy trip home.

Chapter 14

South American Report

To: Gary Green, Chairman of the Board, Art Colonies of America

South America has strong ties with its native artists. I believe imported art will never have a significant share of the South American market.

There is limited potential in the more culturally advanced communities: São Paulo, Buenos Aires, Bogota, and Brasilia. The contracts I secured in the other principal cities of South American are, in my opinion, of marginal long-term value.

The ABC's of Advertising's format of annual catalog mailings really should be changed to quarterly mailings. The old phrase "Out of sight, out of mind" is particularly applicable to our South American clientele.

Our catalog mailings should be followed up by the marketing people, to ensure the catalog had been received and to ask if the recipients need to replenish their stock. *Ask for the order is critically important.*

A number of new South American gallery contract holders plan to accept the Colonies' offer of the three-day, all-expenses paid visit to either Taos or Fort Myers/Naples. I am confident Bud and Kathleen Robitaille and Dick and Gail Boyd will do an excellent job of entertaining them.

Our success in this campaign was due to

1. 20 percent per capita increase in income in South America over the past five years;
2. excellent weather;
3. the ABC's of Advertising's sparkling three-part mailings and newspaper ads;
4. our unique exhibitions in São Paulo and Buenos Aires; and
5. diligence and attention to detail, coupled with the hard work of our Team Buenos.

Frank Creech

Copies to:

Carroll Swanson, President, Art Colonies of America
Bud Robitaille, President, Taos Art Colony
Dick Boyd, President, SW Florida Art Colony

Scoreboard:

June 1: São Paulo, Brazil	9 contracts	14 consignments	22 collector sales
June 17: Rio de Janeiro, Brazil	2 contracts	1 consignment	
July 20: Buenos Aires, Argentina	12 contracts	6 consignments	8 collector sales

This was the first exhibition featuring our sales team. I made a mistake in selling directly to two boutiques. There were complaints from art gallery clients. I asked President Swanson to recall the art and refund the boutiques.

His answer was, "No, and don't do it again."

August 1: Montevideo, Uruguay	1 contract	2 consignments
August 4: Santiago, Chile	nada	
August 7: Asuncion, Paraguay	2 contracts	
August 12: Santa Cruz/La Paz, Bolivia	2 contracts	4 consignments

La Paz, at 12,333-foot elevation, is the highest capital in the world. Compare: Denver is 5,280 feet. Higher altitude cities in South America have cooler temperatures, but the altitude can cause altitude sickness for those, like me, who are not acclimated.

August 16: Lima, Peru	2 consignments	
August 20: Quito, Ecuador	1 contract	
August 29: Bogota, Columbia	3 contracts	3 consignments
September 2 Caracas, Venezuela	nada	

There was an unfortunate incident involving "Yankee Go Home" antagonists. I waded into a group of young vigilantes who were spitting on elderly American tourists. *La policia* escorted *me* to the airport, photographed my passport, and warned me not to return. I really need to start heeding State Department warnings.

September 4: Brasilia, Brazil	2 contracts	1 consignment

Brasilia, the capital of Brazil, has a highly educated, diversified population.

September 8–12: São Paulo/Rio de Janeiro

I made follow-up seen calls on new contract galleries which I had not visited previously, which garnered four additional orders.

Chapter 15

New Assignment

Just back from his long journey in South America, Frank was enjoying a Tex-Mex dinner at the Old Blinking Light restaurant when his cell phone rang. It was Chairman Gary Green.

"Thank you for summarizing our South American campaign, Frank. There are some things we need to discuss. Please come to my office Monday morning at nine."

"Will do, Gary,"

"Well," laughed Frank to himself, "at least I'm not ordered to Vic Lich's office."

He thought the meeting might have to do with his selling to the boutiques directly, or maybe it was about the problem he had in Caracas.

On Sunday evening, after a relaxing weekend at Blue Lake, fishing for bass, trout, and catfish, Frank returned to his Burch Street casita. He called Lola. They had talked about potential dates and places they could be together this fall (spring, in São Paulo).

At nine on the dot, Frank walked into Gary's office.

Mary Ellen brought in a tray of coffee and churros.

She smiled, "Hi, Frank. Call me M.E. I'd bet you are familiar with churros by now."

"Yes, I am. Love 'em, M.E."

"Ahem," said Gary, "you know—"

Frank interrupted. "Yes, time is money. Sorry. Please continue, Gary."

"Your success in South America was covered by the media, resulting in a sudden increase in orders which has seriously depleted our inventory. For the first time since the colonies' inception, we are in a back order or out of stock situation."

Gary continued, "We can't produce art like Ford Motor Company produces automobiles. I read in the *Wall Street Journal* that Ford's worldwide production of automobiles can be as many as ten thousand per day. You, of all people, know that our artists are very deliberate. Some pieces can take months to perfect.

"That's why we have to put on hold your suggestions as to how to increase our sales. We can't meet demand. It's as simple as that."

"Is there anything we can do?"

Carroll stood up, pointing at Frank. "Yes there is. You got us into this untenable predicament, and you're going to get us the hell out of it."

"Whoa, you hired me to sell art, and that's what I have done."

Gary interjected, "Frank, we're not faulting you. You've done a fantastic job. My accountants have already advised me your next increase in draw will likely double your current draw. However, at this critical point in our corporate life, we have to ask you to accept another role for the colonies."

"And that would be?"

"Recruit artists."

"I'm not a headhunter."

"Think about it. Come back at nine o'clock Wednesday morning with a plan."

"Yes, sir." They shook hands.

Frank, bewildered, walked into the closet. "Oops."

Le Cueva Café was within walking distance. But he felt in somewhat of a stupor, so Frank cabbed to the restaurant. He ordered shrimp enchiladas with chipotle cream sauce, cheese and onions, served with rice and beans and garnish, and a glass of unsweetened tea with lime zest.

Lunch helped. Feeling far more stable, Frank walked to his Burch Street residence. Along the way he computed the damage that might be caused if he recruited artists for the art colonies. Art gallery owners who lost their artists would undoubtedly be unhappy. He was filled with uncertainty.

He decided he needed help. From whom? Oh, of course! Marty Freling! He called Marty and left a message, "Marty, hate to bother you, but once again I need your help. I'm in a desperate situation. I need your advice."

Fifteen minutes later Marty returned Frank's call. "Frank, I'm in my Monday poker game, you remember our games. I can't talk now. I'll call you back at 3:30 p.m. your time."

When Marty called back, Frank outlined the problem.

Marty asked, "What triggered the meeting?"

"I submitted my South American report. I thought the meeting was to examine my report."

"Email that report to me, please. I'm reviewing your contract with the colony now to see if I can determine if this order to recruit artists is covered in your contract. I'll call you back in an hour or so."

"Thanks, Marty. I know if there is a solution, you'll find it."

Frank poured himself a Jack Daniel's on the rocks, hoping it would calm his nerves.

Marty called back, "Frank, there is nothing in your contract restricting your duties to sales exclusively. In fact, Vic Lich included a clause that, in short, says you must follow orders legitimately given you by your superiors. The colonies' directors have the right to ask you to recruit artists.

Marty added, "If the colonies cannot supply your clients with art, you'll lose the accounts. The colonies can't continue your draw if there is no income. You'll be out of a job."

Frank slumped in his chair, "Well, what should I do? How do I proceed?"

"Frank, find your South American report. I'll hold."

In a few seconds, Frank said, "I have it in front of me."

"The answer is in the first paragraph. I quote you, 'South America has strong ties with its native artists. I believe imported art will never have a significant share of the South American market.'"

"Oh, I think I see your concept. Because South America has been my least productive area, it will hurt the least to pirate the gallery's South American artists."

"Correct. Are those South American artists as good as you believe them to be?"

"They are totally awesome. As an art critic, I can truthfully tell you I have never seen such gorgeous oils. A Buenos Aires surrealist artist, Roberto Aizenberg, now deceased, was considered the most noted surrealist painter in the world."

"Frank, imagine that you are an owner of a South American art gallery. At first you would be miffed. On reflection, you would realize that the colonies, having a larger variety of art and now with their South American artists paintings included, you'd soon believe this could be a positive thing."

Frank straightened up in his chair, "Thanks, Marty. You are truly a *mensch*."

"I *hope* I'm right. At least it gives you an opportunity to have more art to sell. *Mazel tov*."

Frank worked all day Tuesday outlining as many aspects of his new assignment as he could perceive.

On Wednesday at nine o'clock sharp, Mary Ellen asked, "Coffee, Frank?"

"Thank you, M.E., but I'm already wired up."

Gary and Carroll each shook Frank's hand. Gary asked, "Do you have a plan?"

"I do." Frank gave Marty full credit for the plan to solicit South American artists.

They sat down. Gary said, "Excellent. We'll get together with Vic Lich and draw up contracts for your use. It's entirely possible we may want to form other branches as well. Thank you for being a team player, Frank."

Carroll said, "We've been busy too. Bud has been asked to recruit more area artists and to ask those artists who have pieces in the works to burn a little midnight oil. Bud will meet with the art school owners in Taos, to recruit some of their advanced students."

Gary added, "We are increasing the size of Dick's territory. The SW Florida Art Colony is being expanded beyond Lee and Collier Counties. It will now include Manatee, Sarasota, Charlotte, DeSoto, Glades, and Hendry Counties. Dick will receive contract forms by express mail tomorrow."

Frank asked, "Gentlemen, I believe I should go back to the beginning of our campaign and go to São Paulo. What do you think?"

Gary nodded to Carroll, who said, "Sounds like a plan. When can you start?"

"Give me a day or two to clean up my desk and find a place to stay near the art centers, likely a thirty day condo rental with a Wi-Fi setup."

Gary rose and extended his hand. "Get on with it, Frank. Time is money."

Frank shook hands with both men and left the office. He leaped excitedly.

"Lola, can you find me a thirty-day rental in São Paulo with a Wi-Fi set up near the art centers? I can be there Sunday. Can you meet me at the airport? I'll send my itinerary ASAP."

"*Yes, yes, yes!*"

Chapter 16

Sao Paulo II

Lola DeLicio had found an appropriate residence for Frank. She secured an *apartamento* in the centrally located Jardim district, near the Pan American School of Art and within walking distance of a number of major art galleries. The *apartamento* featured a spacious bedroom, work office, sitting room, kitchenette, and underground parking. It suited Frank's needs and particularly fit Lola's need for privacy.

Frank had come to terms with the colonies' order to solicit art and artists. Dressed in Lola's surprise gift, a luxurious viscose black and gold paisley dressing gown, he sipped his coffee and enjoyed the view of the park below his *apartamento*.

He spent Monday arranging geographically the location of respondents to the marketing department's mailings and integrated those contacts with his lists of prospects.

The ABC's of Advertising, Inc. had prepared four mailings, printed in both English and Portuguese, with RSVP cards enclosed.

The first mailer was to resident artists of São Paulo and its adjacent areas, offering to market their creations internationally. The mailer introduced Frank by biography, his position as senior art critic in the *Washington DC International Art Critics* and his appointment as marketing director for the Art Colonies of America. The bio included awards received and the impressive dollar volume of art Frank had marketed in the past four years.

The second mailer was to area art supply houses asking them to solicit their patrons for an opportunity of marketing their artist's work internationally. Each acceptance to the presentation dinner earned the proprietor or manager R$100 (Brazilian currency, the real). The marketing department had learned that Brazil didn't allow tourists or travelers to use foreign currency bills.

The third mailer was to area art schools. This mailer was similar to the mailer sent the art supply houses.

Mailers addressed to artists and to art galleries offered a dinner presentation for each group, with two seats for each respondent, at the popular Figueira Rubaiyat Restaurant. The clincher was the entertainment to be provided by Lola's famed Samba Troupe.

Frank caught up his email correspondence, which had included an invitation from Judy Freling to attend a party to honor Marty's eightieth birthday. In lieu of gifts, Judy suggested a donation to Marty's favorite charity.

Frank replied to Judy expressing his regret for being unable to attend. He wrote a check for $10,000 to the Jewish Federation of Lee and Charlottte County for their food bank program.

He thought, *What a small price to pay for all that Marty has done for me. I'm probably regarded as a blowhard, somewhat deservedly, but I do recognize that I owe a great deal to Marty Freling and the Art Colonies of America for giving me the opportunity of a lifetime in my chosen field, and for returning me to South America, to Lola, the love of my life.*

Frank had dressed in his casual khaki travel suit, appropriate for the eighty-one-degree, sunny and clear Tuesday morning. His driver had promptly met him in the lobby at 8:30 a.m. They reviewed the chart of calls Frank had prepared. The driver marked his map, set his GPS, and they departed for their farthest contact, in Guaruja, less than an hour away.

The artist he contacted, and his family, cordially greeted Frank. They spoke Portuguese, so Frank had his driver translate. He sat up his SLR on its portrait stand and photographed each piece of art for the marketing catalog. They agreed to selling prices. Frank explained that the colonies' traffic and transportation department would FedEx appropriate packaging materials, prepaid and insured, for the twelve paintings the artist agreed to consign to the art colonies. Frank further explained to the artist that he would receive Brazilian currency in payment for pieces sold.

Contract in hand, Frank pushed his chair back and stood up to leave. Everyone in the family hugged him and his driver. They responded in kind. Frank expressed what Lola had taught him, "Adeus meus amigos."

He recalled that every American visitor to Brazil with whom he was acquainted had told him about the warmth of the Brazilian people.

Frank made five more seen calls that day. He and the driver lunched lightly at noon and pressed on. Three more artists contracted with the Art Colonies of America. He had secured forty-four pieces of high-quality South American oil paintings to market.

"Game on!" shouted Chairman Gary Green, splashing his coffee on his desk, when Mary Ellen told him of the contracts Frank had secured.

Gary had instructed the marketing department to create a new South American art catalog ASAP and expedite it to the colonies' high-end galleries and independent collectors. He wanted to give Frank additional, immediate ammunition for his presentations.

Mindful that he had two separate dinner presentations to prepare for, as well as many seen calls to make beforehand, Frank picked up a takeout taco dinner from the deli near his residence.

He worked the rest of the evening planning calls for the next three days.

Armed with the ammunition from Gary, Frank integrated the accepted contracts and how the new South American art was to be marketed into his presentation.

His excitement was contagious. In the next three days he collected nine more contracts.

The gorgeous oils to be shipped to the colonies now numbered one hundred sixteen!

On Saturday morning, Frank made walking seen calls on art supply houses and art schools in the Jardim district.

Frank texted Gary: "To say the owners and managers were in awe of having someone with my credentials contacting them in person would be an understatement."

They introduced him to their customers and to their students, and they allowed him to recruit on their premises. He contracted three artists and paid the manager or owner the finder's fee in Brazilian reals from his pocket. They gave him signed receipts, which colonies' auditors absolutely required.

Frank made appointments to examine and evaluate the artists' creations.

Lola made reservations for a dinner cruise on Prince William Sound for Saturday evening. She looked forward to the glacier tour, narrated by a park ranger, together with fine dining and entertainment and was so happy to again enjoy Frank's company.

Lola was a nonpracticing Catholic, but she was a true deist. She thanked God for Frank having been sent back to her. They enjoyed a beautiful evening dining and dancing on the calm cruise (the cruise line guaranteed no sea sickness).

When they returned from the cruise they made ardent love, beginning in the elevator and continuing in the *apartamento*.

Lola had to drive to Rio de Janeiro on Sunday morning for a week of instructing Samba Troupe classes. They finished their breakfast, kissed goodbye, and kissed goodbye, and kissed goodbye.

Close to noon, Frank cabbed to the Mercado Municipal de São Paulo, a huge superstore. At the food court he enjoyed the popular mortadella sandwich topped with provolone and pickled hot pepper relish. His waiter suggested a traditional Brazilian quaff, Bradesco beer, which Frank enjoyed immensely.

From the Mercado, Frank cabbed to the São Paulo Museum of Art (MASP). The building is a symbol of modern Brazilian architecture. He appreciated the opportunity of seeing an emphatic assemblage of Brazilian art, prints, and drawings. He dictated the artists' names and locales into his recorder to add to his prospect list.

In bed, Frank thought about the week ahead with some trepidation; he recalled that historically his sales campaigns started strong, faded in the middle, and finished strong. The notepad on his nightstand had the numbers 150 and 50 circled. He wanted a hundred fifty artists in the fold and fifty art galleries on board at the end of the São Paulo campaign.

He snuggled up in his bed and inhaled the aroma of the pillows still redolent with Lola's frangipani perfume.

The city of Campinas was fifty-eight miles north of and about an hour's drive from São Paulo. The marketing department had forwarded to Frank "I'm interested" RSVPs from two artists and, surprisingly, from two art galleries. He had worn his blue silk suit for luck. And luck it brought him! Both RSVP artists contracted.

A prospect artist contracted. Both art galleries contracted. He contracted one artist from an art school and another from an art supply store. Another six artists and one gallery owner were also interested, and he would follow up with them in ten days.

The art galleries Frank had contracted brought a smile to Chairman Gary Green's face.

The one fear that Frank and the board had about the campaign was Director Ken Geelhood's cautionary about possible retribution from the art galleries.

Gary opined in his memo to the board: "The gallery owners are realists, their acquisitions will now be marketed internationally. In the end, business is business."

Frank tripped over his office chair on Friday afternoon of the second week of the campaign when he received an email from the marketing department: "Four of your Guaruja artist's submissions were sold today to an independent collector in Tewkesbury, England."

He grabbed his contact list and forwarded the email to everyone, reflecting, *Those sales will strengthen the campaign immensely*. He then copied the email and made it part of his presentation.

When Frank returned from his Saturday walking program, he opened his laptop and was delighted to learn the marketing department had received four contracts; three from artists, one from an art gallery. These contracts had evidently been generated by his emails.

"No mid-campaign slump," Frank chortled.

He felt things went swimmingly for the rest of the month. The dinner on the last Saturday of the month for the artist group—one hundred twenty-two contracted artists accompanied by one hundred of their guests—was an absolute sensation, topped off by the spectacular performance of Lola's Samba Troupe. Frank, costumed appropriately, joined the troupe for the last segment of the dance.

He renewed his lease for the *apartamento* an additional month. While the artist group had exceeded expectations, it was not so for the gallery group. He had only twenty-three galleries contracted. The board suggested Frank expand his theater of operations to include additional communities in the São Paulo area.

For the next three weeks he met his driver on Monday through Friday at 8:30 a.m., and they drove to nearby communities: Osasco, Santo Andre, Diadema, São Bernardo do Campo, Carapicuíba, Maua, and Embu. He also made second and third calls on galleries in São Paulo, citing results obtained in marketing art for the galleries he had contracted. On Saturdays he continued his visits to the schools and the art supply houses.

In all, Frank ended the São Paulo campaign with thirty-eight galleries and a total of one hundred thirty-six artists.

On the last Saturday evening of his second month in São Paulo, he joined his contracted gallery owners and their guests at the Figueira Rubaiyat restaurant. And once again, Lola's Samba Troupe entertained to great applause.

As he said *adeus meus amigos* to everyone, many gallery owners suggested that other galleries would contract when they learned how sales through the American colonies succeeded.

Earlier in the week, Lola had asked her uncle Fernando to recommend someone to be appointed to the presidency of the new American colonies branch in São Paulo. Without hesitation, he nominated Maria de la Silva, a politically connected relative.

Senhora de la Silva, herself an avid art collector, knew many of the artists; all of the gallery owners contracted.

Carroll Swanson ran a background check on Senhora de la Silva: clear, no lawsuits, widowed, politically active, patron of the arts.

Lola and Frank said their goodbyes on Sunday morning at the *apartamento*.

Gary asked him to accompany Senhora de la Silvia to Taos. His driver would take them to the airport. Frank had to return to Taos to handle many things that had accumulated during his two months in São Paulo. He tipped the driver $R500, receipted, of course.

Senhora Maria de la Silva—a svelte, well-coiffed, and very attractive lady—sat next to Frank on the long flights to Taos.

They talked about the company, about the job, and about art. She was a delightful and knowledgeable companion, and he felt the Art Colonies of America could not have made a better choice for president of the São Paulo branch.

The directors allowed Maria de la Silva to sleep in Monday morning, following her long trip from São Paulo. At 4:00 p.m. Maria and Frank arrived at the Art Colonies of America's building. Frank escorted her to Gary's office. Mary Ellen helped remove Maria's *xale* (shawl), which she had worn because the morning was chilly in Taos at 47°F.

Waiting with Gary were President Carroll Swanson, Director Ken Geelhood, President Dick Boyd of the SW Florida Art Colony, and President Bud Robitaille of the Taos Art Colony. Each man stood and greeted Senhora de la Silva, warmly shook her hand, and welcomed her to Taos.

Mary Ellen brought in the tray of coffee, with tea for Maria, and the familiar churros.

While speaking casually about the trip and the weather, all participated in the tray goodies.

When they began the tour of the facilities, Frank said, "Got a ton of things to do. Please excuse me. I'll pick up Maria and join you at dinner."

Dinner was scheduled for 7:00 p.m. at Gary and Susan Green's home.

Out of earshot, Mary Ellen whispered to Frank, "Nice to have a lady president."

"M.E.," Frank replied, performing a three-count tap riff dance, "she'll keep those fellows on their toes."

Mary Ellen laughed and nodded her head. "I believe she will!"

Chapter 17

Chicago Art Extravaganza

Frank went straightaway to the marketing department, put his jacket on the coat rack, and asked for a progress report for the art colonies' upcoming program, the Chicago Art Extravaganza.

Office Manager Leslie D'Alessandro brought him a thick packet of material. He sat down at the nearest desk and began wading through the material, making pencil notes in the margins for later discussion.

The extravaganza would be at McCormick Place, the largest convention center in North America. Frank knew the rules of display there were firm and unalterable. Bookings were due well in advance; thus, there was a great deal of negotiating to gain adjacent space for the new art colony of São Paulo.

He curled his finger, waved Leslie to his desk, and pointed at the item. He complimented her with a military salute. She had accomplished it somehow and didn't share the nitty-gritty details with Frank.

They'd meet tomorrow morning to go through the packet with the entire department.

Frank met Maria at her El Monte Sagrado Living Resort and Spa lodging. They cabbed to the Green's house, situated just beside the spectacular Sangre de Cristo Mountains. In route he showed her the sights of Taos.

She said, "Incredibly scenic. Now I see why so many artists make their homes here." Then she added, "Frank, may I ask you something?"

"Please do so. Ask me anything at all, Maria."

"I noticed in São Paulo you cabbed everywhere. I can understand the reason when you're there. Why do you not use your own car in Taos?"

"Good question. It's because I don't own a car. When I was the art critic for the *Washington DC International Art Critics*, I could walk to work. In fact, I got into big trouble walking up Constitution Avenue one morning, but that's another story. Seriously, I travel so much a car would simply sit, and that's not a good thing."

He thought to himself, *This lady misses nothing.*

"Maria, it's my turn to ask a question, OK?"

"Certainly you may."

Glancing at her exquisite gold jewelry—matching necklace and earrings—and her fashionable clothing, Frank asked, "Why would a person of your obvious refinement want a very difficult position in a start-up branch?"

"I love challenges, just as I suspect you do. Making my branch successful is a worthwhile endeavor. Moreover, art is my passion. I'm going to make this work."

Frank threw his arms up. "That I believe," he responded.

Susan Green's chef had produced an outstanding meal for her guests: roasted wild duck with a raspberry couscous base served with a salad of pickled beets and asparagus, freshly baked pine nut bread, accompanied by an excellent Bordeaux wine.

After dinner, the ladies—Nancy Swanson, Kathleen Robitaille, Gail Boyd, and Maria de la Silva—cognacs in hand, joined Susan Green in the sitting room. The gentlemen—Carroll Swanson, Bud Robitaille, Dick Boyd, and Frank Creech—cognacs in hand, joined Gary on the deck where Frank could enjoy his Trinidad short Bali cigar.

Frank heard from Gail that the ladies related to Maria how they and their husbands had become involved with the art colonies and how the enterprise had grown astronomically since Frank had been appointed marketing director.

Carroll went over the details of the plan to relocate the colonies' distribution center to Chicago. The move was engineered by FedEx's presentation to him reflecting huge savings in both money and time from separately shipping from the branches. He explained this was because Chicago was a major hub city with direct FedEx flights from Chicago's O'Hare airport to most local and international cities.

He would oversee the purchase or rental of a suitable facility near O'Hare and the relocation of the traffic and transportation department to Chicago. Frank had heard the traffic and transportation department's staffs weren't very happy about moving away from Taos.

Carroll gave printouts to each person, outlining the plan, the anticipated savings, and the necessary time schedule so that Team Chicago could coordinate its participation in the plan—all needed in six weeks—in time for the Art Colonies of America's exhibition at McCormack Place.

Maria told Frank that she was scheduled to meet Gary at 9:00 a.m. in Vic Lich's office to formalize her contract with the colonies and that they planned to lunch together thereafter.

Frank offered to escort her to Vic Lich's office in the morning, which she happily accepted.

At Vic Lich's office, Frank opened the door for Maria. She literally gasped at the rustic splendor of Vic's offices, particularly the waiting room with its gallery of original art colony paintings.

Vic's receptionist, Martha Cunningham, began to escort Maria into Vic's office. Frank stopped them for a moment to ask Maria to meet him in the marketing department office at 2:00 p.m. to join Bud, Dick, and himself in previewing Team Chicago's game plan for the Chicago Art Extravaganza.

Maria came to the marketing department at 1:30 p.m. so she would have an opportunity to chat with Frank before Bud and Dick arrived.

"How'd it go, Maria?"

"It went quite well. The contract was all I expected and more. The directors gave me plenty of leeway in getting my organization off the ground. We had dinner at Le Cueva Café. Janet Lich joined us. What a delightful lady. She made me feel right at home. I understand the Le Cueva Café is one of your favorite places."

"That it is, and I'm glad you met Janet. She is indeed a delightful lady. When do you return to São Paulo?"

"Tomorrow afternoon. You don't have to escort me this time. Carroll arranged for Don Lambrix, the colonies' limo driver, to take Dick, Gail, and me to the airport. You've been an excellent host, which I will happily report to Lola when she meets me at Guarulhos International Airport."

Noting the surprise in Frank's countenance, Maria said, laughingly, "Oh, Frank. Latinas know everything that is going on in the family."

Dick and Bud joined them. The first item on Team Chicago's check-off sheet was obtaining Maria's clothing sizes for her Art Colonies of America uniform (a la Team Buenos), and she was given a size form to complete for her new gallery manager who would work with her in their booth.

Team Chicago went through the entire list: accommodations, space allocation, number of pieces for each booth, reserves, insurance, signage, hours of display, and record keeping.

Unlike Buenos Aires, they would not be allowed to set up their booths or hang their art at McCormick Place. Those functions were the realm of the labor union.

"Details, details," Frank sighed, "how did we live without them?"

Everyone laughed. Continuing, they covered the per diem rate allocated to wives Gail and Kathleen, the ladies who had been indispensable in Buenos's highly successful exhibition. The same rate would be allocated to Maria's nominee. The chamber of commerce could not be involved in this exhibition.

"Questions, anyone?" queried Frank.

There were no questions.

"All right then, everyone has my number and Leslie's number in their speed dial. I quote an old Azerbaijani proverb, 'Shameful is not the one who doesn't know but the one who doesn't ask.'"

Frank and Maria cabbed to the Old Blinking Light restaurant for their final quiet time together.

Once seated, Frank asked, "What has your overall experience been and your evaluation of the Art Colonies of America?"

Between bites, Maria answered, "The work ethic is phenomenal. I've never seen anything like it. No one even noticed it was 7:30 p.m. until we had completed the Team Chicago review.

"Oh, and so thorough! Carroll gave me a huge briefcase to hold all the paperwork I'll be carrying back to São Paulo. Tomorrow I will follow an order from its inception to its fulfillment, its billing, its collection, and its cash distribution.

"I'll have a chart which shows the allocation, the buyer, the artist, the piece number, its location, everything. And I'll be traveling via Fort Myers with Dick and Gail to visit the SW Florida Art Colony facility in the Metro Industrial Park in Fort Myers. Perfect."

In the next three weeks Frank met with Carroll and Gary several times, going over his hidden agenda of recruiting artists and art galleries during the Chicago Art Extravaganza.

The marketing department of the colonies had obtained an exhibitor list with booth locations for freelance artists, art galleries, art schools, and art supply houses. With one hundred forty booths of exhibitors and an expected attendance of over one million people, the extravaganza likely would be a huge success.

Since the colonies would have a distribution center in Chicago, it logically followed that the colonies should establish a branch there.

Frank was elated to learn that Bud and Dick had gained additional colony members and galleries, so the supply of art was now noncritical. And with the addition of Maria's colony in Sao Paulo, sales would again be on an upward trend.

Lola had a break in her schedule and came to visit Frank in Taos during the last week before he was to depart for Chicago.

He had to tell her to dress warmly. She was leaving temperatures in São Paulo, high 77°F, low 55°F; whereas in Taos it was high 60°F, low 22°F.

She said, "You'll keep me warm."

"Of that you may be sure," chortled Frank. He chortled a lot. They spent four days together, sight-seeing, skiing, and making love.

During their visit to the art colonies facilities, Frank introduced her to all the people in each department.

In the marketing department, Frank saw heads swivel and computers quieted as a hushed silence fell upon the department when gorgeous Lola was introduced.

The usual volume of activity resumed when manager Leslie D'Alessandro tapped her pen sharply on her glass-topped desk.

Lola oohed and aahed at the proposed site of Frank's Sangre de Cristo Mountain estate.

Frank admitted to Lola that the home plan and the site had been put on hold.

They went to the airport together on the fifth day via company limo; he to Chicago for the Chicago Art Extravagancy, she to São Paulo.

She was expected back in São Paulo to develop a second group of samba dancers for a Brazilian cultural exchange between Rio de Janeiro, Brazil, and the Blue Danube area of Europe, which had been arranged by her Uncle Fernando.

Frank met Manual Orba, Maria's gallery manager, at the hospitality center of the Hyatt Regency McCormick Place Hotel where Team Chicago stayed during the exhibition. Frank noted that Manual was an energetic and keenly alert young man.

The São Paulo Art Colony display was spectacular. The new colony outsold the SW Florida Art Colony and the Taos Art Colony by a margin of two to one.

Maria and Manual were resupplied daily from the reserve art. They sold ninety-six of the one hundred pieces they had shipped to Chicago.

Frank floated in and out of the colonies' booths, making suggestions and spelling the Team Chicago people when necessary.

He worked the other exhibitor booths doggedly. He attended as many post showtime cocktail parties (a McCormick tradition) as he could manage.

He stayed another two weeks and contracted more artists and galleries.

Enough, he thought, *to establish the art colony of Chicago.*

Carroll begrudgingly conceded to Gary, "Your workhorse pulled us out of the dilemma which *he* created."

Chapter 18

Water Under The Bridge

"**M.E.**, what have I done now?" implored Frank, when he reported to Gary Green's office at 9:00 a.m. the day after his return from Chicago.

"Oh, it's not like that at all. Your old boss Dick Brooks asked Gary for your help in judging an art contest."

"You're on my Christmas list, young lady."

"I'd better be," laughed Mary Ellen, shaking her spoon at Frank.

Gary waved Frank into his office and motioned him to a chair while continuing his phone conversation. Mary Ellen brought in the coffee and churros.

Frank poured a cup of coffee, selected a churro, sat down, nibbled and sipped, and waited while Gary completed his call.

"Frank, the *Washington DC International Art Critics* general manager, Dick Brooks, asked us to help him with an art judging event in Wisconsin next month. I said I would discuss it with you. Would you have a problem doing a favor for the *Washington DC International Art Critics?*"

Brushing crumbs off his slacks, Frank said, "No problem, boss. As they say, that's water under the bridge."

"I think we may be able to use events like this to gain favorable press and possibly to develop new branches."

Squirming in his seat, Frank asked, "Could you elaborate, please?"

"You'll recall that you suggested we establish a branch in Southwest Florida when SOSA disbanded? Then you created a new branch in São Paulo, and you laid the groundwork for the branch in Chicago. Your work took us out of the supply-demand crises we faced, and those branches more than doubled our volume. I don't want to appear greedy. My job is to seek corporate growth opportunities."

Gary handed Frank a file folder labeled *Wisconsin State Art Competition*. "I'll tell Dick Brooks at the *Washington DC International Art Critics* that you'll handle the assignment. Get back to me with your plan ASAP."

Reaching for the file folder, Frank said, "I hope I won't regret this."

The folder contained a copy of the *Milwaukee Journal Sentinel* newspaper article created by Bob Vandewalker, president of the Wisconsin Arts Council, inviting resident Wisconsin artists to participate in the statewide competition.

Submissions would be displayed in accordance with their medium—acrylics, watercolor, mixed media, colored pencil, and pastels.

Each category had three awards. Frank thought the cash prizes were quite high. They were $10,000 for each first prize; $5,000 for each second prize; $2,500 for each third prize for category winners in each medium. There were also $100,000, $50,000 and $25,000 grand prizes for the best of show awards.

"Now," he mused, "I understand the *Washington DC International Art Critics*' interest in this contest."

Contest sponsors were the major art product manufacturers, whose executives would make the presentations. The judges would be the directors of the Milwaukee Art Museum and the Charles Allis Art Museum. The tiebreaker, if needed, would be Frank. And he would arrange the scenario for the entire production. He was ready to manage the event, having done so many times for the *Washington DC International Art Critics*.

Frank phoned Gary the next day. "Good morning, sir. I'm ready to go over the game plan for Milwaukee."

"Frank, we'll get to that later. Right now I've got a problem in Chicago. The labor union is trying to organize our colony warehouse employees."

"Oh, let me make a phone call. I know someone who has legal contacts in Chicago. I'll get back to you."

"Do that, and do it promptly."

Frank called his go-to guy, Marty Freling. "Marty, I recall a poker game one evening when you mentioned your friend, a Chicago attorney, who had experience in union organizing cases. Who was that?"

"Oh yes. He's a retiree here in Fort Myers, Ivan Brownstein. I can get you his cell number, hold on a minute.

"While I have you on the line, thank you so much for your very generous donation to my favorite charity for my birthday gift. The director of the Jewish Lee and Charlotte County Federation, Allen Isaacs, told me your $10,000 gift was the largest single benefaction they had received this year. Who's the *mensch* now?"

"You're welcome, Marty. I have a lot of catching up to do. Oh, maybe it would be better if you checked with Mr. Brownstein to see if he would be interested in handling the case."

"I'll do that, Frank."

"I'm on a short leash. I'll call Gary immediately and give him a heads-up. Thanks to you once again, Marty."

Frank phoned the information to Mary Ellen. She said, "I'll put it under Gary's nose."

He continued researching the Wisconsin state art competition. The event would be held at the Wisconsin State Fair Park in West Allis, a suburb of Milwaukee. The 2014 Wisconsin State Fair drew over a million visitors in eleven days.

The colonies' marketing department told Frank they had updated his bio, which now included his creation of the three new branches. The camera-ready bio, with Frank's photo, was furnished to the *Washington DC International Art Critics* for its coverage of the event.

The Wisconsin Art Council also was furnished the bio for use in its ads for the competition; it would be placed in every major newspaper in Wisconsin.

"Hmm," ideated Frank, "maybe this won't be as difficult an assignment as the first three branches . . . a word here and there to some of the leading artists and art galleries . . . create an atmosphere wherein the artists and galleries approach me."

Two days had passed before Frank heard back from Gary. "Frank, can you come to my office tomorrow morning at nine with your plan for the Wisconsin campaign?"

"Good morning, M.E.," said Frank, with a little flourish of his hand.

"Hello, frequent visitor. Go on in, Gary's waiting for you."

"Good morning, Frank. Before we start on our plan for Wisconsin, I'll bring you up to date on our Chicago union problem. I laid out the whole issue for Ivan Brownstein," Gary said, shaking his head. "He said we could stall through legal estoppels, but eventually, the union would succeed in organizing our distribution center due to the political strength of the unions in Chicago.

"Carroll and the board agreed to allow the union to organize our employees, but not our artists. Ivan wouldn't accept a consultation fee. He said it was a favor for Marty Freling."

"Hope it doesn't spread to the other branches, Gary."

"We don't think it will," Gary said, as he poured fresh coffee in his cup. "Let's hear your Milwaukee plan."

"The contest runs three days, Thursday through Saturday, November 27, 28, and 29. The first two days are for category awards, the final day is for grand prizes. I'm booked at the Ambassador Hotel in Milwaukee on Monday the twenty-fourth through the twenty-ninth.

"I've booked the convention hall for a potential three hundred people the evening of the twenty-ninth for the dinner and presentation. I'll need Team Milwaukee, the same people we had in Chicago, to man the sign-up desks. They'll help me immensely in recruiting artists and during the competition. I have booked them at the Ambassador.

"I'll spend the first three days meeting the judges and other officials of the competition going over the rules. I'll visit the art galleries, and I'll set up the dinner presentation."

"Carroll applauded your work ethic," Gary declared. Nodding his head, he continued, "He called you a workhorse, and I am inclined to agree with him."

Frank laughed, and he and Gary shook hands.

Frank said, "OK, boss, I need to get back to the marketing department. We're in the early stages of our 2015 calendar of events. As I recall, you wanted the complete calendar by December 10."

"Oh," Gary said, raising his hand, forefinger extended. "I almost forgot something. Carroll had a call from your ex, Diane Arnold. She's opening a gallery in Chelsea. She wants to stock our art. Do you have a problem with that?"

"Wow, is this ever the month of water under the bridge for me. No problem. That's an income opportunity for us. As you frequently say, business is business."

While listening to his voice recorder, Frank walked up to the huge 2015 calendar on the wall in the marketing department. He chalked in his entries for the Blue Danube expositions.

Prague: June 14–June 20
Vienna: June 21–June 27
Salzburg: June 28 – July 4

Those dates were tied to Lola's part in the cultural exchange between Brazil and the Blue Danube countries. Her Samba Troupe would perform at their bookings on Fridays. On Saturdays they would perform for the exposition guests at the Art Colonies of America's expense.

Frank felt there would likely be a crossover of guests for the performances.

When Frank explained his entries on the calendar to her, Leslie D'Alessandro softly clapped her hands and whispered, "Amore, amore."

The marketing people worked on the calendar until Frank's stomach began to complain, and he said good night. He walked to Le Cueva Café and ordered his taco dinner.

Just as he took the first bite, his cell phone rang. He didn't recognize the foreign exchange area code. He let his phone take a message.

It was Diane Arnold. Her message pleaded with him to call her back. Not about to have the call overheard, Frank pocketed his phone, finished his meal, and walked home.

At his casita, Frank poured two fingers of Jack Daniel's into his shot glass and took a sip.

"Diane," Frank said, "I'm returning your call."

"Thank you for approving my purchase of colonies' art for my new gallery, and if you have a moment, I have another favor to ask."

"OK."

"I really need an advance to pay the security deposit and the first month's rent of my gallery and to buy my stock. Please, please," Diane purred in her Pussy Galore voice.

"How much do you need?"

"Frank, I need $300,000."

"I'll see Vic Lich tomorrow. Your loan will cost me investment interest and legal fees, so those items will have to be factored into your repayment schedule. The loan will be for twenty-four months with 10 percent interest."

"Anyway you want to handle it, I will accept. Oh, thank you so much."

He visualized Diane's eyelashes fluttering.

Concluding the call, Frank said in his stentorian voice, "Diane, I don't mind helping you this time. But please understand it will not happen again."

"Absolutely not. You have my word on it. I promise."

Shaking his head, Frank left a message on Vic's answering service. He asked for an appointment in the morning.

Pat Napior showed Frank into Vic's office at 9:00 a.m. They went to work on Diane's loan. Vic quickly worked the numbers. His fingers flew across his calculator.

Vic prepared the loan contract. Frank signed it, and Vic said he would FedEx the paperwork to Diane for her signature and her electronic fund transfer data.

Frank left Vic's office, shaking his head, and walked to the colonies' marketing department to continue his 2015 scheduling work.

The time flew by. Team Milwaukee assembled in front of the exhibition tent at the Wisconsin State Fair Park in the chilly 47°F weather.

Frank raised his hands over his head and leaned forward. "Showtime!" he shouted to the team.

Looking directly at Manual Orba (the dynamo from the São Paulo Art Colony), Frank said, "Remember, no pressure. Our approach, I have learned, is called negative selling, which is having the prospect think he or she is being given an opportunity to be a part of the new Milwaukee Art Colony, a branch of the American Art Colonies."

Frank continued, "Introduce yourself, ask if the person you are greeting is an artist, and if so, hand them the packet. Politely answer all questions asked. Tell the artists someone will be at the exit gate to collect the applications."

Bud waved Frank aside, out of earshot, "Need to ask you something, Frank. Kathleen and I have done all we can do in Taos, and as you've probably heard, we're interested in either Chicago or Milwaukee. But we're indecisive. She likes Chicago, and I prefer Milwaukee."

Frank said, "You know Carroll's handling Chicago now, and because of the union problems and the distribution center activity, he may need to stay there. Bud, I think you and Kathleen are better off running things here in Milwaukee, both for yourselves and the colonies. Your experience is irreplaceable, and after all, Chicago is only a hundred miles away."

"You'll support that?" Bud asked.

"I'll clear it with Gary first, and if OK with him, I'll make the announcement at the dinner presentation at the Ambassador."

"Thanks, Frank."

Bob Vandewalker, president of the Wisconsin Art Council, told Frank the art judging competition drew close to seventeen thousand visitors.

Frank said, "Thankfully there were no hitches. Everything went like clockwork. There were no tiebreakers for me to judge."

Frank called Lola, "I enjoyed the emcee role immensely. Maybe I'll change my occupation."

She laughed, "I don't think so, sweetheart."

Frank addressed the Milwaukee Art Colony. "Please meet your president Bud Robitaille and his lovely wife, Kathleen."

Gail Boyd told Frank they had 122 artists on board by the end of the dinner presentation.

Frank barely heard her over the dance band. He danced the Wisconsin dance, the polka.

To standing applause, Frank climbed onto the dais. His arms extended upward, he thanked everyone for coming to the presentation and assured the Milwaukee Art Colony artists that he would be working hard to sell their paintings.

Gary Green emailed Frank, "Your draw for the coming year will be 1.25 million. I have instructed the marketing department to implement the items you requested in your South American report. Catalog mailings will be quarterly rather than annually. We've hired two additional people to follow up the mailings."

Gesturing toward Carroll and Nancy Swanson during the annual holiday party which took place three weeks before Christmas, Gary said, "While they were quite reluctant to move from Taos, the Swansons have accepted the presidency of our Chicago Art Colony for the good of our organization. Let's hear it for them."

Everyone applauded.

Extending his left hand toward Ken Geelhood, Gary continued, "Ken is going to head up the Taos branch."

Everyone applauded.

Gary, with his arms extended and his palms up, continued, "I'm now your president and chairman of your board."

Everyone applauded.

"Mary Ellen is now our executive Secretary and colonies coordinator."

Everyone applauded.

Frank thought it was a logical and orderly change that would benefit everyone. The colonies' top authority functions had been awkwardly overlapping.

He straightened his shoulders, stood up, and said, "Gary, that's all so positive. Thank you, sir."

Chapter 19

Stock Hustler

Frank left a message wishing Marty Freling and his family a happy Hanukkah.

Marty called, "Merry Christmas, Frank. Did Santa give you a nice present?"

Frank replied, "Yes." He continued, "I'm very happy with my increase for the coming year. What I'm not happy with is the return I'm getting on my investments."

"Hmm, what are you doing over the holidays?" Marty asked.

"I'll be with Lola in Miami, our halfway point."

Marty responded, "I'm thinking of something. I'll call you back."

Mike Maxwell called Frank. He said, "I've got another party interested in your house plans. Would you be interested in selling?"

"Let me get back to you."

"Sure."

Frank found the architectural rendering and placed it in the document section of his suitcase. He'd talk with Lola about the house over the holidays.

Marty called back, "Do you remember Sally and Larry Thompson from CYRC?"

"I surely do. Diane and I sat at their table at the last CYRC holiday party."

"They moved to Key Biscayne, in Miami. Sally is redecorating their house and wants some original art. She asked me if I could help. I thought of you immediately. I spoke with Larry about your investment problems. He proposed a trade—his aid in your investment portfolio for your art expertise and your assistance. Lola and you are invited to join us at their holiday dinner party. Is that a deal?"

"That's a deal."

Marty emailed Frank the Thompsons' address and the date and time for the party.

Frank recently had been introduced to a refreshing and inexpensive alternative for his Dom Pérignon champagne—Prosecco, champagne's sexy little Italian cousin. He had a case shipped to the Thompsons' house. He kept the receipt. If the Thompsons bought colonies art, he would expense the gift.

Frank was in awe of Lola's ability to book shows in places where he could be with her if she was given sufficient time.

Her Samba Troupe would perform at the venerable old Fontainebleau Hotel on Miami Beach on New Year's Eve. Frank bought tickets for the Thompsons, the Frelings, and himself for Lola's show. He'd keep those receipts.

When Frank met Lola at Miami International, she was wearing the yellow cling dress she had worn when she met him in Rio. It had the same effect on him as it did then. She looked both alluring and sensual.

Lola was starved. They cabbed to Miami's Versailles Restaurant, a Cuban restaurant highly recommended by Fontainebleau's concierge, Oscar Fernandez. He explained that the restaurant's name had been inherited. They agreed the restaurant lived up to expectations. The huge restaurant took up the entire city block and had two bakeries *inside* its building.

Over dinner, they talked about the nearly two weeks they would enjoy together. Their plans included a visit to the Ichimura Japanese garden and the Morikami Museum just north of Miami, recommended by the concierge.

Back at the Fontainebleau, Frank changed into his Ipanema flip-flops and Speedo swimsuit while Lola changed into her bikini. It was still sunny and warm on the beach. The beach servers brought them refreshing mojitos. They watched a mélange of luxury yachts, jet skis, and sailboats in the bay and freighters and oilers at sea. After sunset, they happily returned to their "Sweet Suite Bleau."

During their room service breakfast, Frank showed Lola the architect's rendering of his home design, set against a background of the Sangre de Cristo Mountains.

"The architect, Mike Maxwell, has another party who could use the design. If I don't plan to build, I could sell the plans. That would depend largely on you."

Lola stood up, walked around to his side of the table, and placed her hand on his arm. She cocked her head, her golden tan eyes wide. Lola wordlessly held the pose, tongue-in-cheek, while Frank began to fidget.

Lola switched her pose. Hands on her hips, she demanded, "Are you proposing?"

Frank stuttered, "I . . . uh . . . I . . . er . . . uh . . . hoebaby, oh hell."

Lola threw her head back and laughed hysterically. Frank joined her.

Lola said, "Honey, we'll get to that in time, I'm sure. Keep the plans. Do you own the property?"

"No, I have an option on the seven-acre site."

"Frank, buy the land. I have a feeling it's an excellent investment."

Judy Freling complimented Sally on her dinner of roasted Rock Cornish game hens, wild rice, glazed tomatoes, peppers, and onions served on individual platters.

Marty stood. Holding his glass of Prosecco at waist level, he said, "I would like to propose a toast to our hosts, Sally and Larry."

Lola, Judy, and Frank stood. All looked directly at their hosts and raised their glasses.

Marty said, "*L'chaim*—that's Yiddish. It means 'to life.'"

On the pleasant lanai, Larry paged through Frank's financial portfolio while Frank puffed on his short Beli cigar.

"Your problem is diversification. I have listed several opportune investments for you, which include ITAU, the huge Brazilian bank's security investment funds, and Voya Financial retirement funds."

Frank thanked Larry and put the list in his portfolio.

Marty and the ladies paged through the colonies' catalog as they walked through the house, initialing their selections for each area.

Larry and Frank joined the others. They reviewed the initialed selections. Frank made only a few changes based on several factors, one of which made Larry's eyes widen: the expected growth in value of certain paintings by artists of the colonies.

Frank filled out the order form. The order came to $385,000. Out of the corner of his eye, he saw Larry shaking his head at Sally.

In the notes section Frank quickly wrote, "Overnight freight and insurance absorbed. Include lockable, self-leveling devices for hanging. Apply 10 percent volume discount."

Larry signed. Laughingly, he asked, "Still feel like trading?"

"Sure," Frank replied, as he faxed the order to the colonies.

"May I have your homeowner's insurance policy, please?"

Frank phoned Leslie. He asked her to prepare certificates of authenticity for each piece purchased and send the packet to the Thompsons' insurance carrier and the copies to the Thompsons.

Larry shook hands with Frank. "You're exactly as advertised—very thorough. Now here's my deal. Help us hang our art, and we'll go on a lunch cruise."

Glancing at Larry's sleek forty-two-foot yacht, *Stock Hustler*, Frank said, "You've got a deal."

Judy chimed in, "We're helping too."

Two days later, after Judy, Marty, Lola, and Frank had toured Biscayne Bay sights, Larry called Frank.

"Ask everyone to be here by nine tomorrow morning, please."

Sally served orange juice and Prosecco wine mimosas. She had very lightly chalked each painting's position on the walls. The crew accurately hung the paintings in just under two hours.

They sailed to Crandon Park, docked the boat, and rented a golf cart to tour the island.

Stopping at the Sony Open Tennis Center, they walked through the facility, which was the site of the Miami Open tennis tournament featuring the world's top ATP men's and WTA women's tennis players.

Larry told Frank, "ITAU, one of the investment firms I referred to you, is the sponsor of this year's Miami tournament."

The next stop was the 100% Natural Restaurant, a popular Mexican-inspired Crandon Island restaurant. After their delicious seafood lunches, served with homemade Saratoga chips, Marty tried to grab the tab.

Frank said, "No, you don't, sir. That's mine, compliments of the colonies, of course. You bought in Washington."

Larry and Frank were on the flying bridge, Marty and the girls on the aft deck as they left the dock.

Larry asked Frank if he would like to take the helm.

"That would make my day, Larry. I miss my boat, the *Artistically Endowed*, from my Washington DC days."

Sally screamed, "Larry, there's a fast boat coming up behind us!"

Larry and Frank saw the boat, a cigarette type. Three men were in the cockpit, one of whom had a grappling hook in his hand.

Leather-lunged Frank yelled, "Everybody hold on tight!"

He put the starboard engine in neutral, the port engine in half throttle reverse.

Frank full throttled both engines forward and rammed the fast boat amidships.

Larry saw the three crewmen swimming toward his boat after their boat flipped on its side; they were thrown overboard.

Marty shouted from the galley, "Judy banged her head on the cabinet door. She'll be OK. No water in the galley but a lot of damage."

Sally went below, while Lola ran forward.

Lola loudly said, "The bow is twisted."

Sally said, "Some damage in the engine room but no water."

Frank tried to restart the engines. "No ignition," he said.

Larry speed dialed the U.S. Coast Guard. He gave them his latitude and longitude and boat name and size. He also reported, "Men trying to board our boat. We're damaged, can't take evasive action."

The coast guard operator had Larry describe nearby landmarks.

"Two boats and our helicopter are on the way. They're 'bout twenty minutes out. We're alerting local authorities as well."

One man swam to the bow, another to the stern.

When the man at the stern climbed aboard the swim platform, Sally hit him on the head with a large frying pan. He fell back in the water.

When the man at the bow got as far as the bow rail, Lola sprayed him with her mace pepper spray. He fell back in the water.

When the man on the port side reached the gunwale, Larry discharged his fire extinguisher in the man's face. He fell back in the water.

The coast guard helicopter crew lowered a sailor with an M16 rifle onto the bridge in two minutes after their arrival. Waving his M16, he directed the men in the water to swim to the stern of the boat.

The coast guard cutter arrived. Its crew took charge of the pirates. The second boat came and took *Stock Hustler*'s crew aboard.

They waited until the tow boat secured *Stock Hustler* and began to tow her to Larry's boat repair facility before sailing to the Thompsons' home.

Everyone profusely thanked the coast guard crew.

The Thompsons and their guests watched the Miami TV live interview of the area coast guard commander. The commander explained to the reporters that if not for Frank Creech's daring action in ramming the fast boat, the people on the *Stock Hustler* could have been injured or even killed.

He stated, "Many large boats are stolen every month by smugglers to use in bringing illegal aliens into the United States. There have been a number of incidents where the smugglers have severely injured or killed our citizens during the seizure of their boats."

The commander, doffing his hat, concluded, "My hat's off to Mr. Creech and to the other heroic people of the *Stock Hustler* for their defiance of the sea pirates."

Happy just to be alive and together, everyone hugged.

Lola said, "Have to go now. Need to start rehearsing my troupe."

On cue, Frank fished up tickets for Lola's show.

The spectacular Samba Troupe performance was a grand finale to everyone's Miami holiday.

Embracing Frank at the Miami International airport on New Year's Day, Lola said "Happy New Year, bonito."

Frank responded, "Happy New Year to you, my bonita."

Frank waved at the enthusiastic crowd at Taos Municipal Airport as they chanted, "Our hero, Frank Creech! Our hero, Frank Creech!"

"Here we go again," Carroll said to Gary.

Gary said, "Yup."

Chapter 20

Lola's Dilemma

Frank called realtor Susan Csikos and left her a message, "Please make a $600,000 offer for parcel 16."

Next, he called his architect, Mike Maxwell. "I've been advised by the most beautiful woman in the world to retain the house plans."

Frank called his bank president, David Pohl. He left a message that he would stop by shortly to discuss a loan.

"Good morning Frank. Would you like some coffee?"

"No coffee, thanks. I need to get an idea of how much I can borrow for a property that I'm trying to purchase."

"Would that be some acreage out by the mountains?"

"How'd you know that?"

"Ha, ha! I'm a mind reader. No, just kidding. It's a small town, really. The owner, Jack Steers, called me ten minutes ago. He asked me if you could handle an $850,000 purchase. I told him I'd get back to him."

"As I recall, Dave, you have a copy of my contract with the colonies?"

"Yes, I have," Dave said, opening a file folder labeled "Frank Creech" while adjusting his glasses.

"This is over three years old. Have there been any changes?"

"Well, yes, quite an increase in my draw since that time," Frank said, as he passed Mr. Pohl a copy of Chairman Green's order to the payroll department to increase Frank's draw to 1.25 million for this year.

With his eyebrows raised, nodding his head, Dave asked, "Do you plan to build on the property?"

"Not at this time," chortled Frank, "but I'm working on it."

A clerk tapped on the see-through glass pane. They stood up and shook hands.

David said, "Get back to me when you have firmed up the purchase price."

"I will do that," Frank replied, as he left the bank.

After lunch at his delightful little Le Cueva Café, he went to his office. He returned phone calls from high-end gallery owners, from the branch executives, and from his beloved Lola.

She asked, "Did you buy the property?"

"Ola, bonita. I'm working on it, yes, I am."

"I recall the plans for the house included a gazebo with piped-in music. I don't recall seeing a dance floor in the house plans?"

"Well, uh, Diane and I danced on social occasions but not at the level you and I have achieved. Does this interest in a dance floor in the house in Taos mean you are considering my, uh, irregular proposal?"

"It most certainly does. Dancing is how we met *meu homem* (my man), and I want to dance with you all the rest of my life."

Frank jumped up and clicked his heels together.

"I'll ask Mike Maxwell to send a copy of the plans to you, complete with where the dance floor should be. Uh-oh, Leslie is in my doorway tapping her foot. Later, honey."

Frank called Susan Csikos back. "How's it going with our offer for lot 16?"

She said, "I was just going to call you. Jack said the price of $850,000 was more than fair, but he would make it $800,000 if you accept his counter within twenty-four hours."

"I'll call you back," Frank responded.

He went to the bank to talk with bank president David Pohl.

"I've been countered for $800,000. What do you think?"

"The comps support that price. Were you aware of the restrictive covenants for that entire range?"

"Yes, Mike Maxwell told me that those properties may not be used for commerce of any kind, and homes constructed on each property must be worth a minimum of two million dollars."

The loan officer shook his head. "I had to meet with the bank's directors to review what the bank could offer you. The problems we need to overcome are serious. Your default in Washington DC on your condominium lease together with the repossession of your yacht for nonpayment of your loan resulted in an unsatisfactory credit report."

Dave continued, "You're essentially a contractor to the colonies, subject to termination for cause at any time or renegotiation of your draw on thirty days' notice. Worse yet, we have to take into account that your contract with the colonies, while renewable annually, is considered temporary employment."

Clasping his hands together, David Pohl continued, "Not meaning to pour salt into your wounds, but that $300,000 wire transfer to Mrs. Arnold was a serious drain on your cash balance. What was that all about?"

"It's a loan to Diane Arnold for her new colonies gallery in Chelsea. She has a two-year 10 percent interest repayment schedule. I'll ask Vick Lich to send you a copy of the contract."

"OK, that'll help. Get me a copy of your finalized deal for lot 16, and let's see what we can do," he said, as he patted Frank's shoulder.

Frank's stride slowed considerably as he left the bank. *Nothing comes easily*, he thought. *Now it appears I am paying for the sins of my past.*

He realized he couldn't go forward with improving the return on his investments by utilizing Larry Thompson's suggested fund investors because to do so, he would have to cash out his remaining CDs held by the bank. If he did that, he felt Dave would surely turn down his loan application.

He left a message with Susan to accept the counter offer, subject to bank financing.

He walked to the bank. When he learned that David was out to lunch, he did a 180° and walked toward the café.

Frank clicked on the realtor's text message: "Jack Steers wants to know if you got the financing."

He replied, "Susan, will let you know soon."

After lunch, Frank walked back to the bank. As he entered the door, he looked through the glass in Dave's office and saw the big smile on his face.

"You got the loan. We'll finance 75 percent of the $800,000, which is $600,000. Five years, one point over prime. There's some catches. We're going to attach your CDs and monitor your checking account activity monthly. Any irregular activity in your checking account could cause your loan to be called. Also, we are stating in the agreement that the property loan must be satisfied before you can begin construction and that we will finance your home construction loan. Is that agreeable?"

"Do I have any options?"

"No. Believe me, Frank, it took quite a selling job just to get your loan approved. Sign these papers."

Frank signed the papers and pocketed his copies. They shook hands. Frank notified Susan that the loan had been approved.

When he got back to his office, he called Lola and left her a voice mail. "We got the parcel. *Amo-te* (I love you)."

She called him back. "That's great, honey. Mike Maxwell sent me the house plans on which he placed a red star indicating the place for a twenty-by-twenty-foot dance floor. I know it's going to take time for us to enjoy that home together. Still, I'm so excited about the prospects!"

Frank didn't tell her how long it was going to take. He thought, *I'll talk with her another time about the provisions of my loan.*

The next morning Lola texted Frank: "Call me. Something drastic to tell you." The message contained a sad-faced emoticon.

"Frank, I've had a terrible scene with my uncle. I demanded a raise in salary and a larger percentage of the profits of Samba Troupe. You'll recall, I get only 20 percent, and I do all of the work. I wanted to help with the cost of our home.

"When he refused, he said something like 'A deal is a deal.' I resigned. He's replacing me with the woman I trained for the second troupe.

"I went to church this morning for the first time in years, and I prayed for guidance. I felt a glow inside, a strange warm feeling. I am not going to give up. I'm going to try to work with the samba dance competitor in Rio. After all, that is my home, not São Paulo or Taos."

Frank couldn't believe what he was listening to. Her discourse was rambling, almost incoherent. At the end he clearly heard, "As you can see, my plan to be with you—to dance with you for the rest of our lives—isn't going to happen. I have found my calling. Forgive me, Frank, please."

"Lola, you were the love of my life. I will always treasure our time together."

"Oh, my bonito. I pray that God will bless you."

Frank sighed, "Whatever will be will be."

Chapter 21

Productivity

Early on the second day of the New Year, Frank thought, *Lots of things to take care of*, as he poured over the notes he made during his flights back to Taos.

He called Leslie D'Alessandro in his marketing department. "Leslie, I need a detailed printout of the last quarter's sales records for each of our branches. Contrast their activity related to their geography-population statistics. Can that be ready by 1:00 p.m.?"

"It can—and will—be ready at one, boss."

Leslie and Frank pored over the statistical data she produced.

"What's your impression?" Frank asked.

"Maria de la Silva is hitting home runs as if she were Babe Ruth. Her reports are a hodgepodge, but who cares? Ken Geelhood has so much going for him in gallery orders from around the world that his numbers are consistently strong. Dick Boyd's making good progress. However his geo-pop area is relatively small compared to the others, and his local gallery sales could improve. Bud Robitaille is making nice gains for a new colony. Carroll Swanson needs help."

"Well, of course, Carroll has the double whammy of dealing with the unions and managing the distribution facility in Chicago together with new colony pressures."

Frank grew silent for a moment, scratching his head.

"Thanks, Leslie. Good job on the statistics."

As he walked home, Frank considered different approaches he might take in finding a way to improve each colony's productivity. He recalled Thomas Edison's publicized statement: "Success is 10 percent inspiration and 90 percent perspiration."

He called Gary and asked, "Could I look at the branch presidents' employment papers?"

"Why?"

"Part of my research on the project you gave me to improve branch sales."

"Employment papers are privileged. I cannot give permission to anyone to see them. They can't be copied or cited, nor taken from the office. I have an appointment off premises in the morning. Be in my anteroom at 9:00 a.m. tomorrow. You have thirty minutes. Understand?"

"Yes, sir."

The next morning, Mary Ellen greeted Frank at the desk in Gary's anteroom. "Hi, Frank. Thanks so much for the beautiful Waterford Crystal decanter and wine glasses you sent me for Christmas. I expected a box of candy."

She leaned forward to give Frank a kiss on the cheek. In that instant, he looked toward her. Their lips met in a gentle kiss.

"Uh-oh," Mary Ellen uttered, "coffee and churros?"

"Yessum."

At 9:30 a.m., Mary Ellen rang her little silver bell. She had been a school teacher. The bell had been a gift from the students of the last class she taught.

"Get what you wanted?"

"I believe I did," Frank chortled. "Thanks, M.E."

Mary Ellen watched Frank striding down the sidewalk. She thought, *Incident or accident? The kiss will not be in my report to Gary, of that I'm certain.*

Frank felt that he was onto something. He needed to make a number of phone calls in total privacy.

Satisfied with his research, Frank dictated on his recording device the program he would suggest to Gary for improving branch productivity. He called M.E. to ask for an appointment with Chairman Green to discuss his findings and to outline the plan he absolutely believed would be necessary to achieve the desired increase in productivity.

Checking his messages, he had a voice mail from M.E. "Gary asked when you'll be ready for the branch improvement meeting."

Returning the call, Frank said, "I need three more working days. How about next Thursday? OK if I bring Leslie D'Alessandro to the meeting?"

Frank had skipped lunch. "Not a good thing," he sighed.

At the café, while placing his order for the dinner special, his phone rang.

"Hi, Frank. Gary said yes to next Thursday at 9:00 a.m. Leslie may come with you."

Mary Ellen giggled, "I'll make it a foursome."

They met on Thursday morning in the anteroom of Gary's office. Without much prologue, Gary said, "Let's hear it, Frank."

"Some of it you're not going to like, but I believe in the end you'll agree that these very necessary changes in some crucial areas will—I'm sure—be worth the time and dollars invested."

Gary said, "If it's really going to be costly, I'll have to run it by the board. I'll need their approval."

Frank flipped on his recorder, inserted his ear plugs, and listened to his presentation recording while sipping his coffee. Then he spoke, "The first item is the marketing department's geo-pop analysis." He nodded to Leslie.

Leslie opened the first of her six binders. She recited the statistical analysis data and added her own take on the branches' shortcomings.

Frank harrumphed, "Where the colonies' galleries are located is, in our opinion, an essential issue for successful branch sales."

Frank continued, "The distribution center at O'Hare airport is an extremely poor choice for an art gallery. I understand it is an economy, but few people of means will come to that industrial area to view fine art. Leslie, please show the department's recommendations."

Leslie opened her gallery location binder. She passed the binder to Gary. Displayed were photos of gallery sites in the Chicago area where buyers of expensive original art would be comfortable shopping. She had listed the sites in accordance with their affluent locations together with lease information, expected utility, and other related expenses.

Frank said, "The Metro Industrial Park in Fort Myers is another poor choice as a gallery location. Naples is one of the wealthiest communities in America. This is where we need our SW Florida colony gallery. Leslie, please show us the preferred locations."

Leslie passed that binder around.

Frank continued, "The Milwaukee and São Paulo gallery locations are very suitable."

"The next subject, curriculum vitae (CV), is going to be a little more difficult. It has to do with the qualifications of our branch presidents."

Gary put his finger up and said tersely, "Be careful, Frank. M.E. is taking notes on this meeting which may have to be revealed to our board."

"Yes, sir."

"I would *guess* that not one manager has taken an art appreciation class. And likely, no one has a BA in art, although Senhora de la Silva could probably teach the classes," Frank exclaimed.

"Certainly they are all competent, dedicated managers. However, I know it would have to be nearly impossible for Dick, Ken, Bud, or Carroll to converse authoritatively in terms of their customer's interests in the field of fine arts."

"Leslie, please show Gary and M.E. your selection of qualified art education sources available to our branch managers."

Leslie opened her next binder and, using her pencil, pointed out the geographically acceptable schools together with their entry requirements, costs per semester, and online availability.

"My next recommendation is that we hire fine arts graduates to manage our galleries and that we hire an accountant for the São Paulo branch," concluded Frank.

Gary adjusted his collar and quietly asked, "What's the bottom line?"

Frank gestured toward Leslie.

She produced her final binder and recited her data, "Relocation costs for both the Chicago and Fort Myers galleries, $40,000. Depending on locations selected, added cost for the upgraded galleries, $250,000 per annum each, equals $500,000. Art education costs for four presidents to obtain their associate degrees, $60,000 each, equal to $240,000.

"Including benefits, the cost for the gallery managers and the accountant is $100,000 per annum each, equals $500,000. This comes to $1,280,000. Add 10 percent for contingencies, $128,000, equals $1,388,000."

"Frank, considering we are working at 10% profit, are you confident that taking these steps will produce an added billion dollars plus in sales? That's the number we will need to offset the costs."

"Yes, sir, I am. I'm equally certain that if these steps aren't taken, improvement in branch efficiency and profitability will not be forthcoming."

Gary stood up and straightened his slacks. "Good job, both of you. Leslie, I need to borrow your binders. Frank, I'll run this by the board and get back to you."

Leslie and Gary continued to chat as Frank and Mary Ellen left the office. Out of earshot Mary Ellen fluttered her eyelashes and whispered to Frank, "Ooh, you da man."

Frank managed a weak smile. "Thank you, M.E. I'm not sure my banker would share your opinion."

Gary called Frank the next Thursday. "You got the deal," he said. "I called each of the branch presidents, summarizing your recommendations. The only snag was Ken refused to take art classes, so his gallery manager will be the primary contact for art buyers in Taos—yes, the gallery manager with a BA in art."

"Sounds good. You won't regret it."

"Frank, I want you to go to each branch. Spend a week with the managers. Implement the plans. Make a few calls on the high-end galleries either with the president or his gallery manager. I'll ask Carroll, Ken, and Dick to interview and select three candidates for their gallery manager positions. You'll conduct the final hiring interviews.

"Keep me informed. OK?"

"Yes, sir. I'll have the marketing department prepare the want ads. I'll leave Sunday, go to Chicago first, then Milwaukee, then Fort Myers, and on down to São Paulo. When I get back, I'll spend a few days with Ken and interview his final candidates for the Taos gallery manager position."

"You know, time is money. Get on with it, Frank."

Chapter 22

Branch Work-Chicago

"Frank, I just don't have the time to attend art classes. Can we get around that? I'm getting a gallery manager."

Well, that's my Carroll, thought Frank. *Not hello, "how about some coffee," or "isn't this snowstorm terrible?"*

Recollecting Gary's warning about citing anything he read in any of the branch president's employment papers, Frank replied, "I assume that your future income depends in great part on the growth of your branch. I don't see that growth coming until you, personally, can interact with high-end art gallery owners and art collectors without your having a firm grounding in the fine arts."

Frank continued, "I'm sure you've heard that Ken Geelhood got a pass on the education requirements. The Taos Art Colony, you'll recall, is quite successful. Moreover, Ken is nearing retirement. His new gallery manager will be a member of Team Blue Danube.

"Gary expects the other branch presidents, their spouses, and their gallery managers to be part of the team in June. The colonies' galleries will be closed that month.

"I realize there isn't enough time for Bud, Dick, or you to be thoroughly grounded in the fine arts by June. Still, the classes you will have taken by then will allow each of you to speak more authoritatively with the people who buy fine art.

"Gary sees the Blue Danube excursion as a reward to his branch presidents. Spouses will receive per diem pay, as they did in Buenos."

Frank fished three forms out of his briefcase. "These forms are size sheets for exhibition attire for you, Nancy, and your gallery manager, to be completed and sent to the marketing department."

Frank saw Carroll's eyes widen as he massaged the back of his neck. Frank had read somewhere that neck massaging is a sure sign of stress.

Working with the marketing department CV binder, they selected Carroll's art school—the one that offered a combination of online and class attendance. Fortunately, that school was closest to Carroll and Nancy's home. Carroll called the office of the registrar and made an appointment to enroll. He would have to audit the course since the class was in session.

Checking his watch, Carroll asked, "Shall we order lunch delivered?"

"Yes, good idea."

Frank pulled the marketing department's Chicago art gallery binder from his briefcase. They made appointments to meet the leasing agents of six of the available galleries over the next two days. They agreed to display at the new gallery one hundred pieces, twenty-five from each branch, which factored into the amount of space they would require.

Frank suggested they go to the current gallery in Carroll's warehouse to select paintings for the new gallery.

Carroll said, "Go ahead—left at the end of the hall and use the freight elevator. I'll join you shortly."

Frank noticed that it took more than average strength to open the steel door of the freight elevator used to go up to the gallery. The option was a steep flight of stairs.

Frank sighed to himself, "Oh my heavens," when he saw dust particles floating in the atrium lighting. There was a layer of dust on everything, including the paintings displayed on steel warehouse racks. Used coffee mugs adorned the ratty old order desk, in front of which were two plastic chairs. A faux fern in a rusted container sat next to the desk. The floor was oil-spotted concrete. The oil heater spewed as much odor and fumes as heat.

Frank texted Gary, copied to Leslie, including photos: "It's worse than Leslie and I could ever have imagined. We'll need the restoration people here to clean up the artwork going to the new facility."

Frank made a note on his cell phone that new furniture would be required at the art colony of Chicago's new gallery.

"Good thing Leslie added the contingency fund to our budget," he sighed.

Carroll joined Frank, and they selected sixty-two oil paintings for transport to the new gallery. Carroll listed the paintings' ID numbers on his notepad. The remaining thirty-eight paintings would come from the colony's distribution center downstairs. Frank would select them in the morning while Carroll was enrolling in art school. The remaining paintings in the to-be-vacated gallery would be taken to Carroll's distribution center on the main floor.

Carroll planned to join his wife, Nancy, for dinner at one of the superb Chicago steak houses on the near north side. She was working part time as a perioperative nurse in that locale. He asked Frank to join them.

Frank readily agreed. "What's better than a Chicago steak," he chortled.

Delicious broiled steak odors wafted through the restaurant, filling the air with savory aromas that enhanced Frank's appetite.

Carroll reviewed his day with Nancy and she her day with him.

He sounds enthusiastic, Frank thought. *I think he's getting with the program.*

He tucked into his dinner: broiled rib eye steak with fresh herb butter, Idaho-baked potato with sour cream, a garden salad dressed with vinegar and oil, and crumbled Castello Alps Hirten cheese, washed down with an oak barrel aged merlot wine.

Frank excused himself and went to the men's room.

Carroll, remembering the expense account issues early in Frank's career with the colony, said to Nancy, "I knew he dines well everywhere. Now we've seen it for ourselves."

Frank grabbed the tab and asked the waiter to order a cab for his trip to his suite at the Wyndham Grand Chicago Riverfront hotel.

Sipping his nightcap, an ounce of Jack Daniel's on the rocks, Frank watched the snow gather on the vaulted roof below his room.

In the morning Frank asked the bell captain to suggest an interesting place for breakfast. The captain didn't hesitate to send him to Lou Mitchell's famed restaurant in downtown Chicago.

The front door wasn't open yet, so Frank walked into the employee's entrance.

"Hey, are you the new owner? We're not open yet. Go back outside, fellow!" shouted a waiter, who was stacking boxes of Milk Duds into a basket at the checkout counter.

Frank stooped over, pulled the $10 bill out of his sleeve, and said, "You must have dropped this." He handed the bill to the waiter.

"Well, it is cold outside. Sit down, sir. How about a cup of coffee?"

Frank murmured, "Chicago."

"What's with the Milk Duds?" he asked.

The waiter told him, "Lou Mitchell has given Milk Duds to ladies and children, and donut holes to everyone since 1958."

Hmm, thought Frank, *that kind of tradition builds a positive image.* He wrote a quick memo in the notes app on his cell phone.

Carroll joined Frank in the distribution center. They completed the tagging of paintings destined for the new gallery.

"How'd the registration in the fine arts class go?" asked Frank.

"I'll have my first in-class session Monday at 9:00 a.m. The curriculum looks to be exactly what I need. I'm actually looking forward to going back to school. I hope I'm not too old to learn what appears to be all new material for me."

Frank lowered his head and closed his eyes for a few seconds. When he looked up, he said, "When Albert Einstein received his Nobel Prize in physics in 1921 he made a historic comment. 'Once you stop learning, you start dying.'"

Carroll called a cab to take them to their first available art gallery rental. He told Frank, "I'm not yet competent to navigate quickly in Chicago."

The floor in the gallery had a noticeable declivity (downward slope). Frank and Carroll looked at each other, shaking their heads. Carroll told the leasing agent, "Thanks, but this won't work for us."

Arriving thirty minutes early at the next gallery, Frank and Carroll used the time to assess the environment. Carroll made a few notes in the gallery binder.

1. The streets are narrow.
2. No parking on street.
3. No nearby public garages.
4. Unrepaired cracks in the concrete steps in the entryway.

When the leasing agent arrived, they didn't allow him to open the door. They thanked him for his time and told him the site was unsuitable.

They had lunch at the Subway restaurant on the corner. The sign above the door said that it was number 7 of Chicago's 372 Subway restaurants.

Carroll called the leasing agent for the third art gallery scheduled for today and secured an earlier appointment.

According to Leslie's gallery binder information, this gallery was in a community called the Gold Coast, part of Chicago's Near North Side community.

They passed the restaurant where Frank enjoyed his steak dinner last night. *That's a plus*, he thought.

Leslie's binder notes noted there were thirty-five hotels in the Gold Coast area, some with five-star ratings.

At their next appointment, Frank and Carroll agreed the building was an alabaster edifice and that the attached three-level parking garages would be crucial to attract fine arts buyers.

They saw on the occupant listing that the vacant gallery was the first unit off the elevator on the second floor.

When leasing agent Jim Sheets opened the door, the vista before Frank and Carroll was so stunning that they both inhaled sharply.

Jim said, "When I heard the Art Colonies of America's branch here in Chicago needed an art gallery, I thought this site would be perfect."

"You'll have ten assigned spaces in the parking garage. The garage uses the stamped receipt method, no charge for your employees and guests."

Jim Sheets pointed toward the Gainesboro gray carpet, soft underfoot, which set the tone for the reception area. Deep see-through windows, nine feet tall, descended from the oak corniced ceiling allowing visitors a view of what would be on display in the open area beyond the foyer.

Walking into the display room, the men stepped on the ash gray textured surface tile floor. They checked out the private office, the restrooms, and the break room, what appeared to be an assembly room, the huge windows, and the freight elevator at the rear of the main gallery.

"Who was the previous tenant?" asked Carroll.

Jim replied, "A German toy manufacturer. It was their showroom. They completed their three-year lease, and we think they returned to Europe. As you can see, they left the facility immaculate."

Frank checked the gallery binder. As he suspected, this gallery was on the high end of the pricing table.

He asked, "Do you have any additional photos of this unit?"

Opening his iPad, the agent showed photos of every part of the facility.

Frank asked, "Can you send me those photos?"

"Sure, give me your email address."

Frank nodded to Carroll, "What do you think?"

"From what we've seen so far, there is no comparison," Carroll replied.

"I think we've got a deal," Frank enthused. He gave Mr. Sheets Chairman Green's fax address to send the lease contract forms.

They returned to Carroll's office. Carroll called the gallery rental contacts scheduled for tomorrow and canceled.

Frank asked Carroll to set up appointments for the next two days with client galleries that he and Carroll would call on in person.

Jim Sheets called Frank to tell him the lease forms and utility change over papers were on the way to Gary Green.

"Thanks. I have a favor to ask. Can you refer me to a good gallery interior decorator?"

"Sure can. How about the lady who decorated for the toy distributor? Their furnishings were gorgeous. If you would like me to, I can meet her at your new gallery and ask her to put together some ideas for you."

Frank said, "That would be great. Give her my number. Carroll and I can meet with her Friday afternoon."

Jim Sheets texted Carroll, forwarding him Pat Witzberger's decorator flyer.

Frank complimented the leasing agent. "I've no doubt you are at the top of your profession, Jim, due to your superb follow through."

The next day at his office, Carroll said, "Moving right along, I'm enrolled in fine arts school. Our new gallery has been acquired. Paintings have been selected for the gallery, decorator working. I'm making appointments for joint client calls for the next two days. Responses to our gallery manager want ads are starting to come in. How do you want to handle them?"

"You can eliminate the improbable applicants. Scan the potentials, forward their resumes to me. I'll select interviewees, and we'll jointly interview the three top candidates next week on my return from Milwaukee."

Carroll went back to work.

In the next two days Carroll and Frank visited the colony's top clients in Chicago. Two of the clients were acquaintances of Frank's from his years as an art critic, so it was like old home week for them.

Carroll listened carefully as they talked art, art, and art. He picked up very quickly the depth the gallery owners had in their field and Frank's ease in communicating with them.

Pat Witzberger, the interior decorator, was wide eyed. She said, "Oh, I remember you, Mr. Creech. My husband and I were on your train in the Chunnel. You're our hero!"

She opened an album and showed Carroll and Frank the toy distributor's furnishings.

"If the reception area pieces and the display room furnishings are to your tastes, you may catch quite a break. They were leased and returned in perfect condition. Half price for the second lease."

Frank stared at the photos. *Unbelievable*, he thought. The white leather sectional furniture in the display area was identical to the furniture in the lobby of the M.E. Hotel in London, which he had admired.

"What do you think, Carroll?"

Carroll said, "As far as I'm concerned, it's perfect."

Frank turned to Pat. "Mrs. Witzberger, I believe I just heard Mr. Swanson give you an order."

Chapter 23

Branch Work-Milwaukee

On Saturday morning, Frank reviewed his marketing department's binder which listed the Milwaukee art gallery clients. He made appointments for Tuesday and Wednesday with four of the owners.

Frank had texted Leslie to purchase him an iPad (after he had seen Jim Sheets employ his iPad in Chicago). Leslie would upload photos and descriptions of the newly received paintings that were not included in the last catalog. She would express FedEx the iPad to him care of Hotel Metro in Milwaukee.

Frank mentioned to Gary that he had ordered an iPad, and it would have the new paintings uploaded for his presentations to gallery accounts in Milwaukee. He suggested Gary should get iPads for the branch presidents to use in the same manner.

Gary responded, "Excellent idea. No doubt that will help in their presentations."

Frank elected to skip the hassle at O'Hare for the trip from Chicago to Milwaukee. Using his cell phone, he booked passage in a Quiet Car on the Amtrak Hiawatha train departing on Sunday at 11:30 a.m.

Boarding a cab at the Amtrak terminal in Milwaukee, Frank asked his driver to take him to Mader's Restaurant. He'd read in the tourist guide at the Metro Hotel that Mader's Restaurant had been voted the most famous German restaurant in North America. He was interested in seeing Mader's three-million-dollar collection of art on display at the restaurant.

The hostess seated him next to a couple. He looked at his menu and, glancing over the top, saw the man hurriedly leaving the table with his hat in hand. He put the menu down and asked, "Everything all right?"

She smiled and said, "My lunch date is an OB/GYN, and wouldn't you know it, he got called away for an emergency delivery. I'm going to give up dating doctors. I'm Emily Hansen. Would you like some company?"

Frank introduced himself, "I'm Frank Creech, and I dislike eating alone. Please join me."

He pulled back a chair at his table for Emily. They chatted while enjoying their lunch of Wiener Schnitzel, red cabbage, and Rueben rolls, washed down with authentic pilsner beer.

He asked Emily, "That's very interesting clothing you're wearing. Is it designer wear?"

"Yes, and I'm the designer," Emily laughed. "I'm the Emily of Emily's Designer Clothing, three doors down from here. Have to get back to my boutique now. Here's my card. Call me, maybe we can get together again. Do you polka?"

"Yes, I do." He handed her his card.

Frank determined that Mader's art was baroque, depicting palaces with ornate detail, in the seventeenth and eighteenth centuries. He opined, "Classic, but not art that would be of interest to the colonies."

That evening Emily called, "I hope you don't think me too bold, but I'm going to ask you anyway to meet me at Kochanski's Concertina Beer Hall Wednesday evening for their traditional polka jam. Say eight o'clock?"

"Yes, I will. Thanks for inviting me." He reflected, *Nice gal, very pretty, and she likes to dance.*

On Monday morning at 9:00 a.m., Frank met Bud at his gallery.

"Hey, Bud, are we ready to go to work?"

"My calendar is clear. Just you and me this week, big guy."

"You've got a nice place here, plenty of parking on your property. Your foyer is cheery and bright and inviting."

Bud said, "I have to admit Kathleen designed the foyer and did all the work except for the framing."

"Let's go through your gallery. I see you have maybe two hundred paintings hanging. You know the colonies have a new balance concept—120 pieces on display, twenty-four from each branch."

As they walked into the gallery Bud acknowledged, "I did get the memo, and we're rearranging our displays now."

"When you get down to a 120 paintings on display, your sales will increase," Frank offered. "We're not unlike high-end car dealers. If we put too much merchandise on the floor, it can create indecision.

"Oh, I love the five-foot-wide carpet runner on the tile floor. It's perfect for a couple walking together. It's easy on the feet and the right distance from the wall for perspective viewing.

"May I make a couple of suggestions regarding your display?" asked Frank.

Bud extended his right arm, palm up, and said, "Absolutely. Please do so."

"Have signs made for each colony to be placed above their groupings. Start with São Paulo Art Colony, next SW Florida Art Colony, followed by Taos Art Colony, then Chicago Art Colony, and finally Milwaukee Art Colony. You'll give your branch the last at bat as baseball home teams have. It's a proven statistical advantage."

Bud said, "Wow, great idea! I'll get on it right now."

Bud came back from the gallery, "Kathleen called. She wants to see what we're up to. She'll bring lunch, if that's all right with you?"

"It certainly is."

Bud said, "Our sign man is on his way to measure the areas and have us select the material for the signs."

"Good. Please look at my notes in the binder for fine arts education opportunities in Milwaukee. I'm tempted to ask Gary to allow Kathleen to attend fine arts classes if that would be her desire."

Kathleen shrugged off her coat, kissed Bud, and gave Frank a hug. She noticed the people arranging art in the gallery.

She set up the lunch she had prepared—sandwiches on whole wheat bread, a salad tray, hot tea, and bottled water.

Kathleen carefully read through the Milwaukee art school binder, including Frank's highlighted notes.

"The morning classes are best for Bud. There isn't much traffic in the gallery until close to lunchtime."

As she spoke, Frank saw a couple walking up the paver block path toward the gallery's brick building. Kathleen greeted the couple and explained to them that the gallery was being rearranged. Frank heard her ask them to please come back next week.

Frank thought, "Kathleen is an integral—no, an essential part of this colony."

The sign man asked, "Please select the materials we are to use for the signs, the stencil, and typeface and paint color."

Bud and Kathleen put their heads together and made the selections. Frank OK'd their choices. The signs would be delivered on Thursday.

Bud circled the courses he would take the first semester.

Frank asked Kathleen, "Would you like to take those courses?"

"Yes, but we can't—"

Frank interrupted. "We'll see. Are you on the colonies' payroll?"

"I did get per diem pay for my work in London, São Paulo, and Buenos Aires. But no, I'm not salaried. Bud and I have always worked together as a team."

"I'll see what I can do."

Bud drove Frank to the Hotel Metro. He would drive them to their appointments tomorrow.

The bell captain, pointing to the guest service desk, told Frank there was a package for him.

Frank didn't open his package; he'd have time to check out his iPad in the morning. He wrote a few notes on his desk pad while he sipped his Jack Daniel's.

Frank updated Gary on his progress and added, "There's another opportunity we need to discuss."

"Why do I suspect this 'opportunity' is going to cost the colonies money?"

"Did you know Kathleen has been working with Bud without compensation? She's covering for him while he makes seen calls, and she's very involved with the work of the colony."

"Well, actually, I did know that. I've been meaning to rectify that situation. I simply haven't got around to it.

"Here's your chance. *You* could appoint her as gallery manager of the Milwaukee colony."

"OK, you tell her that *I* have appointed her as Bud's gallery manager. I'll confirm the appointment. I'll ask Marion Jones in employment to send Kathleen her employment papers."

"Thanks, boss. It's the right move. I'll send you photos of their display, which I think we can use in the other branches. That'll save us a lot of time."

While he ate his room service potato kielbasa skillet, Frank read the résumés Carroll had sent him and selected the three best qualified candidates. All were currently employed.

Frank texted Carroll: "Contact Featherstone, Wawrinka, and Schmitt. Set appointments for them to interview at 10, 2, and 4 in your office Saturday."

Carroll had responded to Frank's query about school. He told Frank the class was extremely informative. He was surprised that the instructor didn't assign homework, but he did have weekly subject reviews, which Carroll said he appreciated.

Frank brought his iPad with him to the METRO Restaurant & Lounge at Hotel Metro. While eating breakfast, he familiarized himself with its functions and usages. He rehearsed showing the newly available paintings until he was comfortable with his new visual presentation device.

At their first appointment, Frank introduced Bud to his old friend Boyd Guard, owner of Guard's Art Gallery.

"Boyd, I have a deal for you today," Frank said, as he opened his iPad. "I received these slides yesterday."

He continued as he slowly paged through the slides, iPad turned so that Boyd and Bud could easily view the presentation, "These are sparkling new pieces from each of our colonies, and you are the first gallery owner in the entire world to view them.

"You get first shot at them, with an added 5 percent volume discount for an order of ten or more pieces."

Frank detailed each piece with the name of the artist, his background, and the likelihood of the paintings increasing rapidly in value.

Boyd summoned his gallery manager. "Phil, come in here, please. Give us a few minutes, Frank. Phil has an iPad, so he knows how to page through your offerings."

Boyd called them back into his office. "Gentlemen, we're going to give you a huge order, forty pieces, which we will use exclusively for two shows we're planning. Close to a million dollars. We want an additional 5 percent discount."

Frank said, "I'll need approval for the extra discount. Let me make a phone call."

He walked outside to make his call to Gary.

Back in Boyd's office, Frank sat down and spoke to both Boyd and Phil, "OK, but the additional 5 percent will be granted if payment is made with the order."

"It's a deal," Boyd said, as they shook hands. "It's nice to do business with you again, Frank."

Smiling, Frank replied, "Likewise."

Calls made on the next three gallery owners were modified to fit Frank's presentation; he proudly told those owners about the order from Guard's gallery.

Frank sold another six hundred thousand dollars' worth of art. Those orders were credited to the Milwaukee Art Colony.

Kathleen danced around the gallery floor, "Oh, Frank, you are terrific! Let's go out and celebrate tonight."

"Thanks, but I have a polka date tonight at Kochanski's Concertina Beer Hall."

"Who's your date?" Kathleen asked.

"Emily Hanson, the Emily of Emily's Designer Clothing."

"Oh, I know her! I've been in her boutique. Bud and I polka. May we join you?"

Emily picked Frank up at his hotel. They met Kathleen and Bud at Kochanski's. They enjoyed an evening of outrageous laughter, dancing, food, and drink.

On the way back to his hotel, Emily pulled into a space in front of her business. "Come in for a moment, Frank. I've something to show you.

"Frank, I have a BA in fine arts. I still paint, and I have a few pieces here. I'd appreciate very much your opinion of my work."

"How did you select these scenes?"

"They're from photos I took of lovely scenery while vacationing."

"There's nothing technically wrong with these paintings. Color, line, perspective, and depth are clean and well represented."

"C'mon, let's hear the other half."

"OK, please don't hate me for it. Remember your trips to the museums, your study of the old masters, Cezanne, Gauguin, Van Gogh, and the latter-day American masters, Rockwell, Grandma Moses?"

Emily said, "Yes, I do. But I don't expect to be in their class."

Frank continued, "What they had in common was *inspiration*. And candidly, that's what your work lacks."

Emily shuddered, and Frank saw tears forming in her eyes.

Frank held her in his arms and patted her back, "It's not the end of the world, really. For every artist who succeeds, ten thousand do not."

They drove to his hotel. Emily walked around to Frank as he exited the car. She put her arms around him and kissed him good night.

Kathleen had coffee ready on Thursday morning. Bud and Frank sat down with her at the lounge table.

"Kathleen, it is my distinct privilege to pass on to you Chairman Green's appointment of you as gallery manager of your colony, salaried, with full benefits and expense account."

"Bud will tell you that I am not usually without words, but I am now."

"Then I'll say them for you," Bud said. "Thank you very much, Frank, from both of us, for all you've done for us."

Frank harrumphed. "Here comes your sign man with the new signs, time for us to go to work."

With the signs expertly installed, Frank supervised while Bud, Kathleen, and their two clerks hung the art in the exact positions where they enjoyed the best light and would draw the attention of the colony's discerning clientele and visitors.

Frank took wide lens photos of the gallery, including the carpet runner. He forwarded them to Gary, to the marketing department, and to the branch executives in the other colonies.

Frank's final instructions to Bud and Kathleen were to prepare and send an invitation, including a photo of the gallery, to their contacts.

He said, "Ask them to join you in a party to celebrate your newly designed gallery. You'll get orders that day."

Back at his hotel, Frank checked his messages. He had a voice message from Emily: "Please call me."

"Frank, I feel such an idiot for my display last night. You simply told me what you felt about my paintings. I was hurt. Fortunately I cook better than I paint. Will you join me for dinner? I'll pick you up around seven."

It took Frank all of a millisecond to accept. "Yes, I will be happy to join you for dinner, Emily. I haven't had a home-cooked meal in ages."

Emily served her dinner: grilled salmon on a bed of arugula, tomato, mushrooms, and avocado, with a light balsamic dressing, paired with an Oregon pinot noir.

Frank said, "Excellent. Emily, you are a very good cook. Pairing the salmon with the pinot noir was a perfect counterpoint to the sweet and savory pink meat of the salmon."

"You continue to amaze me. You're a connoisseur of all you survey," Emily said. Her dark auburn hair brushed his cheek as she refilled Frank's wine glass.

After dinner they sat on her comfortable sofa in front of her glowing fireplace. Emily gently massaged his neck.

She asked, "When do you leave?"

"I'm booked Friday at 2:30 p.m. on the Amtrak Hiawatha Quiet Car to Chicago for applicant interviews with Carroll Swanson for his gallery manager position."

"What a coincidence. I'm booked on the same train. I'm going to the fabric fair to buy materials for my boutique. We can talk then. I want to know all about you."

Emily drove Frank to the Metro Hotel. They kissed. This time it was a lingering, passionate kiss. Frank felt no resistance when he held her buttocks during the kiss.

Emily asked, "Can you meet me at Mader's tomorrow at noon? We can have lunch and cab together to the Amtrak terminal."

Gary called, "Frank, the board of directors was elated by your sales in Milwaukee, and they asked me to pass along their congratulations. You took the pressure off our overstocked situation with those four huge orders. I received a nice thank you note from Kathleen Robitaille. Great job there as well. I backed you up on your gallery designs. Keep up the good work."

Frank didn't have the heart to tell Gary the gallery designs would have to be changed from time to time. He knew it would ruin Gary's day. Instead, he filled Gary in on the interview appointments on Saturday at the Chicago colony.

He checked out of his hotel and cabbed to Mader's. Emily was waiting in the reception area. He believed her smile could have lit up one of the dungeons on Mader's wall.

They heard pinging sounds on the window behind them. "Oh," Emily said. "That's hail. The weather forecast isn't good today for Milwaukee and Chicago. Hope our train isn't delayed." She tried to call Amtrak. The lines were busy.

Frank checked the weather on his cell phone. "Doesn't look good. There are delays everywhere."

At the depot, Frank asked the cab driver to wait a minute while they checked inside. The station appeared to be closed.

Emily read the sign on the door: "All schedules for today canceled due to weather. Hold your tickets for your next trip. For information, call 1-800-888-8000 tomorrow after 9:00 a.m."

"Let's take the lady home first, then you can drop me off at the Metro Hotel," Frank suggested.

The driver replied, "Mister, I'll be lucky to get to the lady's home in this storm. My visibility is near zero."

The driver maneuvered, avoiding collisions, until the cab was sideswiped by an ambulance and careened into a light pole. They smelled the radiator fluid as it spewed from the cracked casing.

The cabbie said, "I'm sure it'll be tomorrow morning before another cab can be dispatched for you. There's a Marriott Hotel one block from here, I'll help you with your bags."

In the lobby Emily said, "Frank, I don't want to sit in this lobby all night. Let's check in. OK?"

At the registration desk the clerk asked them what accommodation they wanted and mentioned they had only one suite left.

Frank said, "We'll need separate rooms."

Emily said, "We'll take the suite."

Emily called Linda McAffee, the girlfriend she was going to stay with in Chicago, and told her she would get back to her when the weather cleared.

Frank called the Wyndham Hotel in Chicago and moved his reservation forward to Saturday.

While Emily used the bathroom, Frank texted Carroll, "Stranded, will get back to you tomorrow morning."

Frank unscrewed the cap from the little Jack Daniel's bottle and poured himself an ounce of bourbon.

When he looked up, Emily came out of the bathroom; she was dressed in a beautiful white nightgown, her pink satin robe draped over her shoulders.

He took his turn in the bathroom. He felt he was betraying the memory of Lola as he donned her gift bathrobe.

Frank joined Emily on the small couch in their suite. "Are you hungry?" he asked.

"Yes, but dinner can wait. I'd like to talk with you while we have no distractions. I want to get to know you better."

He couldn't resist saying to her, "Do you mean knowing me in a biblical way?"

"Well, maybe. We'll see."

"Let me tell you a little about myself." She told him she was married at age seventeen to her nineteen-year-old high school sweetheart and that he was killed in Vietnam. She told him she lost their baby.

She admitted to having several affairs over the years and added that she had never remarried. Tears formed in her eyes as she told him her parents had helped her through her college years and that she had inherited the money for her boutique. She said her biggest fear was growing older without anyone to take care of, or not having someone who will take care of her.

"Now tell me about yourself."

"You encapsulated your background far better than I will. Well, here goes. I was an average student in school. However I did earn four athletic letters—baseball, basketball, football, and wrestling.

"I love art but realized early on I wasn't an artist. I used my GI Bill to continue my education. I edited the Michigan State University paper. I earned a BFA degree. After I graduated I had a number of jobs, one of which was as a stringer journalist in the arts and entertainment field. I gravitated into a position with the *Washington DC International Art Critics* and ultimately became the senior art critic.

"I held that prestigious position for thirteen years until I was discharged for publicly humiliating myself and embarrassing the paper in a foolish melee I got into in Washington. An artist friend, Marty Freling, lined up my present position. I hope it will be my last job."

"C'mon, Frank, get to the part about your women," Emily said, as she tossed her robe over the back of the couch.

"OK, I was married three times, divorced three times. No children, which was not their fault. I learned while married to wife number two that I have a low testosterone problem. I've lived with several women. My most recent love was Lola, who after a traumatic experience returned to a religious life.

Frank took Emily's hand, lifted her off the couch, pulled her close, and kissed her.

He guided her to the first bed in their suite.

Emily flipped off the nightstand lamp as Frank turned down the bed's cover. She thought, *I need to get his mind off Lola.*

In the afterglow of their consummated relationship, Emily said, "I wanted you from the first day we met. I told my doctor friend the next day that I was no longer available."

Emily laughed, "It took this storm to make us a couple."

Frank admitted, "I wanted you as well, but I kept telling myself it wasn't right. I was still in love with Lola."

Frank noticed she kept her eyes on his face while walking to the dining room. *Emily is one fantastic catch. I believe I've struck gold*, he thought.

Emily thought, *I've finally found my man. We are connected in so many ways.*

The weather cleared in the morning. Emily canceled their Amtrak reservations while Frank engaged a chauffeured SUV for their trip to Chicago.

"Frank, I was going to stay with my friend Linda, another clothing designer. Since I know you're leaving Sunday, and I want to spend all the time I can with you."

Carroll called Frank, "Bill Schmitt accepted a position in Cicero, so we're down to Wawrinka and Featherstone. There's a good part, though. Bill will manage an art gallery, and he asked for our catalog. I forwarded the information to marketing. Can you make the two remaining interviews today?"

"I'm in an SUV on I-94 heading to Chicago as we speak. No problem."

Frank felt his stomach churn. Then he heard a rumble that sounded like Mt. Etna. He was hungry, and more coffee wasn't going to satisfy that hunger. Since his first interview had canceled, he recognized he and Emily had time for breakfast at Lou Mitchell's restaurant.

He cocked his head, and with a wry grin, asked, "Emily, do you like Milk Duds?"

Carroll texted Frank, "Wawrinka will be here at two o'clock. Featherstone can't be here until five o'clock at best. He's coming here from another appointment out of town. He'll be in touch to update us on his expected arrival."

Carroll and Frank hired both men they interviewed. Frank thought Jeremy Featherstone was the better candidate for the gallery manager position, and Carroll agreed. Carroll said Paul Wawrinka was perfect for the supervisory position opening in his distribution center.

Carroll told Frank, "You know Paul is Polish, and Polish Americans are the largest European ethnic group in the Chicago area. His ability to relate with our Polish union employees and his knowledge of fine art, I believe, will improve our distribution center enormously."

They both felt exalted—Carroll for the economy of two hires in one day, Frank for the good people the colonies had gained.

Chapter 24

Branch Work-SW Florida

Frank and Emily checked out of their Chicago motel Sunday morning. They cabbed to her friend Linda's condo.

Frank cupped his hands, the flakes of snow melting as soon as they touched.

Emily said, "It's beautiful, so perfect for our farewell. Call me when you arrive in sunny Naples."

"That I will do, designing lady," Frank chortled.

They kissed goodbye very slowly and sensuously.

After clearing TSA screening at O'Hare, Frank sat down at the first bar in the concourse and ordered a Jack Daniel's on the rocks with a water chaser.

During his two-hour-and-twenty-three-minute flight to the Regional Southwest International airport in Fort Myers, Frank reviewed his marketing department gallery sites in Naples. He was intrigued with the area called the Naples Art Center, part of the Artis-Naples complex, home of the Baker Museum and the Naples Philharmonic. Frank thought the museum would be an ideal location for the SW Florida Colony art gallery. An affluent clientele, people of culture and means, would be exactly the right market for the colonies' art gallery.

Frank tipped the Hyatt Regency Naples hotel courtesy driver to take him to the Naples Art Center so that he could survey the complex.

The location was prime, prime, prime, thought Frank. *What approach could I make that would create interest in the colonies sharing space here?*

He took four brochures from the Baker Museum's literature rack.

In his suite at the Hyatt, Frank opened his mini bottle of Jack Daniel's, poured it over ice in a tumbler, and took a sip as he reviewed the Baker Museum programs. The *Art for the Ages* series of lectures caught his attention.

"Emily, I didn't forget to call you. I've been working. How's it going?"

"Other than freezing my buns off and being so envious of you in Florida, I'm fine. Bought some gorgeous fabrics and have a dozen new designer outfits to put together."

"Well, sorry I'm not there and warming your cold buns," Frank chortled.

"Oh, wouldn't it be loverly?" sang Emily. "You'll get your chance soon. My aunt and uncle have a condo in Bonita Springs, and I plan to visit them this week. Can you make time for me this coming weekend?"

"I can't even imagine *not* making time for you."

"Good morning," Frank said to the receptionist at the Baker Museum, "I need to talk with the curator or manager."

"May I tell him what this is in reference to?"

"Of course," Frank replied, handing her a brochure from the Art Colonies of America. "I'm interested in shared space."

"Oh my, you're the Frank Creech who fought the pirates in Biscayne Bay! I recognize your photo from the news. May I keep this brochure to show my family?"

"Yes, you may." Frank fished up another brochure from his attaché case and handed it to her.

"Thank you, Mr. Creech. I'll ask our museum's director if he can see you."

A man walking with the help of an exquisite Malacca cane came out of his office, hand extended.

"Mr. Creech, I'm Ron Romano. I met you fifteen years ago at SeaWorld Orlando. I remember you judged the aquatic art competition for the *Washington DC International Art Critics*. It's nice to see you again. I see you've changed jobs too. Please come back to my office."

"Oh yeah." Frank laughed. "It rained like pouring piss out of a boot that day. The artwork was displayed under your building's eaves, and I got soaked walking to the exhibits. You brought me a towel. It really is a small world, isn't it?"

"Yes, it is. You're interested in shared space?"

Frank filled Ron in on the colonies' desire to relocate their Fort Myers gallery to Naples and that he was hopeful the Baker Museum would have some space available the colonies could rent.

"Our funding is primarily from endowments and donations. I'm not confident the board would have interest in offering a lease to a commercial enterprise."

Ron continued, "Having said that, we just dismantled and shipped an entire exhibition of prehistoric art to a museum in Italy, so we do have an area available. How much space would you need?"

"We'll need about a hundred twenty lineal feet."

"I'll run this by our board and get back to you as soon as possible, OK?"

"Certainly. I'll be in the area for the next week. Hopefully we can get together soon."

Frank called Gary and updated him on his efforts with the Baker Museum. "I'll FedEx you the museum's brochure, so you can get a sense of what we're looking at."

"Do that. Have you met with Dick Boyd?"

"I'm en route to Fort Myers right now."

Frank had hired a transport service for the day.

He called Marty Freling. "Do you still play poker on Monday evening?"

Marty laughed, "Things change slowly at CYRC. Get up here, I'll save you a seat."

Frank's first stop was at the SW Florida Colony's gallery in the Fort Myers Metro Industrial Park.

Dick Boyd, dressed in a business suit with an apron cover, greeted Frank at the door. With a huge grin, he said, "Hey, Mr. Marketing Director. Good to see you."

Frank saw that Dick and his gallery clerk had arranged their exhibits in accordance with his instructions.

"Looks good, Dick," Frank said, waving his hand toward the gallery. "Have you lined up your fine arts courses?"

"Sure have. I'll start attending classes next Monday morning at Florida Gulf Coast University."

Frank asked, "What do you think of moving your gallery to Naples?"

"It's the thing to do, no doubt about it. We tried to save the colonies high rental costs, but it has become apparent we're not drawing the clients we need to be successful."

Dick shook his head, "We've tried very hard to make it work, but the numbers don't lie."

Frank handed Dick the Baker Museum brochure.

"I'm working on renting some space the museum has for your gallery," Frank said. "What do you think about sharing space there?"

"Gail and I have been to the Naples Philharmonic and have toured the Baker Museum. I think it's a fantastic idea," Dick excitedly exclaimed.

Dick's cell phone rang. "Hi, Marty." He listened to Marty and responded, "I'll tell him you said 'get your ass in gear.'"

"Frank, Marty says you've got forty-five minutes before the first hand is dealt."

"Thanks, Dick. I'll get back to you ASAP," Frank said as they shook hands.

He directed his driver to Caloosa Yacht & Racquet Club's clubhouse in south Fort Myers.

Marty was sitting on the bench next to the left side concrete lion outside CYRC's clubhouse. The clubhouse was also home to the most popular private dining club in Fort Myers—the Blue Coyote Business & Social Club, owned by Mitch Schwenke and operated by his partner, Corey Swarthout.

"Hey, Frank, good to see you. Dismiss your driver. You're staying with Judy and me tonight. I'll take you to Naples tomorrow morning."

"We need to catch up."

"How's Lola?"

"Er . . . uh . . . that'll take a while," stammered Frank.

Marty looked quizzically at Frank. "Oh, Judy will want to hear this story firsthand, I'm sure. She's preparing one of your favorites dishes for dinner, beef bourguignon."

They played wild card poker. Frank enjoyed the camaraderie with old friends and new friends.

Judy and the Freling's new puppy, Cody, welcomed Frank to their home.

During dinner, Judy's (and Cody's) ears perked up when Marty said to Frank, "OK, Frank, tell us what's going on between you and Lola."

Frank told them of Lola's set-to with her uncle and of her return to religion, which had seemingly pointed her toward salvaging her career in samba dancing in Rio de Janeiro under the auspices of her church.

He showed them the photo the waiter took of Emily and him at Lou Mitchell's restaurant in Chicago.

"Lovely girl," Judy said, shaking her head. "I wonder if she knows what she's getting into with you. No offense intended, Frank, but your history with the women in your life is a disaster."

Marty cupped his chin and, shaking his head, said, "I noticed Lola was quieter than usual in Miami. This business with her uncle was probably on her mind."

"No doubt it was on her mind. I can only hope everything works out for her."

"And that reminds me, I need to fill Gary Green in on the situation. I certainly don't want to further enrich Lola's uncle for the Samba Troupe performances we contracted for in the Blue Danube countries after his shabby treatment of his niece."

Frank so appreciated sharing his feelings with the Frelings. He felt a catharsis of his soul in relating to them the critical issues in his life. Their help had always been so beneficial to him.

Marty drove Frank to Naples in the morning. They went to the Baker Museum. Frank used the visit to show Marty how appropriate the museum would be for the SW Florida gallery. It was also an opportunity for checking with Ron Romano on the progress of his proposal for sharing space.

They toured the museum, eventually encountering Ron in the atrium lit display area recently vacated.

Marty quietly said to Frank, "It's perfect."

Frank introduced Marty to Ron.

Ron's eyes lit up as he looked at Marty. He enthused, "You're the artist who won the Coming Home art competition at the Regional Southwest airport, and I heard you won first prize at the Normandy 2014 seventieth year art contest. It's so nice to meet you." They shook hands.

Frank asked Ron, "Any progress on my space rental request?"

"You can make your move when it is convenient for you. We'll curtain off your area."

Frank treated Marty and Ron to lunch at Truluck's Seafood Steak and Crab in Naples. The restaurant was noted for its Florida stone crab and fresh-catch seafood menu, with over one hundred wines to choose from. All agreed Truluck's was as good as advertised.

Marty told Frank his Oysters Rockefeller hors d'oeuvres were the best he had ever tasted.

Marty dropped Frank off at his hotel, "See you next trip old friend."

Frank called Gary and laid out the deal for the space at the museum. He mentioned Marty's positive feelings toward the SW Florida colony locating their gallery in the museum.

Gary responded, "I'll ask Vic Lich to draw up the rental contract, which we'll submit together with the first month's rent and the security deposit. I'll express it to you care of your hotel. Can you fit the lecture into your schedule?"

"I'm visiting the branches four times a year minimally. The lectures will draw attention to our galleries. And before you order it, yes, we should include those lectures for the other branches.

"Oh, and one other thing for you to consider." He told Gary of Lola's breakup with her uncle's Samba Troupe and asked him if he would cancel the bookings on the Blue Danube excursion.

"Can't do. There is a no cancellation provision in those bookings. Besides, I believe the Samba Troupe performances will enhance our relationship with the Blue Danube art gallery owners. The cultural exchange thing is a two-way street, and business is business.

"Get on with it, Frank. You know—"

"Yes, sir, time is money."

Frank advised Ron of the chairman's acceptance of the Baker Museum proposal.

Ron called back two hours later, "You've got the deal. Congratulations."

Frank called Dick. "Your SW Florida Art Colony has a new location. Come down in the morning. Bring Gail if she can get away. We'll survey your new gallery.

"Oh, and cancel your lease at the Metro Industrial Park, effective the first of the month. The colonies will pay the cancelation fee."

At nine the next morning, Frank introduced Dick and Gail Boyd to Ron Romano.

After coffee, the Boyds, Frank, and Ron went to the colony's new space.

Gail and Dick measured and photographed the space, preparing for their gallery move.

The Boyds and Frank went to a high-end carpet outlet in Naples and ordered a five-foot runner which was compatible with the colors of the gallery.

"Dick, I'm not sure Gary told you you're getting a gallery manager?"

"He did, and I think that'll be the icing on the cake for my branch."

Back at his suite at the Hyatt, Frank pulled an 8 1/2" x 14" legal pad from his attaché case and began to scribble notes for his lecture series. He did so while sipping his Jack Daniel's on the rocks. Sixteen pages later, he put the pad down.

Before dinner Frank chartered a half-day offshore fishing boat for Wednesday morning.

Frank caught two hog grouper fish. He had enjoyed their flaky white delicious flesh previously and looked forward to having hog grouper for lunch. He took his fish to a small restaurant near the dock that prepared fishermen's catches.

He gave one fish to the restaurant and ate the other one with potatoes O'Brien, paired with a white burgundy wine.

"Dining alone again," Frank mused, "is for the birds. Come to think of it, they rarely dine alone."

Emily called. She had arrived in Bonita Springs and was enjoying a Cuba Libre on the lanai at her aunt and uncle's condo.

They basked in the sun, told each other the things that had happened in their lives, made passionate love, and toured Naples, including the new SW Florida gallery site in the Baker Museum.

They danced their first waltz together during the Hyatt's Sunday midmorning tea. Frank put a hundred-dollar bill in the tip jar and asked the trio of classical musicians to play Johann Strauss II's "The Blue Danube Waltz."

Emily followed Frank's sweeping waltz steps and turns perfectly without taking her eyes from his eyes. Her pale blue maxi dress billowed in the sea breeze that flowed through the open French doors. Tiny blue flower bows adorned with baby's breath accented her auburn hair, sparkling in her turns under the lights.

At the end of the dance, Frank bowed, and Emily curtsied to the musicians. The trio rose and applauded the dancers, joined by the guests in the tea room.

Walking back to their suite, Emily gushed, "I've never been applauded before, and it's a heady feeling. I adore you, my very special man who creates memories that will last all my life."

Frank took her hand, smiled, and nodded his appreciation.

In the suite Frank's cell phone rang. It was Gary.

"I have my photos of São Paulo's gallery, and it is exactly in spec with a beautiful carpet runner installed. She's already hired her accountant and is sending her gallery manager, Manual Orba, to fine arts classes. There is nothing that requires your attention in São Paulo at this time."

Truer words were never spoken, Frank thought, as he recalled meeting Lola in São Paulo.

"Ken has three gallery manager candidates ready to meet you, and he doesn't want to wait another week."

"Yes, sir. I've read their résumés. Ken has exceptional candidates. I'll be in Taos tomorrow morning."

Frank called the airlines and changed his flights. He checked the weather in Taos. It was forty-three degrees.

Emily checked on her flight status, and she checked the weather in Milwaukee. It was thirty-five degrees. Frank's ETD was 4:20 p.m.; Emily's ETD was 5:15 p.m. It was noon in Naples.

"Well," Frank chortled, "it's checkout time. We'll have to leave for the airport in an hour."

Emily said, "Get an extension and let's put that time to good use."

"On the beach, soak up some rays?"

"No," Emily laughed as she undid the buttons of her designer pinstripe lace front blouse, "I have a better use for your extension."

Emily administered her newly learned TT (therapeutic touch), and Frank rose to the occasion.

At the airport, Frank saw tears forming in Emily's eyes. He kissed her eyelids. They parted, he striding toward his concourse, she walking slowly toward her concourse.

Chapter 25

Gallery Managers

Frank cabbed to his Burch Street casita residence.

It's hard to believe I've lived in this little place for five years, Frank thought as he fielded a call from Ken Geelhood,

"Frank, can you be here by ten o'clock? I've scheduled the gallery manager candidates for ten, two, and four as per your Chicago scheduling."

"Can do, Ken. I'm on my way."

"Ken, who do you like for your gallery manager?"

"I'm glad you have the final call. I like all three."

Larry Stahlhut was first up to bat. Frank offered his hand, and Larry smiled and patted Frank on the shoulder.

"You don't shake hands?"

"I was a portrait artist until diabetic neuropathy caused nerve damage in my hands. Now they tingle constantly, and there is occasional pain and numbness. I can no longer paint. The pat on your back was my handshake," Larry said with an even broader smile.

"I know art, Mr. Creech, and I can handle the job."

They chatted for a while. Frank was very impressed with Larry and told him so. He asked Larry to call Ken Geelhood at six this evening.

Ken waved in the next candidate, the young woman in the hallway who had been talking with Leslie D'Alessandro.

"Do you shake hands?" Frank asked.

Blond and perky Lydia Noonan smiled and said, "I certainly do, but I like hugs better." She hugged Frank.

Leafing through her resume, Frank said, "I see you were the top-ranked graduate in your class at the School of the Art Institute of Chicago—very impressive. I believe that's one of the highest rated fine art schools in America?"

"It's second only to Yale, Mr. Creech."

"Lydia, please call me Frank. What was your major in fine art?"

"Good question, Frank. My area is the history of art."

"Hmm," Frank said. "You're a very strong candidate, Lydia. Please call Mr. Geelhood at six fifteen this evening."

Ken left; visitors to the gallery were coming into the building.

Frank made pencil notes on Lydia's application form. When he looked up, Leslie rapped on the door. Frank waved her in.

"Hi, Frank. Welcome back. I had a few questions on your request for data you need for your art lectures. One of my questions was 'What was the earliest known artwork?' When Mrs. Noonan told me about her fine arts major, the history of art, I asked her the question. She unhesitatingly said, 'the Paleolithic era.'"

"My researcher found that was the era in which the skull of earliest man was discovered by anthropologists in Sussex, England, together with broken pieces of bone carvings."

They made headway on her research question list. Leslie left, and Ken came back.

Ken introduced Paul Koenig. Paul shook hands with Frank.

"I see that you are employed by the Art Institute of Chicago. Why do you want to make a change?"

"I'm capped out. I'm the assistant to the vice president, and there are only two moves available to me with no one near retirement age. I seek opportunity, sir. I responded to your ad because of the salary *and* the bonus."

They talked art for the next twenty minutes. It was obvious to Frank that Paul Koenig knew his art and could communicate intelligently.

"Paul, you are a strong candidate for our position. Please call Mr. Geelhood at six thirty this evening.

Ken and Frank put their heads together. "I see what you meant, Ken. All three are strong candidates."

Ken said, "Paul Koenig has experience in a very significant art gallery. Gary would appreciate his ambition, I'm sure."

Frank said, "I really like Lydia, particularly her specialty, the history of art. It's a great talking point for a gallery manager."

Ken said, "Larry is selling Porsches for a living now. They're big ticket automobiles. He's used to interacting with high-end buyers."

Ken put his right arm up and asked, "What do we do, flip a coin?"

Saved by the ringtone, Frank answered his call.

"Frank, I can't seem to catch a break," Carroll said dispiritedly. "Jeremy Featherstone called. His father is gravely ill, and Jeremy is returning to England. I really need to keep Paul Wawrinka in the distribution center."

"Carroll, maybe you will catch a break. I need to talk with Ken a few minutes about the people we've interviewed for his gallery. I'll call you back."

Frank called Leslie, "Would you like having Lydia on our team, even though her primary assignment would be the gallery?"

"*Oh yes*. She could provide an immediate historic background for our art that would strengthen our presentations!"

"Ken, I think I may have a solution. We hire all three. Carroll could have Paul Koenig, who lives in Chicago and has connections there. Larry would fit in perfectly in Naples with Dick Boyd, while you and marketing would gain the delightful Lydia. What do you say?"

Ken said, "Let's run it by Gary. I know he'll appreciate the multiple hire, saves money."

Frank clicked on his speakerphone so Ken could hear the conversation. He laid out the whole situation and asked Gary for his approval of the suggested solutions.

Gary said, "Sounds like a plan. Get on with it, Frank."

Ken took the call, "Congratulations, Larry. Please come here at nine o'clock in the morning for indoctrination."

"Thank you, Mr. Geelhood, and please thank Mr. Creech for me. You won't be sorry."

At 6:15 Ken's phone rang. "Congratulations, Lydia. Please come here at nine o'clock in the morning for indoctrination."

"Yes, sir. Whoopee!"

Ken accepted the call from Paul Koenig. "Congratulations, Paul, you're now on our team. Please come here at nine o'clock in the morning for indoctrination."

"I appreciate the opportunity, Mr. Geelhood. See you in the morning."

Frank filled Carroll in on the appointments. "We'll have Paul Koenig contact you tomorrow."

Frank said, "Ken, I could use a drink."

Ken said, "So could I, and we've earned it." He opened the minibar behind his desk.

"Alice is expecting you for dinner tonight, OK?"

"There's one important thing I need to know," laughed Frank. "What time?"

Alice served her chipotle chili, a garden salad, and her homemade bruschetta with Corona beers.

Frank told Alice her chili on a "chilly" evening was perfect.

They relaxed and chatted about the day and how they hoped everything was going to work out.

Ken admitted he was tired of going to the gallery every time the chamber of commerce gave admission tickets to tourists and was so happy someone else would be in charge of his gallery.

After clearing the dishes Alice disappeared for a few minutes. She returned carrying what appeared to Frank to be a heavy photo album.

"You know, Frank, I haven't always been your biggest fan. I thought you were flamboyant and even a bit hokey. However, in the last few years we have been able to purchase our new home, new cars, designer furnishings, and we're setting aside retirement funds—due entirely to your marketing prowess. So I've done a 180°, and now I keep a scrapbook of your deeds, your heroics, and your accomplishments."

She handed Frank the scrapbook. Frank thumbed through it quickly. It was replete with photos, news stories, commentary, and year-end summaries of colony successes.

"I am impressed, Alice. There are things in here that I didn't remember. Someday I'd like to have this journal."

"Ha, ha," Alice laughed. "Maybe someday."

At headquarters the next morning, Frank and Ken sipped their coffee and munched on Mary Ellen's churros. She had set up a sideboard in the conference room with plates, napkins, silverware, churros, coffee, and juices.

Bill Hasse had furnished the new hires with name-photo badges.

M.E. brought the new gallery managers to the conference room.

Marion Jones introduced herself, "I'm director of the personnel department." She handed the threesome their employment papers, insurance papers, the corporate structure protocol declaration, and the clothing size form, together with the newest catalog of the colonies.

Ken waved them toward the refreshment table.

When they were seated at the conference table, Frank motioned to Ken and said "Mr. Geelhood, president of the Taos colony, will open your indoctrination session."

Ken leaned forward and looked first at Lydia. "Lydia, you've been assigned to manage the gallery here in Taos. You'll report to me. I am so happy to welcome you."

Turning to Larry, Ken said, "Larry, you've been assigned to manage our new Naples gallery. We'll put you in touch with your boss, Dick Boyd."

"Paul, you're going to work in your hometown, Chicago. You've been assigned to manage our new gallery there. We'll put you in touch with your boss, Carroll Swanson."

"Is this OK with everyone?"

He pointed to Lydia.

"Oh yes, this is a dream come true for me."

He pointed to Larry.

"Perfect."

He pointed to Paul.

"I don't even have to move, and I have a lot of contacts in the windy city."

As if on cue, Mary Ellen opened the door, and Gary Green walked in. She said, "Ladies and gentlemen, here to greet you this morning is the Art Colonies of America's chairman of the board, Mr. Gary Green."

Everyone stood and shook hands with Gary as Mary Ellen poured coffee in his cup.

"Sit down, sit down, and enjoy M.E.'s goodies, please. I can only stay for a few minutes. It is my pleasure to meet you and welcome you to our family."

Gary gave them a brief history of the colonies and nodded to Ken.

"Ken will take you on a tour of the facilities. He'll explain our procedures, our requirements, and please remember the only dumb question is the one unasked."

Gary slid his chair back stood up and concluded, "Thanks for joining our team. Best wishes to all. Take a few minutes and fill out your paperwork for Marion."

Ken brought the new gallery managers to the marketing department. Leslie introduced them to her staff, explaining their functions.

Frank saw Lydia's eyes become as large as silver dollars when she looked up at the electronic display of sales activity.

He recalled when the display was a chalkboard.

Frank could see that Larry was intrigued as he watched the catalog staff pasting up the second quarter mailer, including the photographs of the new gallery managers the security officer had taken when they arrived and the bio information furnished by the employment department.

Paul listened to the telemarketers, shaking his head. Frank heard him say, "Fantastic."

As they were leaving, Frank asked Paul if he had spoken with Carroll Swanson.

"Yes, sir. Prior to my application to the colonies, I had notified my superiors at the institute of my intentions, and they are releasing me at the end of this week. I'll report to Carroll next Monday."

"Lydia, when can you report for work?"

"Frank, Ken is giving me the rest of the month to take care of things I need to do for the move. I report the first of next month. I can hardly wait."

"Larry?"

"I talked with Dick Boyd. He's in the process of moving to our new gallery. He said two weeks would be fine. I gave two weeks' notice to my dealership owner."

Frank removed his Burberry boat collar felted wool double-breasted coat from the coat rack. He waved goodbye to everyone.

Warmly wrapped, he walked home.

Chapter 26

Blue Danube

Frank looked at the calendar in the marketing department. The Blue Danube campaign would begin in Prague in one week, on June 15. It would continue the week of June 22 in Vienna and then a week in Salzburg, beginning June 29 and ending July 4 with the final Samba Troupe performance.

The ABC's of Advertising people created a series of three mailers saluting the cultural exchange, asking gallery owners and private collectors to visit the colonies' exhibitions in Prague, Vienna, or Salzburg. RSVPs would receive their tickets from Leslie for the Samba Troupe's Brazilian samba performances at the colonies' exhibition sites or from Frank during his seen calls.

The invitations were printed in both English and Czech or German (the official Austrian language). The mailers included RSVP requests, together with current colonies' catalogs.

Marketing department personnel were making their follow-up calls to recipients. The electronic scoreboard was registering RSVPs.

In addition to the mailers, the marketing department had placed newspaper ads in the Sunday papers of each community.

Frank and Leslie selected 240 for the colonies' display—eighty from São Paulo and forty pieces each from the other four colonies. One hundred twenty pieces would be shipped to Prague, the remaining pieces designated as reserves and readied for air shipment from Chicago to Prague, Vienna, or Salzburg as needed.

Three orders had already been posted, the result of the colonies' current catalog being included in the mailings. They were part of the stock going to Prague to be marked as sold.

Branch São Paulo was favored because it was Brazil's cultural exchange which had ignited the colonies' Blue Danube tour.

Gary had instructed the branch presidents and gallery managers to include their significant others in the Blue Danube exposition. He included Emily.

Emily happily told Frank she would close her shop for the three weeks of that wonderful tour with him.

Leslie continued to amaze Frank with her organizational skill. Once again her rolling cart had been utilized to compartmentalize each segment of the Danube tour.

Frank asked Leslie to remind the contact staff to pack their exhibition clothing. She showed him the folder marked "Weather/Clothing."

He read her memo: "June brings in some of the warmest weather of the year in Prague, Czech Republic, reaching highs of 21°C (that's about 70°F) during the day. Average wet days for June in Prague are higher than most months in the calendar year. It can rain unexpectedly during summer months. Pack accordingly, and please don't forget your exhibition attire."

She had a file for air flight reservations, which included passport applications and visas where required. Frank would fly to Chicago together with all the colonies' people in Taos for their direct flight to Prague via Turkish Airlines. Emily would join him in Chicago.

Leslie showed Frank her own travel documents for herself as group director for the entire tour and for her husband for the week in Vienna; it was a gift from Gary.

To Frank's total surprise, Gary and his wife, Susan, were included in the Salzburg segment.

The colonies' complement was twenty-four people.

Frank commented to Leslie, "That sly fox Gary got the count over twenty and qualified for group pricing and comped hotels and tours for you as director."

Leslie laughed, "Uh, it wasn't entirely his idea."

Frank said, "Well, what about this 'memo to file' that the Blue Danube tour was a business trip and therefore not taxable gifting to colonies' employees?"

Leslie laughed again, "That came from our auditors."

Now it was Frank's turn to laugh, "Uh-huh."

Included in the package were group tours for each of the cities, Monday trips by tour busses.

When Alice Geelhood heard about all the "goodies" the Blue Danube tour included, she very quickly dissuaded Ken of his idea of not being involved.

The marketing department had booked the Blue Danube team in the Expo Hotel, close to the Prague exhibition area where the colonies' artwork would be displayed.

In Vienna the team was booked in Austria Trend Hotel Messe Wien, near the exhibition center.

The Kolpinghaus Salzburg would be their home for the last week of the Blue Danube tour. The tour ended with the final samba performance on July 4.

Leslie and Frank opened the file "Presentation."

Lydia inputted the significant art over the centuries of Blue Danube acrylic paintings, which included the artwork of Czech artists Alphonse Mucha and Anna Chromy along with Austrian artists like Frank Miklis and Marianne Hasenoehrl-Obsieger, their pieces, and the dates of each piece.

He would use Lydia's information in his presentation. Where possible, he would illustrate the similarities and dissimilarities of the Austrian and Czech artwork compared to that of the artwork produced in the New World, using his laser pointer on the projected images.

Frank's presentations at the exhibit halls to RSVPs were scheduled for 1:00 p.m. and 5:00 p.m. on Saturdays and Sundays.

They opened the file "Refreshments."

The exhibition sites operators recommended caterers for the refreshments to be served to the RSVPs in each city on Saturdays and Sunday. The caterers would need firm counts of the expected guests.

The exhibits would be open to the general public from 10:00 a.m. to 7:00 p.m. on Tuesdays through Fridays. Mondays were travel days for the Blue Danube team.

Leslie and Frank selected the dry white wines produced in Austria, along with red wines produced on the Danube at southeast Moravia. They selected the Czech Pilsner Urquell (the world's first pilsner) and two other popular beers. Leslie placed a note in the file: "The Czech Republic has the highest beer consumption per capita in the world."

Appetizers were local favorites, including the Czech potato dumplings and cheese spreads. For Austria they selected cake omelets and lobster dishes, and the locally popular stuffed Vienna bread. Frank was especially interested in the sauerkraut soup.

Next folder was "Free Time Options."

Frank made two teams of the exhibitor staff, mixing veterans with new people.

Team A: Maria, Carroll, Dick, Ken and Larry.

Team B: Paul, Lydia, Bud, Manual and Kathleen.

They would alternate. Team A would work on Tuesdays and Wednesdays on general public days, Saturdays on RSVP days. Team B would work on Thursdays and Fridays on general public days, Sundays on RSVP days. The exhibitor staff would have leisure time to enjoy their tour.

Gary made it quite clear to both Frank and Leslie that free-time expenses would be the responsibility of the buyers, adding that tips are also the responsibility of the givers, not to be expensed. The colonies would pay for the mandatory samba performances.

Gary said, "Mixing socially with the clients and prospects is good business."

The budget had been set at $10,000 per person, a total of $240,000. Gary pointed out that sales, at 10 percent profit to the colonies, would have to be $2,400,000 to break even.

Leslie had emailed the exhibitors regarding their off-time opportunities. She pointed out that these were not expense items and that checks made payable to the colonies had to be submitted with Team Blue Danube's selections.

Frank selected the June offerings of Vienna's Staatsoper and Volksoper opera houses, Tristan and Isolde at Staatsoper and Romeo and Juliet at Volksoper. He also chose the dinner plus concert (Mozart and Strauss) at Schonbrunn Palace.

There were dozens of opportunities for free-time activity in Prague, from beer gardens to trendy cocktail bars, jet set, rock, all the way to black-tie events to choose from. Frank made no reservations in Prague.

Salzburg featured a marionette theater which Frank opted for. He also chose Landestheater's Mozart program. There would be waltzing at Mirabell Gardens, which Frank knew Emily would love. No charge for that program.

Leslie showed Frank a fistful of orders and checks already received. Frank wrote his check to the colonies.

He made a note in the reminders on his smartphone to pack his tuxedo for Mirabell Gardens in the new suit carrier which Ricky Carter had painted palm trees on for easy ID.

Frank and Leslie continued their checklist the next day. The next file was "Health." The Travel Health Clinic had no essential vaccination requirements for either Austria or the Czech Republic. However, for Austria, tetanus-diphtheria vaccination was recommended. Tick-borne encephalitis vaccination was listed as optional.

For the Czech Republic, tetanus-diphtheria and Hepatitis A vaccinations were "Recommended." Tick-borne encephalitis vaccination was listed as optional.

Leslie had sent the memo to all traveling on the Blue Danube tour.

Frank added the note in his reminders, thinking, *Is there anything that remarkable young lady ever overlooks?*

Frank made an appointment with his physician to take the shots tomorrow.

Next up was "Currency."

Leslie's memo explained that the currency of the Czech Republic was the koruna. U.S. dollars may be exchanged at banks for 2 percent of the transaction amount. She suggested the team exchange some currency at their local banks prior to traveling. ATMs were widely available in Prague. All major credit cards were accepted.

In Austria the currency is the euro. U.S. credit cards were widely accepted, and ATMs were also readily available.

Finally, the last file was "Sales." *Phew*, thought Frank.

Leslie had added in her Blue Danube information kit the information regarding sales.

Sales in both Austria and the Czech Republic were taxable. The current rates were structured into the sales receipts of either checks or credit cards. If exempt, the buyer would sign the exemption form required. Large gallery or collector sales would be handled by Frank.

In the mailers there was a check box for gallery owners or managers who wanted to meet with Frank at their businesses. To date, there were six appointments made for Frank by the marketing department.

Wrapping up the preparations, Frank called Gary, "Well begun is half done."

Gary replied, "Aristotle, I believe. Get on with it, Frank. Time is money."

"Yes, sir."

On Sunday, all of the colonies' Team Blue Danube would depart for Prague.

After check-in at the Expo Hotel in Prague on Monday, Frank and Emily met with everyone in the Blue Danube team in the hotel's dining room for lunch.

Introductions were made, handshakes and hugs given (except for Larry, who gave shoulder pats).

Frank reviewed the plans for the exhibitions to be sure everyone was on the same page. He gave his standard lecture on venturing forth in crowds. "Be alert to the possibility someone will try to pick your pocket or steal your purse. It happens."

Team members walked to the exhibition site. They saw the admission signs had been posted.

The site operators had brought the encased artwork into the gallery. The team hung the art, sectioned exactly as their home galleries, except that the art colony of São Paulo had last position for this exhibition.

They adjusted lights and set up the video and audio equipment. Forms and credit card devices were arranged at sales tables. Catalogs were placed at entry and exit doors.

Frank was satisfied that everything that could be done had been done.

Emily and Frank walked around their hotel. He found the art gallery just three blocks away where he had an appointment at ten in the morning.

At the Kolkovna restaurant, they ordered traditional Bohemian cabbage pancakes made from cabbage, smoked home-style sausages, smoked pork shoulder, and potatoes, drizzled with spicy garlic sour cream. They enjoyed the world famous Czech Pilsner Urquell beer with their dinner.

In their suite, they changed clothes. Emily said, "I meant to ask you where you got that dressing gown. It's spectacular—viscose black and gold paisley, I believe. Not something from your usual men's department store, I'm sure."

"Honey, this was a gift from Lola. I just can't throw it away."

Frank opened one of the bottles of Jack Daniel's he had in his suitcase, along with one of the bottles of Prosecco wine. He poured a few ounces of each into their hotel glasses.

He told Emily everything he had learned about what happened to Lola.

"She probably didn't care for that tacky old terry cloth robe I had."

They made love gently and passionately and fell asleep in each other's arms.

Frank tried not to awaken Emily, but she got up with him. They ordered a Czech breakfast delivered to their suite: salami, cheese, honey, rye bread, and coffee.

Frank felt the rush—the adrenaline rush (like the lettered athlete he was at Michigan State University). His energy level escalated to a real high.

"Showtime," Frank chortled, as he kissed Emily goodbye.

He would meet Paul Koenig at the appointed gallery. Each seen call made with Frank would be a learning experience for a new colonies' contact staff member.

Emily shopped for souvenirs and checked out the designer clothes shops while Frank made his first call. They would be in touch by cell phone.

The call was on an elegant avant-garde shop in downtown Prague. Frank nodded to Paul and gestured to the display of beautiful pieces in the gallery.

The owner and his gallery manager invited Frank and Paul into his office.

"Mr. Creech," the owner said, "I have known about you for years, and it is my pleasure to meet you and this young man."

They shook hands, as a young lady rolled in a cart of coffee and cakes.

"I'm flattered, Mr. Novotny."

"When your telephone people called me, I leaped at the chance to meet such an authority as you in the world of fine art."

"When I walked into your gallery, sir, I recognized a man with tastes and fine discernment in art."

They sipped coffee and nibbled on the dainty cakes while continuing their talk about art.

Frank opened his iPad, "Mr. Novotny—"

"Call me Artur, please."

"Of course, and please call me Frank. I know you received a catalog with your invitation to our exhibition, Artur," He paged his iPad. "This device shows even newer pieces available from the colonies. You know, Artur, 60% of list price."

"Yes, I know. And Petr and I are prepared to give you an order. However, I would like to be your exclusive distributor in Prague. Can we do that?"

Frank set his cup down, tightened his lips, and slowly shook his head.

"Some years ago, a Berlin art dealer contracted with the Taos Art Colony for exclusive distribution in Berlin. Things went well for five years until the owner passed away. His wife informed the colony that the family would continue their business.

"Reviewing the annual orders from contracted galleries, our marketing department noticed the scarcity of orders from the Berlin gallery. The sons of the deceased owners had inherited the business. They placed one order each year. The colony sued in the German courts for the right to contract with other distributors. Long story short, the colony lost."

Frank continued, "Since then no contracts are made which feature exclusivity. However, I can tell you that if you give me a substantial order, you will receive favorable treatment."

"I dislike vagueness, Frank. What would be the favorable treatment?"

"In exchange for your one million USD order at list price, instead of our 40 percent discount, you will receive a 50 percent discount and the same for all future orders of that volume. There is one proviso. Payment must be made with the order."

Paul moved his head back and forth as he watched the two old pros haggle.

"I want thirty days."

"No, the chairman won't permit me to do that. I'll throw in ready to hang frames."

"Done deal. Petr, give them the order. I'll have our cashier wire transfer the payment."

They stood up, hugged each other, and smiled.

"Artur, are you planning to attend the samba performance Saturday night?"

"Yes, I am. I like to keep up with my competitors."

"Here are four tickets. *Dekuju* (thank you), Artur, for the nice order."

Petr and Paul completed the contract.

The graveyard shift order takers in Taos received Frank's huge order late that evening. They knew Chairman Green would want to see the order. They placed an enlarged copy of the order on M.E.'s desk.

When M.E. arrived for work the next morning she read the order and screamed, "Frank's done it, He's done it!" She opened Gary Green's door and placed the order on his desk.

Gary read the order. He upset his coffee cup as he jumped up and roared, *"Game on!"*

Frank stopped at a deli and bought sausage sandwiches and soft drinks for Paul and himself.

Paul said, "What a performance. You are the master of the art of selling art!"

"It's all in a day's work. I have to get cracking. My next appointment is at 2:00 p.m. on the outskirts, and I need to pick up Lydia at the hotel."

Lydia and Frank met Mr. Bendik, the owner of a small gallery in the outskirts of Prague.

Mr. Bendik bought a sampling of new world paintings which Frank suggested he call Art of the Americas. He bought a mountain lake scene from São Paulo, a cityscape from Chicago, a field of grain from Milwaukee, an ocean scene from SW Florida, and a pueblo living heritage scene from Taos.

"*Dekuju*, Beda. Here are four tickets to the samba performance Saturday evening."

Lydia and Frank returned to the hotel and walked over to the exhibition.

There were four tables with representatives from the colonies writing orders when they arrived.

Frank asked Leslie, "How's it going, wonder woman?"

"We're writing orders, not like you, but a good steady flow."

Lydia said, "Watching Frank work is an education in itself. He turned a moderately curious gallery owner into a buyer by suggesting pieces from each colony that depicted what Frank labeled the Art of the Americas."

"All in a day's work," Frank chortled.

Emily and Frank joined four Team Blue Danube couples for dinner and an evening of dancing at a sexy Prague club called Dancers.

Frank's week flew by. He put on crowd-pleasing art shows for both Friday and Saturday evening RSVP programs. The team wrote six orders each evening.

On Saturday evening, Frank and Emily mixed with clients and prospects at the samba performance. Some of the guests who had not ordered previously told him they planned to order in the future when their stock level permitted.

On Sunday they went on the Prague city tour.

On Monday they traveled to Vienna. Emily said, "The sights of the old castles, the corn fields, the fields of lilac, and the rivers are memories for a lifetime."

Leslie told Frank that profits from sales in Prague alone, with an additional 20 percent new orders anticipated, would pay for the entire tour.

Frank and Emily agreed Vienna and Salzburg, the home cities of Mozart, were the jewels of Austrian heritage.

Emily hugged Frank in the cab on their way back from waltzing with him at Mirabell Gardens in Salzburg on Sunday afternoon.

She said, "Frank, this has been the most exciting vacation of my lifetime. *Danke schön.*"

On Monday morning they flew out of Salzburg's W. A. Mozart Airport. Emily had to get back to Milwaukee, and Frank was returning to Taos with most of the team.

Frank and Leslie sat together. Frank looked around and asked Leslie, "Did Gary and Susan miss the flight?"

"He told me he'd have a stop to make on the way home, and he'd see everyone Wednesday."

"It was a blockbuster campaign, Leslie. Do you have the numbers?"

"Won't have until Wednesday or Thursday. We're still confirming orders, processing and insuring shipments, and we're trying to exchange substitutes for duplicate orders."

"Leslie, c'mon. How about giving me a ballpark figure, OK?"

"Hold your breath Frank—over ten million!"

"Wow."

"As expected, South American art came in strongest at nearly 60 percent. It was their cultural exchange. SW Forida surprised me with almost 20 percent. Larry Stahlhut scored big."

Frank chortled, "Was it the art of the sale or the sale of the art?"

"I think it is because Larry is a private collector himself, he related to those buyers. So you're correct, and you're correct."

Frank got an email from Emily: "I loved everything about our trip together. The adoration which the art world has for you, the enthusiasm and excitement you generated. The beautiful scenery and wonderful foods we enjoyed together. I mean everything. I love you."

Chapter 27

Lecture Series

Aloft, Frank sipped his Jack Daniel's on the rocks while catching up on his correspondence.

He responded to Emily: "Glad you enjoyed the tour. If you had to name one thing that stood out above everything else, what would it have been?"

"Hmm, now that requires some thought. I think our waltz at Mirabell was outstanding. You were so handsome in your tuxedo. And how you 'stood out' for me was very impressive. LOL."

"Love you, wanton woman."

He emailed a broad outline of his lecture series to Chairman Green, copied to Leslie in the marketing department.

Frank asked Leslie's team to research known dates and highlights of discovered cave art, medieval art, impressionist art, surrealistic art, Nazi stolen art, and a dozen other categories including critical art eras, artists, and art-related events and themes which he planned to expound upon in his lecture series.

This is where Lydia will be essential, he thought.

In order not to overwhelm the department, Frank made notes to use later in exploring the areas of financial support, advertising, slide materials, format, rehearsals, and timing of the lectures.

Of one thing he was certain: Gary would want the lecture series to begin in the branch where increased sales were most needed—Chicago.

It was getting colder. Through the corridor window as he walked to the marketing department Frank saw the weather on the bank's thermometer display—50°F–21°F dropping to 40°F–16°F tomorrow.

Frank listened to the muted tones of the follow-up telemarketers in their quietened booths talking with clients and prospects. His telemarketers were generating 30 to 40 percent of the colonies' sales. Some were bilingual; he heard French and German conversation.

When he first came to the colony, Frank recalled, there were four people in the marketing department. Now there were eighteen people on the day shift. They took their breaks at varying times.

Leslie told him two telemarketers worked a second shift together with two order clerks, and an identical crew worked the graveyard shift due to global time differences.

Frank reflected, *I'm on the road so much I can't really keep up with these changes.*

"Uh-oh, three fingers left in my Jack Daniel's bottle. Have to shop tomorrow, should get some fresh food as well."

He texted Leslie: "Need to structure the lecture series, will be in at nine o'clock tomorrow morning."

Making notes and restaging the lectures, including the backdrops, slide projector, projector operator, pointer, raised dais—he was interrupted by "The Blue Danube Waltz," the ringtone he had assigned exclusively to Emily's calls.

"How's my man doing?"

"I'm fine. How's my woman doing?"

"OK. I'll go first. I have my first new designer casual winter suit on display in my shop window, and it is drawing attention."

Frank said, "I'm now designing my platform, literally—the riser I'll need for my lecture series. Everything starts at the bottom, you know."

"*Oh you.* I caught it. Careful, I'll descend on you as I did in Naples."

They chatted for a while and made plans to get together the following weekend. Emily said she wanted to see "the lion in his den."

Leslie maneuvered her rolling file cart to Frank's desk. He saw the upper tier bore a sign: *Lecture Series*. The files began with "Dais," next was "Audio/Slide Equipment," then "Presentation," followed by "Audience/Invitations," "Advertising," "Facility," and "Lecture Series."

"Leslie, you are doubtlessly the most highly organized person I've ever had the pleasure of working with."

She smiled and said, "And you are the most creative person I've ever had the privilege of working for." She opened her "Dais" file.

"Other than São Paulo, which we're leaving to Senhora de la Silva, we've sourced these risers. We'll need thirty days advance booking. We're recommending the nine-inch models."

Frank declared, "I want to step onto the platform at the rear, facing the audience, as George C. Scott did in the 1970 movie *Patton,* for the dramatic effect."

Leslie made the note in the file and picked up the next folder, "Audio/Slide."

"We've selected the video equipment, also rentable. We'll need some space and size of audience feedback from the gallery managers as to best rentals. I've sent them a memo."

Frank chortled, "Will I get to peddle colonies art during the presentation?"

"Boss, I think you're kidding. But to be on the safe side, no, siree. It's an educational program. We're expecting the type of results Hallmark Hall of Fame has achieved with its award-winning anthology series. As Hallmark does, we'll open the programs with 'presented by the Art Colonies of America.' That's image advertising designed to increase consumer awareness and influence gallery and collector buying behavior."

Frank said, "Yes, I was kidding. Could I have colonies' catalogs on tables at the exits?"

"No problem with that at all." Leslie made notes in the file.

Leslie and Frank moved right along. She pulled up the file on "Audience/Invitations."

They reviewed the newspaper ads and the invitations to the colonies' clients. Only the presentation dates needed to be filled in.

Frank suggested having RSVP fliers made up to give to gallery visitors and for branch presidents to give as handouts on their seen calls.

Leslie made notes in the file.

"Advertising" included posting lecture dates in the quarterly catalog mailing of the colonies.

Leslie asked Frank, "What would you think of using some advertising budget on classical music radio station spots?"

She continued, "Dick Boyd texted me the membership data presented him by their local FM classical music radio station. That station sold out a Blue Danube tour costing an average of $8,000 per person in two days."

"Hmm, that never occurred to me. Keep in mind that Gary will have to approve our budget."

"I think Gary will like their method of funding. The colonies make donations which are charitable tax deductions. The stations give boosters thank-you messages on the air which include endorsements of the donor's products or services."

"Let's try a thousand dollars for each of our branch locations."

Leslie made notes in the file.

"Lunchtime, Leslie. Let's continue at the Le Cueva Café. I have a reservation."

"You're on, boss. Give me fifteen minutes."

Frank returned phone calls, text messages, and emails and called for his ride. Gary had assigned the colonies' limo as Frank's transportation when it wasn't busy with gallery owners and other VIPs.

Frank chuckled. "He probably did that after he reviewed my transportation expenses."

Next up in the "Advertising" folder was prelecture coverage. Leslie reviewed the department's plan to issue press releases with lecture highlights. She recited her contact with Dick Brooks, managing editor of the *Washington DC International Art Critics*. Because Frank had handled the Wisconsin state art competition for the *Post*, Mr. Brooks promised a nice spread in the *Post*'s arts and entertainment section.

After ordering their lunch at the café, Leslie waded into the last item in the "Advertising" folder: the colonies' Web site.

Catching Frank's puzzled look, Leslie laid the folder on the table.

"Frank, I know you recall the department's computer techies created the Web site back in December. We've been testing our hits, as they're called, and trying to measure the effectiveness of our site."

Frank nodded his head, "Oh yes. But as I recall, it wasn't very high on our list."

"Correct. It could be very significant with our new approach. We've created a 'friends' network. We're now getting feedback on purchases, quality evaluations, and ratings of the experience buyers have with the colonies. This month we're getting an average of four stars, five stars being tops. Most feedback is very complimentary.

"We're international, and the internet is widely used around the world," she continued, as she handed him the print copy. We plan to use our site to advertise your lectures."

Frank shook his head. "Guess I'm a little slow on the uptake."

He muttered to himself, "And that's the second time today."

Back at the office, Frank saw that Leslie's pager and smartphone were lit up.

He said, "I'll take the 'Lecture' folders and the 'Date/Place' folder home and let you get to all those messages and your other responsibilities."

"Thanks for lunch, boss. See you in the morning?"

"Nine o'clock, Leslie, and maybe with bells on if the predicted snow comes in."

At home Frank let his fingers do the walking. The liquor store would deliver a case of Jack Daniel's and a case of Prosecco wine. The deli would deliver his edibles.

He tackled "Date/Place."

Frank asked Gary if he could use the Baker Museum scheduling: Saturdays, midmonth for the lectures, so art student children could attend.

Leslie had asked Lydia Noonan to contact her alma mater, the Art Institute of Chicago, to ask if the colonies could use the Rubloff Auditorium for the first lecture site. In forty-eight hours she received permission to use the school's 950-seat auditorium.

The dean called Gary to ask if he could reserve half of the seating for students and faculty and told Gary there would be no charge to the colonies for use of the auditorium.

Gary saw he was in the negotiation phase and countered by asking the dean if the school could furnish the audio and video equipment and the dais. The dean responded, "Not only can we furnish that equipment, we'll furnish the operators and the ushers and ticket takers as well."

Gary said, "We've got a deal. I'll send you your tickets."

The dean told Gary, "We look forward very much to the lecture by your Frank Creech. It will be a first for us."

Gary told Leslie about his arrangement with the Art Institute of Chicago and asked her to produce the tickets; he also told her to send half of them to the dean and to distribute the tickets to area clients, galleries, and collectors and to Frank, Paul, and Carroll.

Keying on that information, she responded, "Great, sir. May I assume the other lecture sites will also furnish the equipment and the operators?"

"Yes, you may. You find the art schools near our branches, send me the contact information and auditorium capacities, and I'll make the deals."

Lydia would assist in selecting the art photos for the slide show once the subjects were agreed upon—slides which could be purchased from historical art publications.

All the dates were set for the series of lectures, each of which would conclude with a video by Gary Green—"a word from our sponsor," thanking the audience for their support and the institution's support. He would ask the lecture attendees to pick up the colonies' current catalogs at the exit doors.

Frank opened the first lecture folder. The procedure would be an introduction of himself by the area branch president, highlighting his background, his work as an art critic, his work as director of marketing for the colonies.

Frank planned to stride onto the riser, cup his hands over his eyes, look around the audience, acknowledge people whom he knew, and welcome all, particularly the children.

He would signal the slide operator using his new laser pointer, and the forty-minute show narrated by Frank would begin.

Frank went through each folder shaking his head at the enormous amount of material the marketing department had assembled. He realized he would have a good deal of memorization ahead to prepare for the lectures.

"Might as well get started," he chortled, pouring himself a Jack Daniel's on the rocks.

The week went well; most of the items needed had been received, and Frank had rehearsed his lecture.

Frank met Emily Hanson at the airport Friday evening. Frank asked the colonies' limo driver, Don Lambrix, to take them to the Old Blinking Light restaurant.

Frank offered to buy dinner for all, but Don said he had some errands to run.

Frank winked at Emily, "A gentleman of the first order."

"Is this where you take all your dates?" playfully asked Emily.

"Only those I hope to make out with," Frank chortled.

They started with OBL's strawberry-mango salad, followed by the King Ranch casserole, green chili, and cheese-stacked enchiladas. They washed the food down with a magnum of Dom Pérignon champagne. Dessert was crispy banana delight for Emily and fried ice cream for Frank.

After dinner they went to Frank's Burch Street casita. He asked Don Lambrix to pick them up at 9:00 a.m. in the morning for a tour of Taos.

Emily walked through the casita. "You actually live in this little place?"

"Well, I'm not here very often. I'm mostly on the road, you know. Tomorrow I'll show you something much more permanent, my home in the future."

The two lovers devoured each other with heroic fervor until they fell asleep. Morning came only a few hours later.

Frank had the café deliver fresh churros for their breakfast.

While they waited for their ride, Frank showed Emily the plans for his estate at the foot of the Sangre de Cristo Mountains.

"Oh My God!" exclaimed Emily. "It has a dance floor!"

Their first stop was the colonies' home office.

Bill Hasse logged them in after photographing Emily and furnishing her a visitor's pass.

They went to the marketing office where Frank introduced Emily to Leslie.

Leslie gave Frank her current checklist of the lecture series items to review. Smiling, she walked Emily through the department.

Even on Saturday morning, Frank thought, *there are four clerks at work, and the electronic sales display board is lit up.*

A light snow began to fall as they were driving to the home site. They passed three ski resorts and Blue Lake, which was iced over.

Emily brought the plans along. She made a few notes on the plans.

At the Le Cueva Café for lunch, Emily said, "Frank, this parcel and the estate plans are the most magnificent I've ever seen. I am surprised, however, at the small space provided for the kitchen and dining areas."

Frank scratched his head, "Oh. To be honest, the women I was with during the planning stages weren't really into cooking. However, you are an excellent cook. Maybe I should ask my architect to enlarge those areas?"

"If you have long-range plans for us, yes, that would be the thing to do. And while we're downtown, could we walk around a little after lunch? I want to do a little window shopping."

Frank rolled his eyes up. He thought, curiously, *Emily is projecting herself into my future.*

They walked around the central town streets for the next two hours. The streets were becoming deserted because the snowfall had increased. They stopped at the café and picked up their take home dinners.

"What was that window shopping all about?"

"I wanted to see if there were any designer clothing shops in downtown Taos. There were franchises but no shops like mine."

Emily put her arms around his neck, "Frank, I love you. I want to spend the rest of our lives together."

Frank brought Emily a glass of Prosecco wine and raised his glass of Jack Daniel's on the rocks to her. "Emily, I haven't had much success with the women in my life in the past. If you're convinced we can make it work, let's go for it."

They hugged and kissed.

Frank flew to Milwaukee on the last week of February. He made calls with Bud. Frank was enthused by Bud's use of his fine arts education language in his presentations. Emily and Frank had dinner with Bud and Kathleen and danced the polka.

Frank asked Emily to come to Chicago to be at his first lecture.

Frank and Carroll made calls during the week, and he was thrilled with Carroll's use of his fine arts education course language in their seen calls on gallery clients. They passed out tickets to the coming lecture.

Paul Kling, Carroll's gallery manager, gave tickets to gallery visitors.

Emily had used the Hiawatha Amtrak train to Chicago to join Frank on the weekend of his trip to the Chicago Art Colony. They had dinner with Nancy and Carroll. Everyone was looking forward to Frank's lecture on Saturday afternoon.

Emily shook her head in amazement as Frank appeared to be speaking with his audience at the lecture as if he was a guest sitting together on couches in their home.

She thought his presentation was spectacular, and she noticed that the audience was agog.

Gary emailed Frank: "Our sales are lighting up the marketing department's electronic scoreboard. It is evident that the revised galleries, the gallery managers, and the fine arts education for our presidents are paying dividends. The feedback I'm getting on your lecture is extremely positive. Keep up the good work."

Chapter 28

'Dance with the one who brung you'

Frank made a layaway deposit on a wedding ring set he selected for Emily. On Saturday morning, Emily and Frank cabbed to the jewelry store in Chicago's loop.

The jewelry consultant opened the locked display case and placed the diamond engagement ring on a velvet cloth on the counter under a lighted display lamp.

Emily gasped when she saw the brilliant emerald-cut, 3.02-carat engagement ring.

She whispered to Frank, "I love my wedding ring set, but I know ring prices, and this set is very expensive. Maybe we should shop around?"

Frank waved his fingers toward the manager, indicating he should come to the counter.

They chatted briefly, and the manager said, "I'll throw in the wedding band and have the rings sized while you wait, no charge."

"Do it."

Frank stroked his chin and looked up to the ceiling. With one eye closed, he said, "I'll have to report this extraordinary expenditure to David Pohl, the president of my bank, ha, ha, a posteriori."

That evening they joined Paul Kling, the Chicago gallery's manager, and his, wife Delores, together with the Swansons at their favorite steak house on the Near North Side.

Nancy, looking with wide eyes at the huge ring on Emily's ring finger, asked, "Is that what I think it is?"

Emily extended her left arm and flexed the fingers of her left hand at the first joint. Her hand appeared to be a huge bird's talon on the shadow of the white tablecloth.

"Yep, I finally nailed him. We haven't set a date yet."

Emily went back to Milwaukee. She didn't tell Frank that she and Linda had come to terms on Linda's purchase of her designer shop, preferring to tell him when the deal was completed.

Gary read the *Chicago Tribune*'s sparkling review of the lecture. The article exalted Frank for his verbal interaction with the young people in the audience and commended the colonies for sponsoring the lecture.

Hearing from others on the staff, Gary learned that the article was picked up by the *New York Times*, the *Wall Street Journal*, and Frank's old employer the *Washington DC International Art Critics*.

Leslie called Mary Ellen. "I need to talk with Gary about how to handle requests we're getting for Frank's lecture."

Gary called Leslie, "Who's requesting the lecture?"

"A number of institutions are making the requests, sir, including Yale University. We have had twenty-six requests this morning."

"Send me the list. For now respond to the interested parties that we are considering their request for the lecture and will advise them of our decision. I'll get back to you."

"Mary Ellen, please take your lunch break a little early. I have to make a private call. I need about thirty minutes."

When she returned, Gary politely said, "M.E., please ask Frank to see me before lunch."

Frank realized Mary Ellen had texted him so their conversation would not be overheard. He texted back, "What's up?"

"Best guess. Art institutions requesting your lecture."

"Thanks, M.E. I won't forget the favor."

"You certainly did not forget me last Christmas."

Frank winked at Mary Ellen as he entered her office, "Hello, beautiful lady."

Mary Ellen batted her eyes, smiled, and said, "The boss is waiting for you. Go on in."

"Frank, you've hit a grand slam in your outstanding Chicago lecture. We're getting requests for catalogs from organizations and individuals not on our contact lists due to the favorable press coverage. We're also getting requests for your lecture from other art institutions, including Yale University. Could you expand your lectures to include additional audiences?"

Frank wiped the now stale churro crumbs off his chin and opened his attaché case. He fished up his schedule.

"Boss, I'm booked from now until August 23, 2016, with the lectures and exhibitions at all five of our branches in addition to the mandatory monthly visits and joint calls scheduled at each branch. I just don't have the time for additional lectures."

"You've done a superb job with the branches, four of which you created. Art education for the branch presidents, the acquisition of gallery managers, the overhaul of our galleries, and your thorough preparation and execution of our exhibitions have paid huge dividends.

"Add to the mix your personal sales, and you have produced a volume of business we never dreamed of five years ago. If we relieved you of all your physical contacts with the branches, including the exhibitions, how many lectures could you present in a year's time?"

"Hmm," Frank mused, "maybe it is time to cut the cord with the branches."

Frank told Gary, "One of the things we would have to do is copyright the lecture material."

Gary tapped his fingers on his desk and said, "Reproduce your lecture transcripts and list your art slides. Vic will handle our copyrights. What else?"

"I want 20 percent of our audiences to be youths between ten and eighteen years of age with art backgrounds. That's another goal, as I see it, to educate those youths and create enthusiasm for their lifetimes of adventure in art. They won't forget our presentations."

"OK, and what's the other thing?"

"How would this affect my income?"

Gary said, gesturing toward the door, "Let's go to lunch at your little café."

Don Lambrix drove them to the Le Cueva Café. Once seated, Gary spoke in low tones. "This is not for publication. On the way home from Salzburg, I stopped in Geneva, Switzerland to meet with an international firm whose board was considering acquiring the colonies. They had our financial statements. The thing that bothered them was your income. Considering their resources, they felt you were no longer needed.

"I just spoke with that corporation's chairman of the board this morning. I quoted him an old Texas adage, *'Dance with the one who brung you.'* Their attempt to acquire the colonies failed.

"Frank, it's time to put you on salary with all the benefits—pension plan, health coverage, profit sharing, private office, secretary, full expenses."

"My salary would be?"

"With the year we're having, your draw would have been $2,500,000 next year. I think that's a good salary, not dependent on sales. By your own admission you are maxed out on available personal sales time."

"Ten million, considering that would be my annual income in the next few years. Major league baseball batters make a lot more than that amount. I score as many hits as they do."

"Ha, ha, that's a different league."

"Judge Judy made forty-seven million last year."

"Once again, that's a different league."

"Ten million, that's my bottom line, with a sweetener."

"What's the sweetener?"

"I need a three-million-dollar signing bonus to build a home for Emily and me."

"Oh yes, I did hear about your engagement. Congratulations. Frank, my original question is still unanswered. How many lectures can you handle each year without losing too much time from your executive input and oversee of our marketing functions?"

Frank made some quick calculations on his iPad, which he shared with Gary.

"I have twenty lectures scheduled this year, four at each of our five branches. If we doubled that to forty lectures, I could handle that, but prep time is a major issue. We'll need to constantly tweak the presentations to fit the audiences."

"Frank, I'll never get your ten million past the board. Will you except five million and profit sharing, say, a quarter point?"

"Throw in the signing bonus payable with the contract, and you've got a deal."

"Meet me tomorrow morning at 9:00 a.m. in Vic's office."

"Yes, sir."

Frank went home, poured himself two ounces of Jack Daniel's on the rocks, and called Emily.

"Honey, I have wonderful news to share."

"So do I, sweetheart."

"Ladies first. Go ahead, Emily."

"Linda is in *her* new shop here in Milwaukee inventorying *her* merchandise, and I've hired a realtor to sell my home."

Frank told Emily of his new deal with the colonies, adding, "We can start building our home now with the signing bonus."

"Oh, that's wonderful. I'm so excited. Since you won't be visiting Chicago or Milwaukee very often in the future, selling my business and my home is very timely. Everything is working out for us.

"Uh, Frank, one question, dear. Did you speak with your architect about increasing the size of our kitchen and dining areas?"

"Sorry, I spaced that. I'm not much of a hand with kitchens or dining areas. You know I eat almost all of my meals in restaurants. Could you meet with Mike Maxwell and explain to him what you want?"

Frank read through the employment papers carefully. He noticed he was bound by a noncompete clause and that his profit-sharing earnings were to be channeled into his pension fund, payable only after a minimum of ten years of continuous employment from the date of the contract.

Per Frank's request, Gary had Vic change the pension disbursement feature of the contract. It would be payable to his estate in the event of his demise with or without the ten years of continuous service requirement.

He silently reflected, *That sly fox is going to keep me in rein and working for profits to share until I retire, which will be exactly at the end of my ten-year tenure.*

Gary drove Frank to the colonies' building.

"Whoa, what's going on?" Frank asked, as he saw the sign: "Pardon our dust and debris. We're expanding your Art Colonies facility." Construction crews and their cranes surrounded the building.

Gary explained, "We're adding a much needed third floor. Gallery and art restoration go to the third floor. A cafeteria will be on the second floor. We're tripling the marketing department space which will include your private office."

Frank cocked his head, "Yeah, boss. To use an old Michigan expression, we're 'elbow to appetite' in the marketing department now."

"We're also adding three elevators, one in the entryway, and freight elevators on either end of the building." Gary laughed. "Ken Geelhood said we should have added the elevators years ago,"

They went to the marketing department. Gary advised Leslie that the colonies had a new salaried arrangement with Frank. He explained that Frank was now executive marketing director. He laid out Frank's new assignments and told Leslie she would henceforth be the primary contact with the branches for their marketing needs.

"Leslie, you've done an excellent job for the colonies since our expansion. I am pleased to inform you that you are now the assistant to the executive marketing director, and your salary is doubled beginning this day. Additionally, we are adding profit sharing to your income. I'll have Marion Jones send you your new employment agreement which you'll need to sign and return."

"Oh," Leslie said as she hugged Gary, "I am so happy. I love this work, the people I work with, and my brilliant bosses."

David Pohl shook Frank's hand and congratulated him on his promotion when Frank stopped at the bank to deposit his signing bonus and pay off his parcel loan.

"Keep us in mind when you're ready to make some investments."

"I'll do that. Thanks for everything, Dave."

Frank visited with his architect, Mike Maxwell. "Mike, I can't thank you enough for your patience with me. The lot is paid for. I'm ready to start building our castle. Will you be my general contractor?"

"I have overseen the construction of most of the buildings that I designed. My fee for your estate would be forty thousand, half up front, balance on completion—no add-on fees, other than for permits. I'll hire the subcontractors who will submit their invoices to me, and I'll stay on top of all phases of the construction process."

Frank said, "I need some changes to the plans. My fiancée, Emily, is an excellent cook. She wants a chef's kitchen and an enlarged dining room."

Mike nodded and said, "I didn't charge for the dance floor I created for Lola. It was an exterior addition. The changes Emily wants will require new plans. I'll need another five thousand."

Frank wrote a check to Mike for twenty-five thousand dollars and advised Mike that Emily would see him on Thursday with her ideas for the kitchen and dining area changes.

The next morning Frank met with his assistant, Leslie. They selected the top five candidates for the lecture series and forwarded the list together with contact information to Gary.

Gary called Yale first. He spoke with the dean of the art school and recounted to the dean the requirement that the lectures are on Saturday afternoons, and the audience must minimally be comprised of 20 percent young art students.

He advised the dean of the colonies' further requirement that the schools furnish the equipment for the lecture and that the first school to meet the terms would be awarded their preference of date for the lecture.

When the dean agreed to the terms, Gary asked for the department head's name and phone number in Yale's honorary degree program. He told the dean he'd get back to him.

Gary told the chairman of the honorary degree department that he had a candidate for an honorary doctor of fine arts degree.

He spoke candidly with the chairman; he would give the next lecture date to the first institution to so honor Frank Creech.

Gary repeated the offer to the other four top candidates.

He instructed Leslie to send Frank's bio to the candidate institutions. He asked her not to mention any of this to Frank.

Leslie responded, "Got it, boss. Thought you'd like to know we're getting requests from artists to place their pieces with the colonies. I am forwarding the contact information to our branch presidents."

Yale came through first with everything Gary had stipulated, including the honorary doctorate for Frank.

Frank and Lydia began tweaking the lecture for Yale. She envisioned what seemed to Frank to be a spectacular concept: juxtapose Michelangelo (1475–1564), thought to be heaven's proponent, with a contemporary artist, Hieronymus Bosch (1450–1516), whose paintings were brilliant.

As she presented the contrasting paintings, however, Frank began to cringe.

"Lydia, your concept is sparkling. But those Bosch paintings which depict horrible scenes of the punishment in hell—some of which have birdlike monsters tearing away chunks of living human sinners—is, in my opinion, too severe for general audiences."

Remembering an experience he had as art critic for the *Washington DC International Art Critics* judging controversial art in a gallery's showplace, Frank shook his head and said, "Lydia, I can just envision the responses to the lecture creating an argumentative atmosphere less than favorable to the colonies, which could result in both of us losing our jobs."

"Oh dear," Lydia sighed, with a tears forming in her eyes. "I was only looking at the quality of the paintings and the obvious contrasts. Good heavens, I didn't for the life of me imagine I could lose my precious job."

Frank patted her on the back. "Lydia, it was still a great idea whose time has not yet come."

They elected to display the works of extraordinary New England painters: James Abbott McNeill Whistler of *Whistler's Mother*; John Singer Sargent, a famous portrait painter; philanthropist Peter Faneuil; Impressionist pioneer Childe Hassam; Winslow Homer, a landscape painter and printmaker; and the fabled Grandma Moses.

At the end of the lecture the audience burst into voracious applause. And as in Chicago, the tributes to Frank's lecture at the Yale campus in New Haven, Connecticut, were effusive.

Gary walked into the new offices of the marketing department. Although not quite finished, he told Leslie and Frank that "it looks good."

"Frank," Gary said, shaking Frank's hand, "The lectures may be your greatest contribution to the colonies."

"Thanks, boss. I think it was a win-win for everyone—the students, Yale University, and the colonies. We're working now on the next two lectures simultaneously. Leslie has assigned two of her top researchers to the team. Lydia is fantastic, and we'll be able now to prepare for coming lectures most efficiently."

Gary turned his head and winked at Leslie. Turning back to Frank, he said, "Oh, Frank, we're having a planning session next Saturday evening in our new company cafeteria. It isn't officially open, but we'll have a catered dinner. Please bring Emily, 6:00 p.m. prompt."

Frank went back into his spacious office and joined Lydia and his researchers.

Leslie said, "Boss, I'm guessing, would this be the presentation of Frank's honorary doctorate by Yale?'

"As usual, you are right on. Let's get to work on the invitation list and the party details."

Chapter 29

Honorary Doctorate

Leslie rolled her cart out and began organizing Frank's Honorary Doctorate presentation party. The header on the cart read Planning Party, a disguise. Frank wouldn't see the presentation folder.

The first hanging folder was labeled "Invitations." She selected the top ten dollar volume gallery clients and their guests. The first names which crossed her mind were Ron Romano, Boyd Guard, and Artur Novotny, She would research her data bank for the others. She added the branch presidents and gallery managers, and their spouses or significant others.

Music: She hired a D.J. (disc jockey) who would spin a variety of dance music during the latter part of the evening.

Next was Presentation Ceremony: She was in touch with Dean Jones of the Yale Honorary Doctorate department. He kindly changed his schedule to be able to personally make the presentation for Yale. He would bring his own advertising people to document the event for the media.

Planning: She wrote, "Part of the program or just camouflage?" "Consult with Gary."

The next day she met with Gary. He added Marty and Judy Freling and Vic and Janet Lich and Leslie and her husband Peter, Mary Ellen and her beau Don to the guest list.

As to "planning," Gary said he did have a program, but wouldn't divulge it in their published party plans.

She thought, "I should have known he wouldn't miss the opportunity of announcing a new marketing plan he had in mind with all of his key people gathered."

Catering: Leslie knew Frank loved the Old Blinking Light Restaurant. She ordered their traditional Tex-Mex dinners with a variety of deserts for her estimated sixty people.

She engaged a popular bar in downtown Taos to cater the liquor, including cocktails, and dinner drinks.

Flowers for the tables were ordered, including a "Congratulations" wreath for Frank.

There still were some details Leslie needed to handle. Once the attendees had all been named, she had the art department's in-house print shop make place cards. The Colonies no longer had to outsource their print requirements. It was one of the improvements Gary made with the added space gained by the addition of the third floor to their building.

Dress: Casual, elegant. She called Emily and told her Gary wanted Frank to wear his Colonies exhibition attire.

Leslie thought, "Gary knows Yale plans to Video the presentation and he wants Frank to wear the exhibition suit so the Colonies patch on the jacket would be seen."

Frank was to arrive at 6 p.m. prompt. Everyone else was directed to be at the enlarged and refurbished building at 4:30 p.m. for a tour conducted by Ken Geelhood. After the tour they would assemble in the new cafeteria at 5:30 p.m. for cocktails.

She detailed the entire presentation program and furnished it to all the invitees except Frank and Emily.

Frank and Emily didn't see the crowd assembled as they entered the cafeteria, because the lights had been dimmed.

When the lights came on fully, everyone began a slow cadenced chant: "Frank Creech, Frank Creech, while stomping their feet and applauding –a greeting Dick Boyd had rehearsed minutes before Frank and Emily arrived.

When the applause ended, Mary Ellen stepped forward and said, "Ooh, you da man."

The guests continued to applaud until Gary stepped forward and quietened them.

"Frank, it's my privilege to introduce you and your lovely fiancée Emily to Dean Edward Jones of Yale's Honorary Doctorate department."

They shook hands. Frank thought, "Oh, could it be…"

The Dean smiled and picked up a framed diploma from the front table. He read the inscription aloud: "Yale University recognizes Frank Creech for his achievements in the field of fine arts and herewith awards him an Honorary Doctorate of Fine Arts."

He handed the diploma to Frank, shook hands again with both Emily and Frank. Then Dean Jones said, solemnly, "Congratulations Doctor Creech."

There was a thunderous round of applause.

Frank thanked the Dean and Gary and the assembly. He and Emily applauded them.

The entire ceremony, beginning with Frank and Emily's entry into the cafeteria, was videoed by Yale's Honorary Doctorate staff. The video/audio operator sent a copy of the video to Chairman Green.

Gary raised his hand and pointed to the caterers opening the lids of their food containers. He announced, "Dinner time."

As everyone was finishing their desserts, Don Lambrix quietly entered the cafeteria and nodded to the head table.

Gary said, "Our limo driver has just clued me that it's time for our Yale people to leave for the airport. Let's give them a round of applause for a job well done."

Everyone stood and applauded. Gary said "Cheers," as the assembly raised their glasses.

Leslie thanked the OBL caterers as they prepared to leave, having already gathered their dishes and packed up their service equipment on their roll-away carts.

The bar's staff gave everyone a heated cloth as they took orders for after dinner drinks.

Leslie had prearranged with the bar people that they were to stop serving when signaled and take a break until the D.J. arrived. She walked over to the bar and said, "Time for the closed session. Please take your break. I'll phone you when to return, and it will be at the same time the D.J. arrives. You're doing a great job."

Gary walked over to the gallery client's tables. He explained that the next segment was a colonies planning session, and they could "take a break." He asked that they return when called to enjoy the rest of the evening.

When only colonies personnel and their companions remained, Mary Ellen locked the cafeteria's doors.

Manual Orba and Paul Kling maneuvered a small table and chair to face the audience.

Chairman Green placed a folder on the table and opened it and announced, "Hey everyone lets thank Leslie, our 'wonder woman,' for putting this entire show together."

There was a round of applause.

"We're going into our planning session now. Most of the time news filters down to the branches via memo or directive. I'm especially pleased to share directly with you some of the things we're all going to participate in to augment our successful adventure in the distribution of fine arts.

"Two days ago, I had a conversation with a programming director from PBS (Public Broadcasting System). He asked me if our lecturer – he waved toward Frank - would deliver a live broadcasted lecture on their national network."

There was a stunned silence for a few seconds, until Lydia Noonan jumped up from her seat and yelled, "Awesome!"

Gary said, "How about it Frank?"

"Mr. Chairman, delivering a live lecture on PBS would be equally significant, or perhaps an even greater honor than the Doctorate *you* arranged to have Yale award to me."

Gary raised his left arm and said, "I learned recently there are 11.5 million visual fine artists in North America. The PBS audience would likely encompass a great number of these artists, together with people who acquire fine art."

"This would be an opportunity for the Colonies to sponsor the program by a donation, and likely the fine art supply manufacturers and distributors would want to be included in that sponsorship. It feels to me as if it is a win-win situation.

"Sra. de la Silva, I know you are well connected politically in South America. Do you think LPB (Latino Public Broadcasting) might have interest in Frank's lecture, and maybe you could translate? Oh, and what would be your estimate of the number of fine artists in South America?"

Maria de la Silva stood up, "Mr. Chairman, I will make the proper inquiries as to the possibility of Doctor Creech's lecture being broadcast by LPB. With the economic growth in South America in the last twenty years, I would imagine there may be a similar number of South American artists as there are in the U.S.

"I would be honored to be the translator of Frank's lecture."

"Excellent. Thank you very much Maria."

"Next item: We need a Public Relations director to handle our PR needs. Does anyone know of a candidate – a person with a fine arts background – not just a 'talking head?'"

Carroll Swanson stood up. "Frank will remember Bill Schmitt, a candidate we had for The Art Colony of Chicago's gallery manager position."

Frank nodded his head.

"Carroll continued, "Bill took a gallery manager position in Cicero, and has given us a few orders. He called me last month. He said he made a mistake in taking that position without being interviewed by us. He is very articulate and has a BA in fine arts. He asked me to let him know of future openings the Colonies might have."

Gary said, "Sounds good, Carroll. Ask Mr. Schmitt to contact Frank about our PR opening. Does anyone else have a candidate?"

Everyone shook their head.

"Leslie, please prepare an interview sheet for Frank outlining the attributes we would require, together with the expected functions of our PR spokesperson."

"Will do, boss."

"Frank, we're going to reduce the number of lectures you have programmed because of the PBS lecture. We'll honor the contractual lectures granted, but I want the dates spread out over the years to free you up for other assignments. OK?"

"Yes Sir."

"Finally, and I know you all need a fresh drink, go to the bathroom, start dancing, whatever, I'll try to make the last item as brief as possible.

"Mary Ellen, whom I think we all call 'M.E.' now, raised a good point when we learned Frank's lecture could be broadcasted by PBS. Her point was that we're likely to enjoy enormous growth of new galleries and Colonies branches.

Under the 'other duties assigned' provision of your contracts, Frank will be assigning our branch presidents a rotating chore of indoctrination and education of those new entities. Is that understood by all?"

There were a few quiet moans.

"Alright, I'm first in line for the men's room, RHIP, you know, ha, ha, *rank hath its privilege.*"

M.E. opened the cafeteria doors.

Leslie first called Boyd Guard and asked him to tell the gallery guests to return to the cafeteria. She told him the bar was open and the dancing would soon begin.

Then she called the bar staff and the D.J and asked that they come into the cafeteria.

The D.J. started with the "Pennsylvania Polka, continuing with "The Chicken Dance Polka," No Beer in Heaven Polka," and finished the polka music with Jimmy Dorsey's "Clarinet Polka." The polkas had been suggested to Leslie by Bud Robitalle.

The Robitaille's, Emily and Frank, and no surprise to anyone, Dick and Gail Boyd were accomplished polka dancers. Everyone else picked up the steps quickly. Even Manual and Maria took their turns.

The D.J. then spun "Golden Oldies," popular dance favorites, beginning with a Frank Sinatra album and concluding with Hoagy Carmichael's "Stardust."

Ending the program, the D.J. waved Emily and Frank onto the floor. They waltzed to Johan Strauss II's "The Blue Danube." The D.J. stood and applauded and the audience and bar tenders joined him.

Gary told everyone to take the flowers from their tables.

He and Frank went to the exit door and bid farewell and thanked all for coming.

Gary asked Frank to come to his office to go over a few things that didn't involve the rest of the staff, at 9:00 a.m. Monday morning.

When they got home, Emily and Frank took their shoes off and talked about the wonderful evening; the Doctorate, the great food and drink, the comradery, the new Colonies plans, and the dancing.

Frank said to Emily, "Honey, I'm concerned with what else Gary has come up with for me. I did not believe I could deliver forty lectures a year, and am happy that the number has been reduced to those lectures we had contracted."

Emily said, "I'm not worried at all, you can handle whatever Gary dishes out; but I would like to have you to myself for longer periods than a mid-week here and there."

Long day tired, they kissed and fell asleep immediately.

"Good Morning, M.E. – I hope that shortened name is acceptable to you?"

"Sure it is Frank, whatever works. Easier to text I'm sure, ha, ha. Great award ceremony, great party, all thanks to you."

"Nah, I had a lot of support."

"Well, go on in Frank, Gary gets nervous at two minutes past his appointment times."

"Good morning Frank, have some fresh coffee and churros."

"Thank you Gary, not just for the churros and coffee, but for all the good things that are happening for me."

"Well, you've earned every bit of it. What was it Carroll said, oh yes; he said you were my 'workhorse.'

"Let me get right to it. What I need to go over with you, but not something the rest of the Colonies need to know at this time, is my plan for European expansion.

"I asked Leslie to prepare a statement for me contrasting gallery sales to direct Colonies sales by ratio and by community."

He handed Leslie's statement to Frank.

I also asked our auditors Tim McClary and Bill McDaniels to prepare a profit analysis contrasting the profitability of the Colonies branches versus client gallery sales.

He handed the auditors statements to Frank.

Frank carefully perused the statements. He arched his eyebrows and widened his eyes and then began to slowly shake his head.

"Boss, I knew the gallery client sales were less profitable than branch sales, but would never have believed the huge difference in Colonies earnings these statements evidence."

"Frank, it only occurred to me as our growth afforded the opportunity to check the profits comparatively. You know, when parents watch their toddler take his first steps they are delighted, and are not then concerned with improvement.

"Private collector sales are obviously quite profitable, and would be even more profitable if sold by our branches.

"On top of that I'm sure you're sick and tired of negotiating for space for our exhibitions in both the U.S. and Europe.

"Let's start with the affluent European communities:

He read from his list, "London, Paris, Rome, Stockholm, Istanbul, Madrid, Vienna, Zurich, Geneva, Munich, and Brussels. I'll exclude Prague for now because of the huge orders we get from your Mr. Novotny.

"Checking with Leslie, I learned it had been two years since we've received an order from our exclusive dealer in Berlin. That's a violation of that gallery's contract. I've asked Vic Lich to petition the courts in Germany to permit the establishment of our own branch in Berlin.

"When that's cleared up, we'll add Berlin to the list.

"Now I know this assignment may appear daunting. However, we have years to get it accomplished before your employment term is completed.

"Let's start with planning your lectures in the targeted cities and simultaneously developing Colonies branches in those cities, after your PBS lecture."

"Yes Sir."

Chapter 30

Two Marriages

Gary advised the PBS program director, Kerry Heinz, that the colonies would donate $500,000 to the network and that he was in touch with the agent for the artists' supply manufacturers and distributors, who likely would make a matching donation. He gave the agent's phone number to Mr. Heinz.

He said, "Mr. Heinz, you will need to coordinate with Leslie D'Alessandro, Frank Creech's executive marketing assistant. Her extension is 2012.

"May I transfer your call to her?" Gary fumbled a moment; the colonies new automated telephone system had only been installed a few days ago.

"Yes, please."

Kerry Heinz spoke with Leslie. He explained to her that PBS wanted to schedule Frank's lecture as soon as possible while the media coverage of Yale University's award of Frank's honorary doctorate was fresh in the public's mind. They talked about how the programming worked and mentioned that the lecture would have forty minutes, and sponsor commentary would have three minutes.

"I'll call you back shortly, Mr. Heinz."

She called Frank through the intercom. "PBS wants a quick schedule for your lecture. I'll have Gary's three-minute commentary and the time sequencing ready in two days. Your lecture time is forty minutes. How many days will you need to prepare your lecture?"

He pressed the speaker feature on the new phone. "Lydia, what time will we need to alter the localized version to Art of the Americas?"

"A week, I think," she turned to the researchers, who nodded their heads.

Leslie thanked them, hung up, and called Mr. Heinz.

"Ten days, Mr. Heinz." She stretched the lecture prep time with her instinctual safety valve. She asked Mr. Heinz if the lecture could be scheduled for a Saturday afternoon.

"I'll check into that and let you know. Oh," he said, "one other thing. We're required by the FCC to clear the material to be broadcast. Can you submit a transcript, please?" FCC stood for Federal Communication Commission, which regulated the television, radio, and telephone industries.

Leslie replied, "We'll do better than that. We'll give you a video of our final rehearsal. It may only be used for censorship viewing. Is that agreed to?"

"Perfect. Now I know why Gary Green referred me to you. Thank you so much. I'll be in touch."

Leslie had taped the conversation for her PBS folder.

Frank was thankful for the new phone system. Now the caller had to state his needs and speak with a knowledgeable person in the department selected.

He changed his cell number so as to no longer receive calls directly. The responding colonies people could handle the caller's needs in most cases.

The marketing department's complex issues were referred to Leslie. If she needed Frank's approval or input, she would contact him.

Things are getting so much better than in the early days of chalkboard tallies and me individually handling all the calls from clients, Frank thought. *I no longer have to turn the phone off in order to eat, shower, go to the toilet, or try to sleep undisturbed. Emily is thankful as well. Har, har.*

Utilizing the cafeteria, Frank and his research team worked through lunch with the basic outline of the lecture.

Gary saw them working at their table. He stopped by and said, "How's it going?"

Lydia nodded toward Frank. He said, "We're going to make our schedule with time to spare boss."

"Good."

Emily and Mike Maxwell had agreed on the size and the locations in the house for the kitchen and the dining room. They also selected the appliances, the cabinets, the granite, and the flooring.

She asked him for a favor. "Mike, could you possibly build the guesthouse first? I could use it to store my furniture and my shop equipment, things I won't have room for in the casita."

"I'll have to start with the road into the property, and the next thing will be your guesthouse."

Emily's next trip was to see the leasing agent at the small mall she selected for her Western designer clothing shop. An appropriate space would be available in the newest building on September 1. She executed a three-year lease and paid for the first and last months.

While he waited for Emily at the casita, Frank called Diane Arnold. She told Frank she had a very good quarter. She accepted his offer to pay the balance of her loan in two installments, interest free. He would formalize the deal at Vic Lich's office that afternoon.

Frank sighed with relief. "Diane, from my experience, is a disaster waiting to happen. I can't have that looming over my head. I don't believe Emily would appreciate nor condone my continuing relationship with Diane, even though it was strictly an arm's-length business arrangement."

Since Leslie would now have the marketing chores with Diane's gallery, Frank saw no reason or need for further communication with Diane Arnold.

As Frank left Vic's office, he saw workmen on scaffolding applying adobe to the exterior of the colonies' building.

Frank saw Gary on the lawn, head cocked and one hand on his hip; his eyes were shielded by the other hand. He was watching the workman apply the adobe.

"Hi, boss. That new adobe coating looks great."

"Well, Frank, when we built this building after the directors decided to make the colony a commercial enterprise, we sought to hold down the cost by using less expensive adobe. Old story, you get what you pay for. This material is 'sustainable' adobe.

"Oh, and while you're here, Art of the Americas is perfect for use in the PBS lecture and for use in both the U.S. and in European lectures to follow.

"For the new lecture, you won't need the European or Asian comparatives. I think just authenticating New World art from a historic base will be our most opportune approach because that's what we sell."

"I couldn't agree more. That's the way we'll go, boss."

Lydia, the two marketing researchers, and Frank began to put together the lecture with the recently discovered cave art in Tennessee—American Indian hunters stalking buffalo and other prey. With permission, they reproduced the six-thousand-year-old charcoal drawings for the lecture's opening scene slides.

Frank apprised Leslie of the researcher's agenda. She developed the press releases of the colonies on that information, and she cleared her releases with PBS's Kerry Heinz. He in turn shared his program ads with Leslie and invited her input on his material as well.

Leslie learned PBS would schedule the lecture Saturday afternoon two weeks hence for the live performance and reserves the right to the videoed version for prime time presentation at a later date.

Simultaneously (using her faithful rolling cart with its hanging files), Leslie prepared Chairman Green's opening commentary, citing Frank's bio credentials and highlighting the importance to the art community and to art students, teachers, and institutions of this never-before-aired New World art history.

Senhora de la Silva called Frank, "Dr. Creech, I was successful in having your lecture broadcast by Latin Public Broadcasting. They will use the video, and I will translate."

"Terrific, Maria. I'll pass this information on to everyone. Gary and the directors will be so pleased."

"Thank you, Frank."

Emily and Frank flew to PBS's headquarters in Arlington, Virginia, two days before the live broadcast. The final rehearsal was videoed for the censorship test. The rehearsal served Frank well. He became acquainted with the lighting, the audience positioning, and the climate of the live broadcast area.

The *Washington DC International Art Critics* Sunday edition headlined the arts and entertainment section column: "*Stunning—Overdue*—Frank Creech reached a huge audience with his sparkling lecture Art of the Americas, broadcast live yesterday on PBS."

The article outlined the lecture's high points and praised PBS for broadcasting on Saturday to the advantage of art students. The reviewer noted that the audience consisted of over 20 percent young artists. She also thanked the Art Colonies of America for sponsoring the lecture.

Emily photographed Frank talking with the young artists and their families after the lecture. *This is his finest hour*, she thought.

Reflecting that while everyone thought they really understood her fiancé's thoughts and actions, Emily believed that she alone knew why Frank insisted children be at least 20 percent of the audience at each lecture. She was certain it was his parenting instincts, which he could never enjoy as a natural father. She never mentioned it either to him or to anyone else.

Gary messaged Frank: "I agree with the *Washington DC International Art Critics* reporter, *stunning* and *overdue*. Good work. Please see me Monday morning at nine o'clock."

Frank called Mary Ellen, "M.E., what's up with my 9:00 a.m. Monday summons?"

She answered, "This time I don't have a clue, but there was no alarm warning. Don and I watched your show Saturday. We both thought it was your best lecture. Your presentation was electric."

"Thanks, M.E."

She was on the phone, waiting, so she put her finger on her lips and nodded Frank toward Gary's anteroom.

Frank walked into Gary's anteroom, surprised to see Ken Geelhood and three other board members, as well as auditors Tim McClary and Bill McDaniel sitting with Frank at his post-remodeled huge conference table.

"Good morning, Frank," Gary said. "Please sit, and I believe you know everyone."

"Yes, sir." He poured himself a cup of coffee and selected a churro, carefully placing a napkin on his lap.

Gary excitedly stated, "As our executive marketing director, we think you should know of our decision to take the colonies public." He waited a second for this to sink in.

"We've incurred considerable debt in the reconstruction of our building, with its new facilities, our sponsorship of your lectures, and other mounting expenses. With that in mind and to secure additional funds for your development of new branches, we've had Vic Lich prepare an IPO of our shares of stock in the colonies.

"We didn't include you in our study of entering a speculative market because of the intensity of your preparation for your best lecture yet—"

He stopped as everyone stood up and applauded Frank.

"We're offering one million shares at an initial price of $23 per share. We're going to suggest our officers and employees buy on Wednesday, the first day of the offering, with the expectation the stock will double in price within three working days.

"Everyone here is going to make a substantial investment. What do you think?"

"I'm going to put my money where my mouth is. I'll buy ten thousand shares."

"Well done, Frank."

Bill McDaniel wrote Frank's number down on his full-page list.

Gary said, "Get on with your lectures and development of more branches, Frank. You know time is money."

"Yes, sir."

Emily and Frank were married in their gazebo the following spring. There were 140 people in attendance, not counting ushers caters, band, photographers, and valet parking attendants.

The maid of honor was Linda McAffee, Emily's best friend. The best men were Chip Drueding, Frank's buddy from the Vietnam War, and the ever faithful Marty Freling.

Frank waved his hand around the estate and the huge gathering of friends. He said, "Marty, thank you for making all of this happen."

Ken Blitch, retired minister and tennis player from CYRC, performed the wedding. His wife, Tina, rehearsed the bridesmaids and other wedding parties in their roles.

Emily had designed a special Western dress with small boots, a leather vest, a ten-gallon hat with sprigs of flowers in the band, and a loose-fitting blouse with big sagebrush imprints.

At the last hour before the ceremony, she changed her mind. "This outfit looks like a walking advertisement for my shop. It appears to be too self-serving."

She switched to the blue maxi dress with tiny flowers, matching the flowers in her hair; the dress was the one she wore to the tea party in Naples, because Frank wore his blue silk suit.

Ever the showman, Frank sang Lou Rawls's "You'll Never Find Another Love Like Mine" to Emily after their wedding vows.

Emily and Frank, accompanied by their musicians, waltzed to the tune of "The Blue Danube" in the traditional first dance.

She said, "Frank, as strange as it may sound, I still get a thrill from the applause of our audiences when we dance."

Frank started to say, "All in a day's work," but thought better of it.

Fred Zebley and his wife, Sharon, stopped the reception line for a moment after shaking hands with Frank and kissing Emily. Fred said in a quiet voice, "Frank, thank you for inviting us to your wedding. Just to close the chapter on the desert misadventure, we settled with the camel tour people for pennies on the dollar. In fact, we sold five additional airships because of the publicity."

Frank said, "I'm glad there are no hard feelings about my inability to help."

"Ha, ha, none at all. We're happy you didn't ask for a commission on the sales."

Judy Freling kissed Emily and Frank. Judy said, "It took a very special person to bring in the reins of our very own wild horse. And you are the extraordinary lady who did just that! Marty bought me one of your Western designer outfits. When I wear it, I'll remember you and our dear Frank's wedding."

Marty said, "Mazel tov."

Emily said, "Frank speaks of you and Marty often in a most respectful manner."

"Well, we love him, and we're so proud of what he has accomplished," Judy responded.

Frank waved excitedly to the caterers. "Getting a little warm out here for the people waiting in line. Please bring trays of champagne and hors d'oeuvres."

Gary Green and his wife, Susan, came up next. Gary saluted Frank; Susan kissed them.

Gary, arms extended heavenward, said to both, "If your marriage is as successful as Frank has been in our business, you'll have a great deal to look forward to."

Emily blushed and squeezed Frank's hand.

Mary Ellen and her new husband, Don Scherzer, congratulated the newlyweds. Mary Ellen said to Frank, "Ooh, you da man."

Frank laughed, "Looks like you didn't do so badly yourself. Don, your bride bailed my big ass out so many times I can't even keep track."

Ron Romano and his wife, Rosemary, greeted the new couple. Ron said, "Congratulations to both of you. Frank, I can't thank you enough for forging the deal to house your SW Florida gallery in my museum. Our attendance is up, and our revenue is beyond our expectations."

"You're too kind, Ron. Actually, as I recall, you were the driving force in our successful deal."

Rosemary said, "My husband is a happy man, not nearly the grouch he used to be. Oh, Ron, I'm just kidding."

"Please remember that a successful marriage is an edifice that must be rebuilt every day," Robert di Grazi reminded Emily and Frank as he and his wife, Donna, congratulated the couple.

Looking down the line of people, Frank saw the groups which had been together during the wedding.

The ABC's of Advertising, Cecillia Albrecht, Ron Bradley, Neil Chartrand, and their significant others danced by Emily and Frank, blowing kisses and singing, "For they're a jolly good couple, for they're a jolly good couple, for they're a jolly good couple, which nobody can deny."

Emily and Frank blew kisses back to them.

The caterers brought out folding chairs for everyone and moved the reception line under the trees onto the circular driveway in front of the house. Frank saw they were no longer serving hors d'oeuvres, but the champagne continued to flow.

Next in line were customers, gallery owners, and private collectors. Each made congratulatory expressions in their native language and in English.

Ken and Alice Geelhood; the Taos staff, friends, and associates; Bill Hasse, Leslie D'Alessandro, Don Lambrix, Jack Murtha, David Pohl, Marion Jones, Pat Napior, Martha Cunningham, Betty James, Allan Isaacs, Mike Maxwell, and their significant others, together with Janet and Vic Lich and Sally and Larry Thompson moved through the reception line. Eyeing the people behind them, they expressed their heartfelt feelings as briefly as possible.

Emily and Frank were now responding with less effusiveness, as they began to tire.

Two groups were still to come: the first of which was the desert rescue team, Barbara and Ladd Orr, Kathy and Tal Leonard, Derrill Dare, and Nona Bennett.

Barbara was the spokesperson. She said, wiping a tear, "We just want you to know that even though we learned our rescue of Diane was under false pretenses, we were there for you. We wish you a long and happy marriage."

All applauded, and Emily and Frank returned their applause.

The final group, the branch presidents, Maria de la Silva, Dick Boyd, Bud Robitaille, Carroll Swanson, Ken Geelhood, and their families together with gallery managers Manual Urba, Larry Stahlhut, Gail Robitaille, Paul Kling, Lydia Noonan, and their families came up to bat.

Dick, before he became SW Florida colony president, had a part-time theater background. Not to be outdone by the ABC's of Advertising, the presidents, their wives, and the gallery managers and their wives sang "It Had To Be You." Dick had modified it for the occasion:

> It had to be you, Frank Creech. It had to be you. I wandered around and finally found the man who could make me be true. Could make me be blue or even be glad, just to be sad thinking of you.

Some others I've seen might never be mean. Might never be cross or be a bad boss. But they wouldn't do for nobody else, gave me a thrill with all your faults. I love you still. It had to be you wonderful you, Frank. It had to be you, and we love Emily too.

Everyone hugged and kissed, and they adjourned to the dinner buffet.

Emily laughed, tapped her spoon on her glass, and addressed her guests. "My mother told me to marry a doctor. Are you listening, Mom? Well, that I did. Frank has an honorary doctorate from Yale, thanks to Chairman Green."

Most of the guests partied the entire weekend. Buffet lines were set up three times a day to feed the huge entourage. The open bar began service at noon each day and shut down on Saturday night at midnight.

All of the guests left by Sunday afternoon. Emily and Frank, hand in hand, said goodbye and thanked every guest for coming to their wedding.

Frank loved his lecture series. He had worked very hard with the marketing department's unending assistance in keeping the material fresh, sparkling, and interesting—even for repeat audiences.

Emily's shop was successful. Her Western designer clothing was both fun and profitable.

The shop gave her a lot to do while Frank traveled.

Over the years Frank and Emily had collected twenty-two spectacular colonies' paintings. They were displayed in both their main and guest houses to their particular delight and to the awe of their guests.

Emily and he thoroughly enjoyed entertaining at the estate Mike Maxwell had created for them, despite the demands of Frank's position.

Chapter 31

Home

Emily and Gary received the news in a joint message from the Polizia di Stato Commissariato in Rome, Italy.

"We obtained your telephone numbers from the ICE (in case of emergency) listings on Frank Creech's cell phone. Mr. Creech fell off a riser in the auditorium at the Lorenzo de Medici art school. He has been ambulanced to Ospedale Santo Spirto hospital. When we have the medical report, we will recontact you."

Emily reasoned the Italian officials would be more responsive to a corporate chairman than to an anxious wife. She called Gary.

"Chairman Green's office, Mary Ellen speaking. How may I help you?"

"M.E., this is Emily—"

Interrupting, M.E. said, "Oh, Emily, I am so sorry. Gary's on the line with the hospital now. I'll ask him to call you when he knows the extent of Frank's injuries."

"Thank you, M.E."

Gary called Emily. "Emily, the news is good and bad. First off, Frank's injuries are not life threatening."

He heard her exhale deeply. "What's the bad news, Gary?"

"His right hip is injured, and his right elbow is shattered. When he is out of surgery and moved to the ICU, they're going to help him call us.

"Emily, my call is being returned from the Rome police department. I'll call you back." He hung up.

Gary asked the police investigator for the report of Frank's fall, and the officer faxed it to him. He read it and called Mary Ellen through the intercom. "M.E., please call Vic Lich right away."

When Vic was in line, Gary said, "Vic, the police report indicates Frank tripped over a loose board walking off the riser at the end of his lecture at Rome's leading art institution."

"Yes, it does. I'm looking at the report M.E. faxed me."

"This could cost us millions of dollars if Frank is no longer able to provide the lectures that have been so very beneficial to the colonies."

"Gary, it wouldn't be prudent to tip our hand that a lawsuit may be in the works. It would give the university too much time to prepare a response. Let's see how it goes with Frank and take it from there. One good thing, alcohol was not found in Frank's system from the analysis of his blood drawn at the scene of the accident."

"Thanks, Vic."

The next day, Emily received her call from Frank. "Honey, don't worry. I'm going to be fine. They're treating me great here. My surgeon says the hip likely won't need replacement, just rehab. The elbow though is pretty bad. I'll learn more about the elbow tomorrow or the next day."

His voice sounded hoarse, so she said, "Get some rest, my very special love. Call me tomorrow when you can."

Emily called Gary and filled him in on the information Frank had given her.

Gary didn't talk about reparations with Emily; he felt that would seem too pecuniary.

Leslie advised the branch presidents of Frank's fall and his injuries and promised to update them when she learned of his prognosis. She couldn't furnish any contact information as he was still in ICU.

She would know tomorrow whether or not Frank could make his next scheduled lecture in Madrid two weeks ahead.

Frank called Leslie. "Can you set up a conference call—you, me, Gary, and Emily?"

"Yes, I can. Give me one hour. I'll originate the call. Is your cell phone OK?"

Frank chortled, but then he coughed and said quietly, "Yes, it was on the side that didn't hit the floor."

With the conference call set up, Frank said, "Hi, everyone. My doctors say I have a hip labral tear. The nurses are applying ice packs every fifteen or twenty minutes. I am using ibuprofen for the pain. My doctors said that will be the treatment for the next three days, after which I'll go to the swimming pool for some resistance work. I'm using a walker now and should be walking on my own in the next few weeks.

"The elbow is a different thing. The x-rays show a fracture. I heard a snap when I fell. The elbow joint is dislocated. The surgeons removed the bone fragments and decided I didn't need nails or a cast. The arm's in a splint. Next week I start rehabilitation to decrease the chance of getting elbow stiffness. This includes exercises, scar massage, ultrasound, heat, ice, and use of a sling on the arm.

"My doctors said my dancing and walking will make my recovery less difficult. They think I can eat normally and use my arm—you know as the pointer arm I use in the lectures in two or three weeks. Maybe we should reschedule Madrid?"

Gary said, "That's good news. We really were worried about you. No question, Madrid has to be rescheduled."

Leslie said, "I'll take care of it. And Frank, you'll let me know when you can make your next lecture. May I have your room number, please?"

"Sure, 234. Thanks, Leslie."

"OK, no problem. Get well soon, Frank. I'm hanging up now."

"Em and Gary, I'm feeling better now. And I'll get back to work in a few weeks, I feel certain."

Gary said, "I'm hanging up now too. Take care, Frank, and I'm sure you know I'll always be in your corner.

"Emily, are you still there, honey?"

"Yes. Leslie and Gary hung up, so I could speak with you privately."

"They're good people, Emily, really. Sometimes I wonder about Gary, but over the years things have worked out."

"Honey, I'm so sorry this has happened to you. Maybe you should come home. You can rehab here."

"You mean give up the lectures?"

"Uh . . . well, yes, I do. You have performed for the colonies, giving lectures for five years and still taking time to supervise the marketing department as executive director. Maybe it's time for you to retire. I'd like to have you spend more time with me in our beautiful home. You could fish on Blue Lake, ski when your limbs are healthy, entertain your friends, have dinner and dance parties here."

"I'll think about it, sweetheart. Here comes the ice pack lady and the masseuse. We'll talk later. Love you."

Two weeks, and it wasn't that bad—pain only when I try to walk, Frank thought. *I have some flexibility in the elbow. I can eat with a fork using my right hand without spilling too much. I can walk without a walker or a cane cautiously and slowly. My jacket hides the sling I'll need to wear for two or three more months.*

The get well cards and flowers were crowded into his room. Frank was grateful for the attention and the remembrances. He thought long and hard about what Emily had asked him to do—to hang it up and come home.

Frank called Gary and asked him to cancel Madrid and the balance of his lectures for that year. He would remain in the hospital until he was able to walk without a walker and was formerly released by the medical staff.

Without comment, Gary said, "OK, Frank. That I will do." He sensed that Frank's career was concluded.

Gary agreed to pay Frank's salary for the remainder of the year and to pay his accumulated share profits over the next five years.

Frank and Emily were well satisfied.

Gary wasn't satisfied. He called Vic and asked him to sue the Lorenzo de Medici art school.

Emily was especially delighted that she would have Frank at home for their retirement. She had hired an ambitious young clothing designer to manage her store so she could be at home for Frank.

The store was so successful Emily leased the unit next door when it became available. She had a double door installed between the units. The initial unit was the showroom and customer fitting room. The second unit housed her two full-time tailors and storage areas.

Vic Lich built his lawsuit carefully. He had engaged a highly reputable trial firm headquartered in Rome to pursue the suit.

They hired a photographer who took pictures of Frank with his bandaged limbs exposed and pictures of him using the walker with his arm in a sling. The photographer made a video of Frank hobbling pathetically and of him doing his painful rehab exercises.

Vic furnished his Roman colleagues canceled lecture notices and a written resignation letter from Frank. He gave them copies of the police report, which included photos of the broken riser that Frank had tripped over.

He itemized the near double cost to the colonies for their health insurance due to the huge expense of Frank's hospitalization, surgeries, and care.

With financial charts prepared by auditors Tim McClary and Bill McDaniels, the severity of Frank's injuries and his retirement were shown to potentially cost the colonies billions of dollars in sales.

Frank had reluctantly joined in the lawsuit, which he was asked to do by Gary.

The Lorenzo de Medici art school's law firm advised their client to settle rather than go to court.

The settlement came to $25 million for Frank, the amount he would have earned over the next five years of his contract. The colonies received $125 million. Sums received were less attorney's fees of 30 percent.

"Boss, I'm so glad now that you insisted I join the civil action against the Roman art school. Truthfully—and please don't tell Emily—my hip hurts every day. I probably couldn't climb the dais without assistance.

"Between you and me, I think the lectures had pretty much run their course."

Gary surprised Frank. "Actually, I did know that. The lectures were very effective, and I'm glad we developed that program. I think they truly made us an important source of fine art sales both nationally and internationally. However, I did see an erosion of interest in the lectures by audiences and the media a couple of years ago."

Frank felt his mission was completed when the colonies' sales had become *ten* billion dollars annually.

He had successfully pleaded out of his ten-year contract with the colonies at the end of the fifth year. He was comfortable with the settlement. He placed ten million dollars with the investment firms Larry Thompson had recommended.

Frank retained his shares in the colonies because they were paying generous dividends. His settlement funds and investments, together with Emily's income from her shop, made them financially comfortable.

They added a swimming pool and cabana outside the main house. Emily thought the pool would help his rehabilitation, and the view of the Sangria de Cristo Mountains was breathtaking.

Leslie put together Frank's retirement party. It was to be held in the colonies' cafeteria. She invited everyone she knew who had a working relationship with Frank.

Leslie used the colonies' Web site, Twitter and Facebook accounts, and the now monthly catalogs and newsletters to tell everyone of Frank's retirement.

The theme Leslie selected for Frank's retirement was "best memories," which she passed on to the invitees.

Gary insisted the party be held on a Saturday afternoon, the day Frank used for his lectures.

When Leslie told Frank of the details of the party for his retirement, he chortled and said, "That sly old fox wasn't just tying together my lectures to my retirement party, he was making sure the party wasn't on the colonies' clock."

Leslie prepared the guest list. Guests who would speak of their best memories of Frank were assigned their position in the lineup and the approximate time slots for their presentations.

She had her print shop make place cards for the seats and personalized name labels.

She ordered the plaque Gary would present to Frank, the inscription of which she had written and had been approved by Gary.

Leslie asked Janet Lich to help with the luncheon to be provided at the party.

Janet ordered lunch for approximately one-hundred people from the Tex-Mex diner, La Cueva Café, which she knew would please Frank. It was served by the colonies' cafeteria staff.

Beer, soft drinks, and teas were on ice on large metal bins separate from the serving line. Wines of various varieties were on tables together with plastic wine glasses and plastic goblets.

Janet had placed flowers on each table together with the seat place cards.

Frank walked slowly into the cafeteria. Emily's arm supported his elbow. The couple greeted everyone throughout the luncheon.

When the tables had been cleared, Gary loudly cleared his throat. When he had everyone's attention, he said, "Let's honor our executive marketing director, Frank Creech, on the occasion of his retirement."

Leslie said, "First up, by lottery, is Alice Geelhood, wife of Taos Art Colony president Ken Geelhood."

Everyone applauded.

Alice and Ken Geelhood joined Gary at the front of the audience. She presented Frank her treasured scrapbook which he had admired at her dinner party years ago. Alice had a cover made for the scrapbook. The title, in raised letters, was *The Legend of Frank Creech*.

Ken stroked his chin and said, "Many, many things to consider, but the most memorable for me was the growth of the colonies to the point where elevators were added to the building."

Everyone laughed.

Frank said, "Alice, I am so flattered that you have chronicled my career. And thank you for your precious collection of the events of my thirteen years with the colonies."

Alice said, "You are so welcome. Best wishes on your retirement, Frank."

Bud Robitaille and his wife, Kathleen, were next. They arose together.

Bud told the story of Frank's standing up to the thugs in London. Kathleen waved her arms around the room and said, "Frank has enriched all of our lives."

Marty Freling recalled to the assembly how he had first met Frank. "Frank was then the *Washington DC International Art Critics'* senior art critic who was sent to judge an RSW art contest depicting American soldiers returning from Desert Storm. The paintings were hung in Concourse B. Frank judged my painting of a soldier in camos, prone, kissing the tile floor at the airport to be the best of show.

"I won that contest thanks to Frank, and we have become fast friends." He mentioned Frank's generous gift to his favorite charity as a birthday gift to him. When Marty began to cry, Judy pulled him back to his seat and addressed Frank.

"Frank, you and Emily will always be welcome in our home, so don't be strangers."

Frank and Emily nodded their heads and hugged the Frelings.

Artur Novotny, a Prague art gallery owner, honored Frank. "If it weren't for you, Frank, we would not be a valued customer. I believe I am speaking for most of the colonies' gallery owners."

There was a round of applause as Frank shook Artur's hand.

Boyd Guard said, "Artur stole my lines," laughed, and then said, "Frank's knowledge of art transcends that of anyone in our field, without question. And that will be my 'best memory' of Frank Creech.

"Frank, it has been my pleasure, and my family and I thank you for the good advice you always gave and the business we have enjoyed together."

"Same here, Boyd. Thank you, sir."

Ron Romano related his secretary's excitement at meeting Frank, whom she had called the "hero of the Battle of Biscayne Bay." Ron turned toward Frank, left hand extended and palm up, and said, "I'm sure you all recall the episode when Frank rammed the pirates' boat to prevent them from seizing Larry Thompson's boat for their use in illegally sneaking immigrants into the United States."

Ron gave Frank an exact duplicate of his Malacca cane which Frank had admired, saying, "I hope you never have to use this to walk, but if you do, you'll be very stylish."

Carroll Swanson stood and raised his glass. "Please join me in wishing Frank and Emily a happy and long retirement."

After they sipped their drinks, Carroll continued, "Frank, I was your antagonist for the first years of our relationship. I was always on your case for this infraction or another of colonies' procedures or protocols."

Carroll smiled as he watched Frank who was nodding his head.

"The time has come for me to say I apologize. I didn't understand what you meant to the colonies and how your boldness— some might call it your audacity —actually moved the colonies ahead at the speed of an SST.

"Speaking for all of the colonies' presidents, you're upgrading our galleries, and your insistence on our fine arts education have proven very profitable for everyone.

"Thank you, from all of us," Carroll said, as the presidents rose and applauded.

Dick Boyd stood up, "My turn."

He looked around the room and said, "There are so many things I can recall about interacting with Frank. My best memory of Frank was his support of his artist friends in the fray on Constitution Avenue in Washington DC. Our marchers were being attacked by the flash mob, and he waded into the crowd to defend us.

"It was an unfortunate incident for Frank, but thankfully, it all worked out well in the end. Marty Freling secured his marketing position with the Taos Art Colony. We all know how well we have done since Frank came to the colonies.

"Another thing that is most memorable is when Frank helped make my branch the first colony created after Taos. Folks, those are just a couple of highlights. And since Leslie is motioning toward me, I believe it's break time.

"Thank you, Frank, for the pleasure of your company over these years."

Following the break, Gail Boyd passed out copies of the lyrics of the New Year's Eve tune, Robert Burns's traditional folk song "Auld Lang Syne."

Dick Boyd said, "Hey, guys and girls, everyone sings 'Auld Lang Syne' at the end of New Year's parties, and no one ever knows exactly what that means. It literally translates to 'times gone by' and is about remembering friends and not letting them be forgotten. Will everyone please rise and join me in singing this beautiful old tune to Frank and his lovely wife, Emily."

They sang:

> Should auld acquaintance be forgot
> And never brought to mind?
> Should auld acquaintance be forgot,
> And auld lang syne?
> For auld lang syne, my dear
> For auld lang syne.
> We'll take a cup o' kindness yet,
> For auld lang syne.

The assembly solemnly raised their glasses and drank a silent toast to Frank.

The final speaker was Gary. He motioned Frank toward the front of the audience.

"Frank, this plaque is presented to you for what you have done for the colonies. Without doubt, no one else could have ever accomplished what you have done for the colonies in your thirteen years of service."

He shook hands with Frank and read the inscription on the plaque.

> To Frank Creech, Executive Marketing Director
> The Art Colonies of America
> We searched long and hard for just the right words
> To tell you how much we love you and appreciate
> What you have done for us
> Mary Ellen said it best
> *Oh, you da man*

Gary handed the plaque to Frank.

Emily wiped the tears from Frank's cheeks with her handkerchief.

Frank shook his head and said, "Thank you, Chairman Green. And thanks, everyone, for coming today. I am so proud of all of you."

As they were leaving, Carroll stopped Gary. "Did I hear correctly that you are planning to have a statue of Frank erected in the colonies' building entryway?"

"Yup, and we're going to have a copy of Frank's plaque engraved on the statue's pedestal."